I0831162

THE CLOCK KEEPER

MELISSA DELPORT

First published by Melissa Delport, 2016

www.melissadelport.com

Cover design by Apple Pie Graphics

Edited by Catherine Eberle of WordWeavers

Printed by Pinetown Printers

ALSO BY MELISSA DELPORT

URBAN FANTASY

GUARDIANS OF SUMMERFELD SERIES

The Cathedral of Cliffdale (Book 1)

The Fight of the Fallen (Book 2)

The Hope of Hawkstone (Book 3)

The Balance of the Blood (Book 4)

Full Series Boxed Set (Books 1-4)

SHADOW MAGIC SERIES

The Witchborn Curse (Book 1)

The Shadow Huntress (Book 2)

The Charmed Quarter (Book 3)

The Rogue Coven (Book 4)

The Darkest Realm (Book 5)

The Hybrid's Fate (Book 6)

Full Series Boxed Set (Books 1-6)

THE TRAVELER DUOLOGY

The Traveler (Book 1)

The Survivor (Book 1.5)

The Saviour (Book 2)

Full Boxed Set

TIME TRAVEL FANTASY

The Clock Keeper

DYSTOPIAN

THE LEGACY TRILOGY

The Legacy (Legacy Trilogy Book 1)

The Legion (Legacy Trilogy Book 2)

The Legend (Legacy Trilogy Book 3)

CONTEMPORARY WOMENS FICTION (as Lissa Del)

Rainfall

Riven

A Life Made of Lava

ROMANCE & ROMANTIC COMEDY (as Rachel Rhodes)

Awkward in Print

Awkward Abroad

Awkward Infidelity

Awkward in Trouble

ANTHOLOGIES

The Space Between Dreams & Chaos

The Space Between Magic & Mayhem

For my kids, for affording me the time to write about... well, time.

PART 1

ONE
THE DEATH OF HENRY ABBOTT

THE TRAIN HURTLED toward Henry Abbott at one hundred and twenty-five miles per hour. His youthful face, illuminated in the mega-watt beam of the halogen cyclops, reflected unadulterated terror, a stark contrast to the fists clenched determinedly at his side.

Bystanders would later say that Henry had been screaming - that he had called for help - but this was not the case. Nineteen-year-old Henry Abbot had been mute for the past three years, ever since his entire family had been killed at a railway crossing on their way to visit him. Henry, battling a drug addiction, had been in rehab at the time.

Mere feet from where Henry stood, the gathered crowd yelled at him to move, to get out of the way, to do something – anything – rather than simply stand in the way of the oncoming train. Most were so focused on the horrific sight that they failed to notice the slim girl elbowing her way through the crowd. She drew little attention, a tight braid containing her thick copper hair, a baseball cap pulled low over her grey-green eyes. Her clothing was non-descript at best - a pair of frayed jeans, a grey sweater two sizes too big and a pair of canvas sneakers caked in days-old mud.

Only when she reached the front of the crush of bodies did she lift her gaze to study the youth. Henry had begun to shudder, his fists unclenching. The blinding light of the train lit the sheen of perspiration on his brow and filled the spaces between the sparse stubble on his jaw. His tongue darted out to lick bloodless lips and his throat bobbed as he attempted to swallow his fear. It was obvious to everyone watching that young Henry's resolve was wavering.

Stay, the girl urged.

Oblivious to her silent plea, Henry suddenly snapped his head back, a low keening wail of despair sounding in his throat, audible only to him beneath the deathly wail of the train's approach. Like a drunken sailor Henry stumbled off the tracks to the collective relief of everyone watching. Everyone except the girl, that is. A stream of profanity danced through her wickedly curved lips as she leapt nimbly from the platform. Henry held out his hands to her, desperate and uncertain, craving human solace.

The girl's extraordinary eyes glistened with empathy as her hands mirrored Henry's, reaching up and towards him, as though she would bring him to her breast and soothe away his fears. Instead, she moved suddenly, forcefully, her hands shoving ruthlessly at Henry's chest, pushing him away – away from her, away from the safe haven of the platform – and into the path of the oncoming train.

It happened so quickly, so violently, that for a moment nobody moved, nobody but the girl, whose cap had been blown off by the wind of the train thundering past. She turned back to the platform and lifted her face. Blood was splattered across her cheeks and had soaked through her sweater, tinting the grey an ugly scarlet hue. The lit carriages of the train flashed by behind her, a ceaselessly moving backdrop.

The keening screech of the train's brakes rent the air then, fingernails down a blackboard on an unbearably magnified scale. Too little, too late for Henry Abbott.

The silence that followed was deafening. Like the calm before the storm, nobody reacted for a few seconds; their voices stunned into silence. Until one roused the rest.

"Get her!" a lone female voice shrieked, galvanising the heroes among the men who stood motionless. Hands reached for the girl, hauling her up onto the platform, cutting deep into her flesh and bruising her skin. Wordlessly, she complied, eyes once again downcast, absorbing every revolting insult hurled at her. Those watching would later recall that she was as meek as a lamb in those few moments before all hell broke loose.

One man watching from the shadows knew otherwise. This girl was no gentle lamb, but a hissing wildcat, lethal when threatened. He waited, arms crossed over his black-clad chest, dark curls falling across eyes as dark blue as the winter sky, eyeing the scene with mild curiosity. He wore a newsboy cap, fashionable in the twenties among the lower working classes, but, on closer inspection, the label on his black jeans was of designer origin and the leather of his shoes could only be genuine.

"I don't know what you find so amusing!" a middle-aged woman in floral print rebuked him, catching sight of his expression. "A young man was just murdered before our eyes!" In response, a small smirk played about the man's lips and she turned away in disgust, muttering under her tannin-laced breath.

Unperturbed, the man uncrossed his arms and glanced at the antique pocket watch he held in his hand - a fine, 18 karat gold timepiece dating back to the 1850s. It was accurate to the second. 10:24 p.m. As if on cue, four armed police officers arrived on the scene, flashing official badges in the faces of the men restraining the girl.

"Detective Harrison, LAPD," said the shortest – a thick-set man in an impeccable suit. His face was set in a scowl, a permanent affliction if the deep grooves in his forehead were any indication, but a sense of power radiated from him. He was not a man to be questioned or disobeyed. "We'll take it from here."

"She pushed him!" shouted the woman who had first demanded

justice from the crowd. "That little bitch pushed the boy onto the tracks. He's dead because of her!"

"Murderer!" cursed one of the men restraining the girl. He spat at her and she dodged to avoid the spittle flying from his lips, colliding with his stomach. Only Detective Harrison noticed the girl's slim hand slip within the pockets of the man's pants, withdrawing an embossed leather wallet which disappeared into the oversized sleeve of her hoodie.

Seizing her, Detective Harrison shoved the girl into the arms of one of his men before jerking a thumb at the remaining two.

"My men will take your statements," he announced authoritatively. The two policemen moved forward, pulling notebooks from their pockets. They showed signs of fatigue after a long night and, faced with the frenzied crowd before them, they cast dark looks at the girl.

"Nice to see you again, Truman," the girl murmured up at the officer who led her away. Truman didn't reply, but valiantly tried to hide his grin. Harrison clumped along behind them muttering under his breath while the streetlights glinted off his balding pate. "You too, Harrison," the girl continued cheerily.

In response, Jonathan Harrison reached for her sleeve, his podgy hand searching inside it for a full minute before he shook it free, clutching the leather wallet.

"I see you're still behaving like a common criminal." He tossed the wallet into the air and the girl's fingers caught it nimbly, a grin spreading across her face.

"Finders Keepers." The wallet disappeared, her sleight of hand remarkable, as always.

"You expect me to be impressed that a member of the Guild resorts to petty thievery when she has the resources of a god?"

"I don't need the Guild's money," the girl snarled. "I make my own way."

"And yet how quickly you go through the documentation we provide you with."

"That's different. Passports and visas aren't so easy to steal."

They emerged from the train station onto the street where a black SUV awaited.

A weary sigh slid from Harrison's lips.

"Just get in the car, Clara."

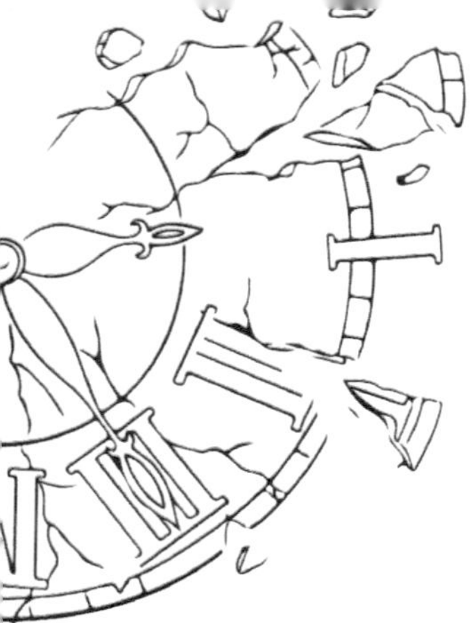

TWO
THE REAL RESOLUTE DESK

I WAIT in Harrison's office, gnawing my bottom lip and cursing the loss of my favourite cap. It's so hard to find one that fits well. I hate this office. You would think someone would redecorate every few decades, but this room hasn't changed since the first time I stepped inside it. The excessive wooden panelling gives me a headache. I focus instead on the modern skyscraper visible through the plate-glass window – the grand glass design marred only by the gaudy red neon light which boldly displays the company name: *Perpetual Life.* The conglomerate is international – an insurance corporation which specialises in life policies. This is the Tempus Guild's neighbour. I can't help but smile at the irony.

My stomach churns as a fresh wave of the metallic stench of Henry Abbot's blood fills my nostrils. I shed the grey sweater, balling what little clean fabric remains and wiping at my bloodied face, but the result, I suspect, is that I now have a fine coat of blood smeared across my entire face, rather than the liberal spray across my cheeks.

Truman, whose name is actually Jason Truman, but who has been known simply as Truman for as long as I can remember, sits beside me in an identical leather chair, his fingers resting lightly on the desk before us. It's a resolute desk, filled with secret compartments and hidden messages. It's also, quite possibly, the ugliest desk I've ever seen. Its very existence is denied by the Royal Collection Trust of the British royal family, but it is the identical twin to the desk currently used in the White House's oval office. Both desks were gifts from Queen Victoria in the 1800s. One was given to the second most powerful man on the planet – the President of the United States of America. This one, the most superior in craftsmanship, was presented to the Grandmaster of the Tempus Guild and here it has stayed, passed down from Grand Master to Grand Master. It currently belongs to Jonathan Harrison.

Truman looks over at me and gets to his feet, digging in his pocket until he pulls out a small square of microfibre cloth which he hands to me.

"Why didn't you run?" he asks, as I wipe my face.

I shrug. "Didn't have time."

"Couldn't you fight your way out?" He eyes the belt at my waist which I had revealed when I removed the hoodie. The daggers I have carried with me for half a century are clearly visible. The cold sensation of steel against my hips has become so reassuring that I hardly ever remove them.

"There was no need for innocent people to get hurt."

"If you knew you'd be caught you should've left well alone."

"Left well alone? And risk yet another anomaly that I'd be blamed for? I'd rather take my chances with Harrison's foul mood." I lift my feet and place them disrespectfully on the desk. Truman flinches but he doesn't comment.

"Nobody blames you, Clara..."

"I go by Clarke now," I remind him. It comes out harsher than I had intended, but it's been two decades since I went by the name of Clara. The Guild is a creature of habit, much to my annoyance. Truman doesn't call me out for the interruption. Instead, he gives me a look that is almost apologetic.

"Yeah, well, I guess that's in keeping with the times."

Neither of us speaks for some time and then he heaves a sigh.

"They don't blame you, you know. I know you feel disconnected from the Guild but you're still a Kennedy."

Kennedy. Once upon a time, the name was revered, along with Truman, Harrison, Lincoln, Washington, Jefferson and Cleveland. The Kennedys were one of seven powerful families, seven sanctified bloodlines that had endured through the ages with one sole purpose - to protect time itself. The Sovereign himself had chosen us at the very beginning, and we had continued to serve him centuries after he had disappeared, none more loyally than the Kennedys. Mine was a name that had struck fear into the hearts of men. My uncle, Jeremiah, had served as Grand Master over a hundred years ago and my great-grandfather before him. Never had one family so predominantly presided over the Guild. But that was before our fall from grace. Now, the Kennedy name was mentioned only in whispers, a stain on Tempus, one that could not be erased. Not even the minor triumph of a distant nephew who had risen through the ranks of the American political system to take up office had excused us. All they remembered was that messy Monroe business.

Truman is still waiting for a response and I take a moment to consider his comment. *They don't blame you.* Perhaps it's true for him. I certainly find no judgement in his eyes, but it's hard to believe that his impression of me isn't influenced by my family's shameful history or the condemnation of so many of Tempus's members.

"Did you know our families used to be close?" Truman announces suddenly, in an attempt to ease the tension. "My Uncle Tobias told me over the weekend that the Kennedys and the Trumans used to be close."

I give him a look that is part mocking, part-disbelieving.

"Oh, right." He grins sheepishly. "Of course you would."

"Anna and Mary were childhood friends," I say, relenting slightly. As always, just mentioning my sister's name sends a pang through my chest. Truman's eyes widen.

"Really? My sister was named after great-granny Mary, you

know. I don't think she's ever forgiven my mother. Says it makes her sound like a virginal prude."

"Yes, well, you should tell her that Mary wasn't a virgin when she got married," I tease. "That might make her feel better. In fact, Mary Truman was the life of the party before women knew how to party. I don't know how she made it through the Prohibition without getting arrested." Unbidden, an image of Anna and Mary as sixteen-year-olds, giggling behind their lovingly embroidered handkerchiefs, comes to mind.

Truman's laugh is infectious. "And you? What were you doing during the Prohibition?"

The smile dies on my lips. Anna didn't live to see Mary's wild antics in the twenties.

"I was trying to clean up my sister's mess."

Before Truman can utter the apology that washes over his face, the door is yanked open behind us and Harrison enters, holding an impressive sheaf of papers.

"Clara," he booms, giving me the benefit of his perpetual scowl, "I've had all record of the incident and your presence there deleted." He waits a full thirty seconds for an expression of gratitude that will never come before continuing. "Do you want to tell me what in God's name you thought you were doing?"

"Henry Abbott," I recite. "Nineteen years old, from Pittsburgh, Pennsylvania. Born 2nd January 1997. Died 19th of March 2016 at 22h28." I glance at my watch. "Two hours, eighteen minutes ago."

"You're still trying to stop the anomalies?" Harrison has been arguing with me about this for the better part of three decades. I'm pretty sure that he welcomes his own death, if only so that he can pass the responsibility of keeping me in line on to his successor. I try to control my rising temper, reminding myself that it can't be easy being the Grand Master of a secret society that protects life and death. Still, I stopped worrying about the Grand Master's respect the day my mortal life ended. Harrison is the fourth Grand Master I have known personally and although he is slightly more lenient than his predecessors, like them, he has no real idea what to do with me.

"If I don't stop them, who will?" I counter. "Besides, you should be thanking me. It was no easy feat finding him and I didn't even ask Techno Truman over here for help." Truman is an information technology genius. There's nothing he can't do with a computer and an internet connection.

"Dammit Clara!" Harrison throws the paperwork down on the smooth, age-worn surface of the desk. A single sheet glides across the smooth surface and dances through Truman's grasping hand to rest innocently on the floor. A quick glimpse shows a list of three names that cut me to my core. Henry Abbott's is at the bottom. I reach for the sheet, slapping it face down on the desk before Harrison can continue.

"Firstly, it's Clarke," I say, although why I bother, I have no idea. I've told him this on at least three separate occasions but the man will not address me as anything but Clara. "Secondly," I continue, stabbing at the list with a bladed finger, "*this* is the reason I was at the station tonight. Because for every name *not* added to this list my sister's memory is trampled further into the mud."

"Your sister made the most monumentally destructive decision in the history of time," Harrison points out. I bite down on my tongue before I say something I might later regret. "I understand you feel responsible," Harrison continues more gently, "and I understand that you feel helpless, but you cannot keep doing this. There is an easier way to do this as I keep reminding you."

"If it's so easy, why do you need me to do it?" I snap. "Why don't you find him yourself?"

Harrison looks uncomfortable, but he takes a deep, courageous breath.

"Because you are the same and you're the only one who can. He has to be found, Clara." Another determined breath. "You know that your very existence is a stain upon humanity."

"Please, Harrison," I say sarcastically, "don't hold back on my account."

An awkward silence follows and Truman stares pointedly at the desk, as though memorising the ornamental etchings is his life's pursuit.

"You need to find Fletcher," Harrison resumes the conversation as if I haven't spoken. It's his standard response to my flippancy. "That should be your top priority."

I drop the sarcasm, too weary to wind him up any further. It's no fun when he's in a temper.

"You think I don't know that? What exactly do you think I've been doing for the past hundred years?"

"Finding Fletcher is far more important than stopping the anomalies," Harrison growls. "He's an abomination. He needs to brought to the Guild so that we can try to fix the mistake your sister made a century ago!"

"Fix it?" I croak, my voice hoarse with humourless laughter, my chest aching with the heartache of the memories overwhelming me. "How do you propose we fix it, Harrison? When Anna stabbed Fletcher's clock something happened to it. It changed. How many names have been etched into that plaque since Fletcher's?" *Three*, my subconscious answers, and the list of names taunts me again. "There's no way to make Fletcher mortal again."

"There has to be a way." Typical Harrison, putting his faith in the establishment. "We won't know for sure until he's brought into custody."

"And me?" I retort. "Once you have Fletcher, I assume you'll take me into custody too? After all, he's not the only abomination Anna's actions created."

"No," Harrison replies gently, and the pitiful look he bestows upon me makes my face flush hot with shame. "He's not."

"Fine," I snap, "seeing as you're the expert, do you want to tell me how you expect me to find a man who doesn't want to be found? In almost a hundred years we've never come close to him – not even a trace. Fletcher has literally vanished. So tell me, Harrison - how exactly does the Guild expect me to find a ghost?"

"Fletcher Kincaid may be immortal, but he's made of flesh and blood."

"As am I." The words ring accusingly in the air.

"We have access to the most technologically advanced tracking systems in the world," Truman interrupts, forgetting to pretend he's not listening. "We've come a long way in the past century. I could allocate a team to finding him – we can use facial recognition software, spyware, hack into..."

He doesn't finish.

"That would require involving civilians," Harrison points out, not unkindly. "This is a matter for the Guild."

Truman's face falls, but he nods his acceptance, ever respectful.

"Where do you think you're going?" Harrison asks as I get to my feet.

"Home." I say, heading for the door.

"You can't just walk out! We're not done here."

"Yes, we are." I stop at the door and turn back to face him. "I am doing everything I can to right the wrong of my sister's mistake, Harrison. I could disappear just as easily as Fletcher, but I'm here - I'm trying - and I will keep trying, no matter how long it takes. But," I pause and meet his furious gaze, "the Guild lost its control over me the same day that Fletcher made me immortal. You would be wise to remember that."

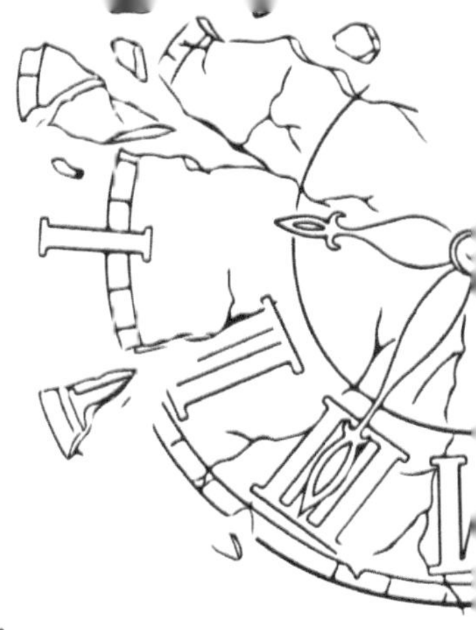

THREE
A DARING STREET RAT

THE TEMPUS GUILD operates covertly under the front of an international corporation called Tempus Trading. Rather unoriginal, if you ask me, but no one ever has. Thankfully, unlike Harrison's office, the exterior of the building has been revolutionised over the years and now blends perfectly with the modern commercialism surrounding it in the Phoenix Metropolitan Area. Unlike *Perpetual Life* across the street, the only branding on the building is an understated block-lettered sign which reads *Tempus Trading*. As far as the rest of the world is concerned, the multi-billion-dollar enterprise is involved in global trade, technological advancement, and has a penchant for successful mergers and acquisitions. Which, incidentally, it does. It's just that that isn't exactly Tempus's primary function.

In reality, the Tempus Guild is run by six Masters who form the High Council and report only to the Grand Master – currently Jonathan Harrison. Under these seven people, the rest of the Guild is comprised of all the living members of the seven families. We are born into a tradition and are honour-bound to serve. Once a Grand Master is selected, his High Council is formed – with one person from each of the remaining six families. These council members are strategically placed in positions of power across the continents, masterminding and manipulating everything from declarations of war to the performance of the stock exchange. Over the course of humanity's existence, many conspiracy theories have cropped up surrounding the Guild, none of which have ever been proven. The council have been called gods, legends, or, more recently, the Illuminati, but no one has ever discovered their true identities or real purpose.

"Clarke!" Truman catches me as I step into the marble foyer. "You're heading for the canyon, aren't you?"

"Yes." Each time I resolve an anomaly I return to visit Fletcher's clock, to write down the new name which has appeared.

"Be careful," Truman warns. "A private organisation just applied for a permit to investigate a six-mile stretch of the Colorado River, in the Marble Canyon region."

The implication of his words is not lost on me. Every few years since 1917, some institution or private entrepreneur stumbles across a digital record of Fletcher's article and tries to find the 'High Cavern' of legend. Fletcher had been missing a year when the article appeared in the Arizona Gazette, claiming that the Smithsonian Institute had discovered a network of tunnels in the heart of the Grand Canyon. Considering what really exists within the walls of the canyon, the Guild immediately suspected Fletcher, particularly since the author was named as one G.E Kincaid. As if any further proof was needed, the date of publication was April 5th – exactly a year to the day that Anna died and Fletcher disappeared. The Smithsonian denied all and any knowledge of the article, and claimed to have no record of the author, but the damage had been done. Scores of archaeological teams descended upon the canyon, creating havoc for the Guild which went on for months.

"I can't believe that, with all the resources at our disposal, we can't just make that article go away," I tell Truman. As head of our Tech department I suspect he takes it as a personal insult.

"We do," he insists. "We delete all digital imprints of the blasted thing and you won't find it in any public records, but every now and again it crops up to haunt us. The internet is a big place."

"You've got to love the digital age."

"I still wonder why he did it," Truman muses.

"Revenge - a whim, it could've been for any number of reasons. Knowing Fletcher, he probably thought it was funny."

Truman's eyes widen and he glances around as if to check we're not being overheard, which is ludicrous considering how many surveillance cameras are installed inside the building.

"What was he like?"

"Fletcher?" I pause, recalling the man I once knew. "He was sweet. Charming and too smart for his own good. He was ambitious but it made him frustrated. He wanted more from life."

"More?" Truman is practically salivating. Fletcher may be an abomination, but his story is legendary.

"He didn't have much," I explain. "He was the orphan son of a coal miner."

I allow myself a small smile.

"You know what's funny, Truman? The fact that the mighty Tempus Guild was bested by a simple street rat."

Leaving him with that parting thought, I turn to go, unfastening my belt as I do and wrapping it in my ruined hoodie.

"Tell Vincent I say hi," Truman calls after me and I wave my hand noncommittally over my shoulder. As always, speaking of Fletcher has stirred up memories that, try as I might, I cannot banish from my mind.

1913, *The Kennedy Estate, Charleston, West Virginia*

"FATHER!" My cry carried down the stairs and my father paused in the open doorway. I lifted my skirts and practically flew down the stairs, fearful of keeping him waiting. It took me only a few seconds but it was enough time for him to pull the pocket watch from his breast and examine it.

"Your scarf, father! You forgot your scarf." I waved it before me as if he might not take me at my word.

The sunlight streamed in through the open doorway behind him, creating a bear-like silhouette. My father was a strapping man, although his paunch had expanded vastly in recent years. His whiskery grey moustache pulled tight as his lips pursed in annoyance.

"I'm late, Clara," he grunted, stowing the watch back in his waistcoat. His trousers were cuffed, ankle-length and perfectly creased, his morning coat thick, heavy and uninviting. My father had always been a stern man, but more so since my mother had passed away two years ago. Secretly I wondered if it was her he missed or the stillborn son who had been buried beside her. In my father's mind, sons were something to be prized. Daughters, on the other hand, were something to be ordered about.

"The Guild doesn't like to be kept waiting," he sniffed, straightening his white tie.

The Guild. A mixture of fear and awe rose up to merge magnificently in my chest. Newly sixteen, I had only recently learned of my family's heritage and the crucial role it played in mankind's history. The Kennedys were only one of seven founding families, but the way my father told it you would be excused for thinking only ours mattered.

"Yes, Papa," I said, forgetting for a moment how he loathed the French endearment. Anna and I had picked it up on our most recent trip to France, thinking it quaint, but father hadn't agreed. Eager for him to be gone, I handed him the scarf and followed him out onto the porch and down the front path, walking, as ever, in his shadow.

"Mister Kennedy." A voice both prickly and velvet called out in greeting when we reached the cobbled street. Fletcher Kincaid doffed his cap as he passed, his blue eyes the only splash of colour on the palette of his sooty face. "Miss Clara," he added, daring to grin as his eyes met mine and held them insolently. His behaviour was shameless. He, an urchin orphan who worked the mines, should never so blatantly ogle the daughter of the wealthiest man in Charleston, West Virginia.

"Get out of here, street rat!" my father bellowed, raising his arm. I cringed, waiting to hear the meaty slap of fist meeting flesh, but none was forthcoming. Fletcher dodged easily, bobbing under father's arm and using his temporary distraction to wink at me. I looked away, my cheeks flaming, but had to raise my hand to hide a smile.

By the time I had recovered my composure, Fletcher had fled.

"I'll get you, boy!" Father roared after his departing back.

I HEAD for the train station but I keep far from the tracks. Earlier today I had stowed my backpack in a locker and I only take the time to retrieve it and stash my daggers inside it before I am back on the street, heading uptown. I fleece the stolen wallet as I walk, not even feeling a twinge of guilt for the man who tried to spit on me. It contains a couple of hundred dollars which I shove into my back pocket and a Visa Card which will no doubt have been reported stolen by now. If only Harrison hadn't delayed me so long. I toss the card, along with the wallet and the bloodstained hoodie, into a trash can and survey the streets around me. I take a left and then two right turns until I stand in the shadow of a familiar warehouse building. Wearily, I climb the metal steps of the fire escape and, with one final leap and a short climb, I emerge onto the roof. The grill of an air vent pulls loose easily and I retrieve a thick woollen blanket and a surprisingly comfortable, if grubby, feather pillow. Taking up my usual spot, I curl up on my side and try not to think of the heinous act of Henry Abbott's death.

Waking early the following morning, I stow the blanket and pillow in the vent once more and climb back down to the road. I have slept on more rooftops than I care to count, but I feel safer above the street, away from the prying eyes of the police or vagrants looking to pilfer my hard-won cash. I wander aimlessly around until mid-morning, and then I enter a local shopping mall. Phoenix may be short on rain, but it's brimming with wealthy housewives. The naked gleam of diamonds catches my eye and I stumble against a slim, suntanned woman yapping into her phone.

"Excuse me!" She admonishes nothing but empty air as I disappear into the mall's foot traffic, clutching a Tiffany's necklace. The weight of it in my palm suggests that it's platinum and I stuff it into my pocket with a smirk. This day just got a whole lot better. I walk into a department store and walk out wearing a new hoodie and, best of all, a perfectly fitting Diamondbacks baseball cap, the security tags still lying in the fitting room stall.

Harrison may revile my petty thievery, but I feel no guilt in taking what I need from people who have so much they won't even miss it. In truth, it gives me a certain satisfaction to take from the rich. It's the same satisfaction Fletcher felt stealing from my father. I know this, because I learned everything I know from him.

"Where are you, you son-of-a-bitch?" I murmur, a blind fury coming over me at the thought of him. A passer-by stares at me in confusion, but I disappear once more into the throng, a wraith, no sooner seen than forgotten. I've become used to going unnoticed – blending into a crowd. I could disappear for seconds, minutes, even hours if I needed to, to evade being caught. Fletcher Kincaid, however, had disappeared for a century.

The last time I'd seen him was almost a hundred years ago, in the spring of 1916. It had been a devastating end to a promising friendship, torn apart by the selfish actions of a love-lost girl who committed the ultimate sin. As a man, Fletcher had been charming and intelligent, if a little fickle in affairs of the heart. As an immortal, Fletcher was dangerous. A darkness had settled over him. I could understand, given what Anna had done to him. His rage I could deal with. It was his revenge that I couldn't forgive – a revenge that had turned two mortal friends into immortal enemies.

FOUR
THE HIGH CAVERN OF LEGEND

THE GRAND CANYON stretches 277 miles through the state of Arizona reaching a depth of over a mile. It is one of the world's most remarkable attractions and draws close on five million visitors every year. Tourists flock to marvel at the impressive views, or to indulge in a multitude of activities – rafting, hiking and adventuring their inconvenient asses off, creating a nightmare for the Guild when they trespass on what is believed to be government land, but which is actually owned by the Guild.

In the dead of night, however, in the heart of this natural wonder, there is no one to witness my journey downstream the mighty Colorado River. It is eerily quiet and, alone with my thoughts for the first time since leaving Harrison's office yesterday, I finally face the consequences of Henry Abbott's death. The smug flippancy I displayed at the scene of the accident was for Harrison's benefit only. In truth, my heart aches, my chest is tight and the blood on my hands runs far deeper than the stains I washed away last night. Nineteen-year-old Henry Abbot is not the first innocent I have killed, nor will he be the last, but that doesn't make it any easier. Sinking down into the bottom of the small rubber dinghy, I let the tears flow freely.

Henry's face, terrified and determined, is crystal clear behind my closed eyelids. He had been so close – so very close – to doing what he was supposed to do but then he had faltered. Henry had faltered and made an alternate choice, all because of a decision my sister Anna had made almost a hundred years ago. A decision that I have paid for every single day between then and now. A decision I will be paying for, for the rest of eternity, if I don't find Fletcher.

My tears run dry, eventually. As they always do, eventually. I kill the engine and less than five minutes later, the prow of the dinghy bumps gently against the cliff face, as though my emotions have been trained to endure only the relatively short distance between where I entered the river and my arrival at this point. The current swirls into an almost invisible crevice in the rock, creating a small but powerful whirlpool that keeps the dinghy in place. I replace my belt and, slinging my tattered leather backpack over my shoulders, I glance up at the imposing, sheer wall before me. There are footholds, if one knows where to look, but they would test even the most intrepid explorer.

Higher and higher I climb, sure-footed and swift, my hands finding purchase in the layered bands of red rock which is still warm, holding the heat of the sun's rays even though the night air is crisp and cool. The upward climb is familiar and I barely raise a sweat, the physical exercise doing much to distract me from the sadness that Henry's death has wrought. About fifteen hundred feet from the top I reach a small hollow set back in a crevice and I pull myself up onto the ledge, my legs dangling over the edge. I take a moment to catch my breath and enjoy the sight of an endless blanket of stars above me before I turn and crawl through a narrow opening in the rock. I experience a familiar sense of mild claustrophobia and then the path opens up ahead and I'm able to stand.

The passageway is narrow and dark, but the air is neither dank nor oppressive. The muted, musky scent of wood and lilac wafts toward me and I press on. A few yards in, the corridor splits and I take a left turn, winding deeper into the depths of the canyon itself.

Left, right, left again, I walk for a full fifteen minutes, never needing to check my bearings; the smooth walls as familiar as if they bounded my own backyard. The entrance to the cavern is a maze of tunnels, impossible to navigate unless you have been shown the way. Without knowing you could stumble around for days, never advancing further than a hundred feet from the entrance.

When I reach the end of the labyrinth, I step out of the corridor onto the edge of a vertical cliff, a sheer drop through nothing but a thousand feet of empty air if I fall. A few decades back, a member of the Cleveland family delivering food stores plummeted to his death. The Guild classified it as an accident, but I happen to know that the boy had feelings for his sister's arrogant, homophobic husband and I suspect he had decided to put himself out of his misery. After all, the food supplies had been found neatly packed against the far wall of the ledge, along with the boy's torch and his jacket.

I pull a bottle of water from my pack taking a few sips before stashing it and withdrawing my torch. Across the divide a cliff-face looms, as high as the canyon wall outside. I shine the beam directly on it. The red rock is more vibrant here, away from the dulling effect of the elements, and gemstones twinkle under the powerful LED light as it sweeps across the surface.

Setting the torch between my teeth, I shoulder my backpack once more and turn to face the tunnel opening. Confidently, I slide my legs over the edge of the cliff, lowering myself down. I am hanging on by my fingertips when my feet find the first step and I rest my weight on the top rung of a ladder that is impossible to spot from above.

It takes only a few minutes to descend to the dusty floor below, and a few more to cross the pitch black space between this side of the ravine and the other. Finally, I duck through yet another opening, this one the entrance to the final passageway. As I walk, the darkness gives way to light, a soft amber glow that brightens with each step. A low hum becomes audible, a vibration that fills the space around me, enveloping me in the sanctity of this hallowed place. The passageway expands and enlarges, gradually widening until, finally, I reach the end. Above my head the word *Tempus* is etched into the smooth stone.

"Time," I murmur, translating the ancient word and then I step out of the passage and into the Hall of Clocks.

The slow countdown of over seven billion clocks creates a crackling energy that permeates the air. The cavern is enormous, the size of a city and stretches away from me as far as the eye can see. The Hall was created by the Sovereign when he gave mankind life. Whether magic or miracle, I can't begin to guess, but since the Hall was established, the clocks record all human life, counting down the years, days, hours, minutes and seconds of every person on the planet. For every death there is a new life and the clock of the deceased will begin again, a new name etched on its face, a new life to be counted down. No numbers mark the perfect spheres, only simple dials, moving at different speeds, depending on the life expectancy and a few words, branded in fiery golden ink. As the human population had grown, so more clocks appeared on the walls, simply winking into existence as if someone had come along and hung them there.

"It's about time you got here," a deep voice croaks, husky as a result of going too long without use. My eyes slide left to find Vincent standing only a few feet away, hand outstretched. His black robe is dusty and, with a pang, I notice the additional grey streaks in his hair that weren't there when I last saw him only a few months ago. This place ages people prematurely, as if the Hall steals life from the only living entity in a city full of death. Still, his eyes, crinkle at the corners as he grins at me expectantly, twinkling with the mischievous light of the eternal prankster.

I smile back at him automatically.

"Hello, Clock Keeper," I say.

Vincent doesn't respond to my teasing greeting. Instead, he waggles his fingers at me.

"I thought you would have forgotten by now," I huff, slipping the backpack from my shoulders.

"Never," Vincent replies. "Now hand them over."

I scrabble through the meagre contents of my pack, tossing aside a black sweater, my mobile phone, purse, torch and water bottle. Finally I find what I'm looking for in the zippered compartment at the front. With great ceremony I present Vincent with a couple of squashed chocolate bars. He snatches them from my hand, tearing the packaging of a Butterfinger and cramming half the bar into his mouth.

"Well that's charming," I say, and then, bending to retrieve the wrapper, "you know you shouldn't be littering in here, right?" Vincent grins, chocolate dribbling down his chin and I turn away, covering my eyes in mock disgust.

"Do you want something to drink?" he asks. "Delivery came yesterday so I think there may still be some caffeinated drinks left."

"I'm okay, thanks."

He nods, opening the small refrigerator in the corner of the room and pulling out a soda for himself.

"You have no idea how lucky you are to have power down here," I say, remembering the Hall as I first saw it – dark and ominous with no creature comforts.

"I wouldn't have served if we didn't," he burps. "I don't know how you survived down here in the dark with no light or running water. Thank the Sovereign for generators and gas."

"You do know you wouldn't have had a choice," I remind him. The Guild dictates who serves as Clock Keeper. It's not something you can turn down, even now, in the twenty-first century.

"I would've run," he grins.

I have known Vincent Washington for almost ten years, ever since he was selected to replace Rebecca Jefferson as the keeper of the clocks. Rebecca and I had been close – one might almost have called us friends – and I had been sad to see her go. It had taken years for us to strike up our unlikely camaraderie. Vincent, however, had taken approximately thirty minutes to break through the defensive wall I kept permanently erected around myself. It was 2008 and I had just celebrated my hundred and tenth birthday, although I'd officially stopped ageing at the age of eighteen.

. . .

2008, *The Hall of Clocks, Grand Canyon, Arizona*

"YOU'RE NOT SUPPOSED to be in here," Vincent announced the second he clapped eyes on me and noticed that my hands were empty, thus not bearing supplies for him. He said this with the utmost calm, as though strange women appeared in the Hall of Clocks every other day.

"My name is Clara Kennedy," I replied, not in the mood to explain myself. I already missed Rebecca – Vincent's predecessor - who was no doubt catching up on a decade of technological advancement. I hoped she had finally gotten herself a decent haircut.

Vincent barely batted an eyelash.

"Oh, right. Well in that case, you wouldn't happen to have any candy, would you?"

That was just how he was, I soon realised. Vincent was unflappable, steadfast, dependable and took everything in his stride. To be fair, he obviously knew who I was. No member of the Guild could plead ignorance at the mention of Clara Kennedy – the infamous Clock Keeper whose sister had created the first immortal and set in motion a sequence of events that would create anomalies in the very fabric of time for all eternity and had then killed herself so she couldn't be held accountable.

"You've done this job, then?" Vincent had asked, and his curiosity had been sincere, although I didn't know why at the time.

"For about a week," I replied darkly. I didn't feel up to re-telling the whole tragic story for the benefit of some snot-nosed kid who wanted to hear about the Kennedy curse first-hand. Instead, Vincent surprised me once again.

"Great! Have you got any pointers? I'm bored to death and I've only been here a few weeks."

And so began an unlikely friendship. Vincent had never pushed me to speak of the past, but I had told him anyway. It had felt good to confide in someone who genuinely didn't care one way or another. It was liberating, but also oddly cathartic. Vincent didn't judge Anna for her actions. In fact, he found something beautiful in her sacrifice, and for the first time I considered the fact that I was not necessarily the enemy – the monster that everyone believed me to be. Vincent made me feel that perhaps I wasn't quite as alone as I had thought.

VINCENT HAS FINALLY EATEN his full and he stows the few remaining chocolate bars in the top drawer of his desk. Harrison would have a heart attack if he knew that the priceless antique was cluttered with candy and dirty magazines, but I don't have the heart to deny Vincent these small favours -not when he's sacrificed ten years of his life in service to the Guild. That is the exact amount of time each Clock Keeper protects the Hall of Clocks. Ten years, spent in isolation, watching over time and death. It is the burden of being chosen. There is beauty here. The hideous brutality of death is observed outside these hallowed halls, while within them, death is simply an endless, peaceful hum of billions of ticking dials; but it is a lonely life. The only perk of being the Clock Keeper is that, once you have served your time, you are no longer required to serve the Guild. They leave you alone for the rest of your life.

"So," Vincent turns to me, a caramel smear running from lip to chin. "Henry Abbott. Did you do it?"

"You should know."

"You know I won't look at it," he rebukes. "It's against the rules."

I heave a sigh and walk across the antechamber. On the far wall, hidden from view by an ancient wooden screen is the only clock in this hall that matters. The clock which had once belonged to Fletcher.

Vincent turns aside as I pull the screen away from the wall, the grating screech of wood against rock all too familiar. I take a deep breath, bracing myself, and then I raise my eyes. The clock is identical to the others in the Hall save for a small, narrow slit the length of a dagger's blade, just left of the pin of the rotating dial. I cannot look upon the imperfection without thinking of my sister, for she was the one who damaged it. I focus on the dial, golden and glinting, ticking backward, constant, inevitable and delaying the moment when I will have to look at the words engraved in golden letters in the middle of the clock face. My mind registers that something is different, but before I can place my finger on it I am distracted.

"Could you hurry it up, Clarke?" Vincent calls. He still has his back to me, his foot tapping impatiently on the floor. I watch that foot, mesmerised, as my mind takes me back.

1914, *The Kennedy Estate, Charleston, West Virginia*

"WHERE ARE YOU GOING?" I grabbed Anna's arm, wrenching her around to face me. I had been watching Sophie Lincoln playing the piano, her hands dancing across the keys with a grace I could never emulate despite hours of tutoring, when I had spotted my sister sneaking out of the room. Her scarlet skirt was a dead giveaway among the sober and muted colours worn by my father's guests. After the outbreak of the war, many women had stopped wearing jewellery and lavish clothing had fallen by the wayside, but my sister had insisted, claiming that whether or not she lived a plainer lifestyle would hardly influence the outcome. Young, spoilt society girls that we were, neither Anna nor I had ever truly appreciated the horror of the war, although Anna had been nothing short of devastated when father had cancelled our annual shopping trips to Paris.

"Where are you going?" I asked again.

"I need some air," Anna replied. The roses blooming on her cheeks and the sparkle in her eyes had belied her words. I should have known she would try to sneak off the second my back was turned.

"Anna, you know what father will do if he catches you outside!"

"He won't know," Anna had replied smugly, inclining her head across the room to where father stood smoking a cigar. "He's been buttonholed by Sir Rawlings for the past ten minutes and I expect he won't escape the man's clutches for some time to come."

She had gathered her skirts and continued on, her slippered feet making no sound as the feathers fell from her hair, leaving a trail of breadcrumbs for father to follow. I had hesitated only a moment before rushing after her, scooping up the evidence as I went.

When we left the grounds my heart started to stutter in my chest.

"Anna, we shouldn't be out here."

"Hush, Clara. We're almost there!"

I heard the music before we turned the corner - a playful birdsong, tranquil and teasing. The lilting melody of the harmonica pierced the quiet night drawing us toward it.

A small group had gathered around the warmth of a fire. A few couples were dancing, their soot-streaked faces more beautiful than any of the painted ladies currently ensconced in our drawing room vying for father's affections. Others sat, feet tapping in time to the music, the firelight flickering red-gold over their drab clothing, bringing it to life.

"There he is," Anna had breathed. I hadn't needed to ask her who she was talking about. My eyes were drawn to him without any prompting. Fletcher Kincaid.

Fletcher stood alone, his left leg propped on a stump of wood, tapping his beat as he summoned the tune. The harmonica obscured the wicked curve of his lips and his newsboy cap was pulled low over his head, but his devilish eyes danced beneath its brim, watching everything. They were the eyes, not quite of a sinner, but of a saint who simply hadn't sinned yet.

The melody lilted, slowing in tempo until the harmonica dropped to his side, forlorn as the silence that broke Fletcher's spell. I blinked, becoming aware of our surroundings as if coming out of a trance. The curious gaze of a dozen pairs of eyes prickled my skin.

"Miss Anna, Miss Clara," Fletcher inclined his head toward us in greeting, breaking the silence. My name lingered on his lips, deeper, more velvet than my sister's. Anna didn't seem to notice.

"Mister Kincaid." She curtsied low before him, her skirts sending up eddies of dust.

"You shouldn't be out here at this time," Fletcher cautioned, but his smiling lips defied his words. He was happy to see us.

"You're right," I said, snatching at Anna's sleeve and turning away from the heat of his gaze. "Come, Anna."

"I'll walk with you," Fletcher offered, ignoring the vehement shaking of my head behind her back

"Why, how kind of you, Mister Kincaid," Anna said, taking the arm he offered.

The walk back to the Kennedy Estate was brief, but, treated to the sight of Fletcher's broad back and my sister's perfect profile, her face constantly turned up toward him, it felt longer. We were almost at the front path when the sound of voices reached us.

"People are leaving!" I whispered, horror-struck. "Quickly, Anna, go around the house. We'll enter through the kitchen and pray that papa hasn't noticed our absence!"

Fear lent her feet wings and she slipped away, disappearing into the shadows of the Red Maple trees. I made to follow her, but a strong hand gripped my arm.

"Fletcher!" Alone now, I automatically reverted to the familiarity of using his first name. Still, despite the friendship we had cultivated over the past year, away from the prying eyes of my father, I was stunned that he would lay his hand on me. At my harsh tone, he immediately released me.

"I am sorry, Clara, but I must speak with you before you leave."

"I have to go, my father..."

"Then let me be quick," he interrupted, pulling me deeper into the trees, "for I do not know when we will see one another again."

"That's very dramatic, Fletcher, considering how often we find ourselves in one another's company." Even after all this time, I found myself blushing. My friendship with Fletcher was one borne of mutual fondness and a deep-seated need to defy my father, but it still weighed heavily on my conscience.

"Besides which," I added, "you see me every Sunday morning in church!"

"And oh, how I do adore the rare sight of the back of your head through the congregation," he teased.

"It is not my fault that my family's pew is at the front and you are relegated to the back with your lot."

He chuckled at that.

"Oh, Clara. How far you have come, but you are still not entirely able to forsake your snobbery. I do wonder, while admiring the intricate weave of your pompadour, if you are perhaps praying for your sins."

"Don't!" I lifted my finger at him.

"Did old Sir Radley ever discover what happened to his pocket watch?" Fletcher sniped.

"For your information, the watch was on his dresser when he returned home."

Fletcher clutched his chest in mocking surprise.

"An honest thief! I am impressed, Clara. How did you manage to sneak it into his house?"

The sounds of yet more guests leaving brought me fearfully to my senses.

"I must go! Anna will be wondering where I am and if father finds me here with you he'll certainly kill me for it!"

He nodded, once, and then retreated, melding into the shadows while I fled up the path.

"CLARKE?" Vincent's foot has stopped tapping and he's watching me quizzically. "Is this going to take all day?"

"Sorry!" I stammer, shaking my head to clear it and turning back to the clock. This time I zoom straight to the words.

"Oh God!" My hand flies to my mouth, the blood draining from my face. No wonder something felt wrong. It's the dial. The dial is moving too fast. The room seems to spin, contracting and flowing, pulling everything around me into the space of a two-inch section of golden text. "Oh God no!"

"What?" Vincent's panic is muted, his voice seeming to come from far away, as my mind tries to block out the awful truth.

"Clarke, what's wrong?"

"It's a baby," I croak, turning to look at him with haunted eyes. "The next name on Fletcher's clock is a baby."

FIVE
ELEVEN CLOCK KEEPERS

"YOU CAN'T KILL A BABY, CLARKE." Vincent says it for the third time, still trying to elicit a response from me. He hands me a Snickers Bar and I take it automatically, but I don't eat it. I'd throw up if I tried. "I mean, there's no way you can kill a baby, right?"

"Of course I can't kill a baby!" I yell, the words racing out of the antechamber and into the hall, dancing and morphing until they return in an ugly echo: *baby, baby, baby*.

"What are you going to do?"

"I don't know." I drop my head into my hands, smearing chocolate in my hair. "I can't eat this." I hand it back and, unthinking, Vincent shoves it into his mouth. "According to the clock, this child will die in eight months. Which means I have eight months to find a miracle."

"It would probably be easier to find Fletcher Kincaid."

I throw him a look that would strike fear into the heart of lesser mortals – those not half-delirious with loneliness and hyped up on Reese's Peanut Butter Cups.

"Look, Clarke, I get what you're trying to do and I support it for the most part, but you better do something fast. There's no way I'm letting you hurt an innocent child."

"Do you think that this has been fun for me?" I snap. "Do you think dealing with these anomalies is just part of the job – faceless, nameless people who I can just forget?" I take a deep breath and then recite, by heart: "Viktor Ivanov, 48 years old, died in Saint Petersburg, January 10th 1964. Celine Dubois, 33 years old, died in Paris, September 21st 1997. Henry Abbott, 19 years old, died 18th March 2016, right here in Arizona. Cody Johnson," My voice grows smaller, the name still burned into my vision, even with my eyes closed, "8 months old, dies November 6th, 2016."

Empathy shines in Vincent's green eyes, his hands resting near his ears, as if he had wanted to block out my words but couldn't bring himself to do it.

"He's not dead yet, Clarke."

"He's supposed to die." I can feel a sob welling up inside of me, building momentum with each second that I try to contain it.

"You don't have to do this... maybe we could just leave him alone and let him..."

"I have to stop the anomalies!"

"Why?"

"Because my sister screwed up! If Anna hadn't tried to interfere – if she hadn't damaged Fletcher's clock – none of this would've happened." I stride across the antechamber and prise the clock from the wall, wishing for all the world I could smash it into oblivion.

"Put it down!" Vincent's voice has lost all trace of softness, all hint of light and familiarity. This is the voice of the Clock Keeper – the one oath-bound to protect the clocks at any cost. I feel the prick of a blade at my neck, the cool edge of steel on skin.

"You should know better than to draw a sword on me," I growl.

"Don't make me do this, Clara." The use of my old name is proof of how serious he is. "Please, put it back."

My daggers are at my hips, but, holding the clock as I am with both hands, I cannot reach for them without dropping it. The weight of Fletcher's clock is my burden, both literally and figuratively, and I have grown to hate it, but damaging it further will only cause another rift – another fracture in the timeline. I lift my arms and hang it back in place, hearing the small click as the grooved wood slots into place. Vincent slowly withdraws his blade, keeping his eyes averted. It is the cardinal rule of all Clock Keepers – never to look at the clocks – never to know when death is coming. The Clock Keepers are only here to protect the hall, not to interfere with time or death. It was the only rule my sister had had to follow and the only rule she had ever broken.

"Cover it back up," Vincent pleads, but he has regained some of his usual flippancy. "That thing gives me the creeps."

I slide the wooden screen back into place and the set of his shoulders relaxes.

"Are you okay?"

"No."

"You have to find Fletcher." Vincent musters a confidence I certainly don't feel. "And before you say it, I know you've searched for decades, but this is different. You no longer have a choice." He glances at the screen, his thoughts obviously on what lies beyond it. A child, who, unless I find Fletcher, will die by my hand in a little over eight months.

"Six weeks," Vincent mused, checking the calendar on his desk. The modern desk-pad is completely out of place in this ancient setting, but we've evolved. Large black crosses have been drawn through the days gone by. "I have less than six weeks before I get out of here. Why did this have to happen on my watch?"

"Technically you'll be gone by the time I have to decide," I remind him. Vincent's ten years are almost up. On the sixteenth of April a new Clock Keeper will be appointed. It's a date I will always remember, given that it was the date I became immortal. The date I was replaced as the Clock Keeper and charged with finding Fletcher Kincaid – the man who cursed me with longevity.

"You think that I'll be able to go about a normal life not knowing how this unfolds?" Vincent asks. "I want to help, Clarke."

"You can't." I reply, without thinking, my attention caught by the calendar and the small black asterisk marking the sixteenth. I wonder which of the seven families' turn it is. I've lost track, but I suspect it might be the Lincoln's.

"What does that mean?" Vincent sounds hurt and I try to cheer him up.

"Look on the bright side: In six weeks you get to go back to your life with a fat bank balance and anything your heart desires." *Unlike me*, I fail to add. *I'll still be stuck in this private hell trying to find a ghost and set right the wrongs of my love-sick sister.*

This brings him up short, as if he's only just considered something.

"Do you ever see Rebecca?"

I consider lying, but quickly decide against it. I shake my head.

"No. Not since she left this place."

"But, *I'll* still see you, right? I mean, you'll visit?"

"The Guild doesn't tell me where you end up." It's a pathetic excuse and he calls me out on it instantly.

"That's bullshit, Clarke. You're not only good at picking pockets. Let's not pretend you don't have access to all the Guild's information. There's not a member of Tempus alive who wouldn't move heaven and earth to help Clara Kennedy." That's true. As much as the Guild dislikes me, they know the importance of the mission I've been tasked with.

"It's complicated, Vincent. When you leave here, you are given a fresh start – the chance to make a real life for yourself. You don't need to be burdened with this."

His face hardens.

"How many Clock Keepers have you known in your lifetime?" he asks.

"Including myself?" My feeble attempt at a joke.

"You don't count – you only served for what, a month?"

"More like a week," I admit, recalling the disastrous incident that occurred on my watch. I heave a sigh and do a quick mental calculation. "Eleven, including Anna."

"Your sister doesn't count either. She never left this place."

"Ten, then."

"And how many of those ten did you ever see again once they'd served their time here?"

I pretend to count.

"None."

His involuntary intake of breath makes me wince, but I meet his gaze levelly.

"You know what, Clarke? You're a shitty friend."

"I know." I retrieve my backpack.

"Thanks for the candy. I'd offer to walk you out but, you know, rules and all."

At the entrance to the Hall I stop, not wanting things to end like this.

"I'll see you, Vincent."

"No," he says sadly. "You probably won't."

My journey out of the canyon is different from any other time I've made it. My heart is heavy with the guilt that Vincent's words have evoked. In truth, over the years the Clock Keepers have been my only friends, the only people who take the time to talk to me without rushing, without reminding me that my sole purpose in life is to find Fletcher and bring him in. I try to console myself with the fact that my occasional visits have provided companionship they would otherwise not have had, but it's no use. Vincent is right. I am a shitty friend.

SIX
REGULAR LITTLE ROBIN HOOD

MY FOUL MOOD shadows me all the way to Aunt Elizabeth's – my home when I'm in Arizona. Technically, Elizabeth isn't my aunt, but rather a distant cousin a few times removed. Neither my sister nor I had had children, but my father's brother Jeremy, who had served as Grand Master of the Guild until our family's spectacular fall from grace, had had two strapping sons. Ironically, they had produced between them only a single daughter. Frail and weak-chested like her mother, the child had survived the influenza pandemic of the twenties, only to fall victim to a fatal lung disease twenty years later, but not before she had born her husband a bouncing baby girl with the constitution of an ox. Elizabeth Kennedy was as immune to illness as her mother had been predisposed.

The last remaining Kennedy besides myself, Elizabeth is also, technically, our family's representative on the High Council. She has held her seat for most of her adult life despite the fact that she refuses to attend council meetings or play any role in Tempus whatsoever. The council can do nothing about it. According to tradition, they have to allow her the Kennedy seat as long as she lives. Like Anna and I, Elizabeth had never had children and the Kennedy line would die with her. As I was likely to live forever, technically, it lived on with me, but I don't think I count. No one can say for sure what it means to the Guild, to lose one of the seven families. All we know for certain is that it isn't supposed to happen. It's a consequence, another anomaly, caused by my sister's actions.

It's late afternoon by the time I let myself in to the modest, but warm little house. Elizabeth emerges from the kitchen as I slam the front door shut.

"Bad day, Clarke?" She asks wryly. Her white hair is neatly pinned, flour falling soft as snow from her trembling hands. Elizabeth is always baking. She may be eighty years old, but in her twinkling green eyes I can still see the child I had watched grow up.

"You could say that." Despite my dour mood, I drop a dutiful kiss on her leathery cheek.

"Did you get the boy?"

"I did. Henry Abbott is dead."

"Good girl." She pats my cheek fondly.

"I'm not sure 'good' is the word I'd use."

"Henry's time was up – that was decided by someone far more powerful than you before time began. Now stop moping child and go and get cleaned up. You smell awful."

"I'm older than you, Aunt Elizabeth, in case you've forgotten," I grumble, but I oblige, heading for the stairs.

"Yes, but you're ridiculously youthful," she teases.

I scrub myself until my skin is pink and raw, letting the warm water wash away the dust along with the suds of shampoo from my hair. I dump my filthy clothes in the bin in my room and pull on an identical pair of faded jeans and a nondescript T-shirt before trudging back down the stairs.

I'm combing my fingers through my damp hair when I enter the kitchen and take a seat at the table.

"You should dry your hair," Elizabeth scolds. "You'll catch your death of cold."

I raise my brow and she grins, her sagging skin pulling around her eyes in a plethora of wrinkles. I don't get sick. I haven't been sick since 1916, and she knows it. One of the many perks of immortality. I can be hurt, I can bleed, but I always recover and I never get sick.

"I saw Harrison today," I say, pinching a ripe peach from the wire rack beside me.

Elizabeth snorts.

"How is the miserable old git?"

"Miserable."

"Not surprising. I think everyone's on edge, especially with the anniversary coming up." April 5th will mark the centennial of the day Fletcher became immortal.

"You'd think he'd get tired of hiding after a hundred years," I say, wiping a trickle of peach juice from my chin with the back of my hand. "Maybe he'll turn himself in and save me the trouble of finding him."

She ignores that, as she often does when I mention Fletcher.

"What happened?" she asks instead. I knew my bad mood wouldn't go without repercussions.

My petulance vanishes, replaced by the heavy weight of my discovery.

"There's a new name on Fletcher's clock. It's a baby."

Even Elizabeth can't hide her emotional response to that. She gives a small gasp and her hand flies to her mouth. I focus on the familiar liver spots and perfectly trimmed fingernails.

"I'm so sorry, Clarke." Unlike Harrison, Aunt Elizabeth rolled quite comfortably with my new name at the turn of the century.

"He's not dead yet," I say, echoing Vincent's words.

"He's as good as."

"I really don't want to hear that."

"I know," she relents slightly, "but what else can you do?"

"I'm going to find Fletcher." Perhaps if I say the words often enough I might actually start to believe them.

Aunt Elizabeth doffs her apron and comes to sit across from me at the cracked wooden table. She interlaces her fingers, twiddling her thumbs, a thoughtful expression on her face. I wait, knowing that she'll speak when she's arranged her thoughts.

"Let's go through it again," she mutters, and I drop my head in frustration.

"Aunt Elizabeth, we've been through this about a hundred times."

"Well then we'll make it a hundred and one," she snaps. "Maybe we missed something. Start at the beginning."

I close my eyes knowing it's pointless to argue with her. Then I take a deep breath and begin.

"Anna must have seen Fletcher's clock. I don't know if she went looking for it, or if she stumbled across it by accident, but she knew he was going to die..."

"No," Aunt Elizabeth interrupts firmly. "Let's go back to the very beginning. Before your sister was chosen as the Clock Keeper. I want to examine Fletcher as the man he was before."

My mind conjures up the image all too easily: a pair of winter blue eyes hooded beneath the familiar newsboy cap.

"Flagstaff?" I ask.

"No. You were only in Arizona for a few weeks before it happened. I want to know what happened before that. Tell me about West Virginia."

1915, *Charleston, West Virginia*

THE WHEELS of our carriage clattered over the gravel street, announcing our impending arrival to all and sundry. Beneath my parasol, I peeked out at the crowd, able to observe them without anyone knowing.

"Hurry up, Clara!" my father barked, climbing down onto the street the second we stopped. Anna was already beside him, her lace collar adorned with mother's locket.

I hastily closed the parasol, feeling the warmth of the sunlight on my cheeks. I didn't need Anna's surprise squeeze of my hand to alert me to Fletcher's presence. He stood among the working class, separated from high society by a no-man's land of dusty earth. In his hands, the beaten harmonica, which he clutched with as much reverence as my father did his Bible. Members of Tempus held a variety of beliefs, but they all agreed on one thing. The creator existed. We knew him as the Sovereign, but God worked just as well.

"Inside," father instructed, casting a disapproving glance at the crowd around Fletcher and ushering us in the opposite direction, as if he thought that simple proximity might taint us.

During the long sermon I found it impossible to concentrate on the Pastor's words. I could feel Fletcher's eyes boring into the back of me. My hands strayed nervously to my hair and the jewelled pins holding it in place and I fidgeted incessantly.

"Sit still!" Father hissed after a few minutes, and I instantly became a statue of devout attentiveness. I would never admit it to Fletcher, but I had prayed for forgiveness for stealing old Mister Radley's pocket watch. I hadn't taken it from his person, as I'd led Fletcher to believe in my boasting, but had simply picked it up when he'd dropped it in the dirt after service one Sunday and stowed it in my skirts. Fletcher had been teaching me how to pickpocket for months, although he did it mostly in jest, claiming I would never be able to do it. I had wanted to wipe the smug expression from his face.

"HE'D BE mighty proud of you now," Elizabeth interrupts and I glance up to find her lips puckered in disapproval. I had never admitted to stealing, not since the first time when she had given me the dressing-down of my life, but Elizabeth always seemed to know, whether due to her uncanny intuition, or probably just as a result of her annoying habit of going through my stuff.

"You need to stop going through my room."

"I don't need to. That was a JC Penney hoodie you walked in with this morning. I'm assuming Miss Penney didn't give it to you?"

My jaw drops.

"Really? JC Penney was a man, Aunt Elizabeth. I swear anyone would think you lived under a rock."

"Don't sass me," she warns. "And don't change the subject. You need to stop stealing. It's dishonest."

"I only steal from the rich. They have insurance." Probably with *Perpetual Life*, I think wryly.

"Oh, so you're a regular little Robin Hood, are you?" Her acid tongue stings.

"Do you want to hear the rest or not?"

She waves her hand in a circular motion and I continue.

"NICE HAIR," Fletcher's voice at my ear almost scared me to death and I dropped the book I was holding. My low chignon was not quite yet fashionable enough to go unnoticed, but I had deliberately dressed it down to avoid his teasing.

"Do you think God forgave you?" he asked, coming to sit beside me. Even hidden as we were by the trees in father's orchard, I still felt a thrill of fear.

"For what?" I feigned innocence, but Fletcher was far too shrewd to be fooled.

"For stealing the watch. I know you prayed about it. Rather intently, from what I could see."

"You're just jealous that I succeeded."

"I'm impressed, actually." He stuck his hand into his pocket and withdrew a familiar white glove. "Here." he handed it to me casually.

I recognised it instantly.

"Why do you have Anna's glove?"

He shrugged. "She dropped it in the dirt near my feet after service."

I pressed my lips together to keep from smiling.

"What?" Fletcher asked warily.

"I think my sister has a crush on you."

I waited for his surprise but instead he shrugged again.

"You knew?"

"It's not uncommon for a girl to drop her glove at a man's feet in the hope that that man will return it."

"And yet you didn't? You're giving it to me."

"It wouldn't be fair to entertain your sister's whims."

"Why not?"

"Because she's a Kennedy. There can be nothing between us."

"I'm a Kennedy," I pointed out, my voice small and pained.

"Yes, but you don't want anything more than friendship." The words sounded forced, formal. "That is something I can offer."

"YOU NEVER TOLD ME THAT," Elizabeth's interruption is more emotive this time.

"Told you what?"

"That Fletcher said that to you."

I shrug. "Fletcher said a lot of things. We were friends for years. I couldn't possibly tell you every single conversation we ever had."

"But this one is important!"

"Why? Anna did care for Fletcher, far more deeply than any of us suspected. She loved him. We learned that the hard way."

"Yes," Elizabeth agrees impatiently, "I know that – although I still think Anna's feelings for Fletcher were more childish obsession than genuine love. What I didn't know was that Fletcher cared for *you*."

SEVEN
AN ADMISSION OF AFFECTION

"HOW CAN YOU KNOW THAT?" I ask, the words slipping from my mouth before, too late, I realise my mistake. For so many years I have guarded this one secret – kept it from her, from the Guild, from even Anna when she was alive, and now, in the blink of an eye, that secret has unravelled. Elizabeth's expression morphs slowly from intrigue to stunned comprehension.

"Clarke?" her voice is a low warning.

"Fletcher doesn't care for me," I scramble quickly to deny it. "He hates me."

"He hates you *now*," she corrects. "You better tell me what really happened."

I open my mouth but no words come out. Shaking my head, I get to my feet, wanting to get away from her. These memories are too painful to dredge up. They are stored in the most secret part of myself, under lock and key, covered with so many layers of guilt and regret that I cannot simply sweep them aside.

"Clarke!" Elizabeth has followed me into the hall, her frail hand displaying surprising strength as she seizes hold of my arm and pulls me away from the front door, away from my means of escape.

"I can't," I say, refusing to look at her.

"Clarke," she is pleading now. Elizabeth has only ever tried to help, providing the love and support I so desperately needed. She's the only family I have, but I can't tell her this. I can't tell her that it wasn't Anna's fault after all. That I am the one to blame for everything.

I wrench my arm free. The sudden movement unbalances Elizabeth and she staggers back a few steps but I use the distraction to yank open the front door. She calls my name but I'm already running, my sneakers pounding the pavement, a monotonous drumming that merges with the sound of the click-clack of court shoes down the steps of my memories.

1915, *Charleston, West Virginia*

"ANNA, you can't sneak off again! Father will notice and he'll punish us both!"

My sister snatched her hand away from mine, two bright spots of anger reddening her cheeks.

"This is about Fletcher, isn't it?" I demanded. "You're going to see him."

Her lack of response was as good as an omission.

"Anna, when are you going to realise there's nothing to be gained from this foolishness? Fletcher Kincaid is not of our station." The words were hypocrisy at its best, considering how much time I had been spending with Fletcher over the past year, but my sister didn't know that.

"You don't understand," Anna's chest rose and fell with emotion.

"Understand what?"

"I love him, Clara!" No sooner had the words left her lips than she tried to force them back, covering her mouth with one white-gloved hand.

"You can't... you don't... Anna you can't mean that!" The very thought that she might act on her feelings and incur our father's wrath was terrifying. And beneath that fear, in the darkest corner of me, bloomed an irrational anger at Anna, a green-eyed jealousy that I wouldn't have believed possible. Fletcher was my friend, nothing more, so why did her admission cut me to the bone?

"I do mean it," Anna said, her eyes - so startlingly like my own - more grey than green. A storm brewing. "I love him, Clara."

"You don't even know him!" My protest died on my lips as tears welled in her eyes, plump and perfect, too heavy for her fragile lashes to endure. She was my sister and I could never bear to see her in pain. Desperately I reached for her, pulling her slim frame to my chest. "Oh, Anna," I whispered, my own loss reflected in her agony.

I CAN SEE Anna in my mind's eye as clearly as if it was yesterday, and slowly, my pounding feet slow to a walk. *Where am I running to*? There is nowhere on Earth I can run to escape the truth. I rub savagely at my eyes trying to wipe away the pain and then I turn back to face Aunt Elizabeth's interrogation.

She opens the door immediately after my timid knock.

"Not like you to be so polite," she remarks dryly.

"I'm sorry." I hang my head, ashamed of my earlier behaviour.

"And so you should be." It is all the remonstration I'm going to get, but I hug her anyway, squeezing her bony frame and putting as much apology into the embrace as I can.

"That's quite enough, Clarke." She disentangles herself and looks me right in the eye. I daren't look away. "Come," she instructs, and meekly I follow.

Five minutes later I am back at the kitchen table, my hands cupping the strong cup of coffee Aunt Elizabeth sets before me. She takes the seat opposite and falls silent, waiting for me to find the right words.

"He told me only a few hours after Anna's admission," I begin hesitantly. "I met him in the orchard, as I always did, but something was different. He was different. I suppose I was too, knowing what I did about how Anna felt, but Fletcher was on edge – fidgety and pacing."

"He told you how he felt?" Elizabeth guesses and I nod. "And what did you say?"

This was the moment. After all these years, it would come to light – the part I had played and I take a steadying breath before I can bring myself to speak.

"It came out of nowhere. One minute he was silent and brooding and the next, he was kissing me. It happened so quickly I didn't know how to respond. I was still reeling from Anna's truths and the guilt and the shame overwhelmed me. He was the love of my sister's life!"

A small, sad smile tugs at Aunt Elizabeth's lips.

"You still don't believe she loved him," I say.

"It's not that. It's just that I finally understand something. You claim Fletcher was the love of Anna's life, but it sounds to me like he was the love of yours too, Clarke."

1915, *Charleston, West Virginia*

"WILL YOU PLAY FOR ME?" I asked, gesturing at the harmonica in Fletcher's hand. The tense silence between us was making me uncomfortable, so far removed from our usual light conversation. Anna's admission earlier had me all mixed up, and I wasn't sure I could withstand the guilt I felt that I was spending so much time with him behind her back. There was only friendship between us, but it still felt like a betrayal.

Fletcher stared down at the instrument as though he'd never seen it before and then he dropped it into the soft grass. His eyes met mine, a blazing expression on his face that took me by complete surprise.

"No," he said, determined. "I want to give you something new to pray for in Church on Sunday." His voice was a velvet blend of trepidation and devilry. Before I could react, his lips brushed mine. Soft, sweet and only the briefest of kisses it was, but a kiss nonetheless. My very first and the only one that ever mattered. For just a second, Fletcher wasn't a poor, lower class urchin, but a man of flesh and bone, a man who made me feel that anything was possible, who ignited a fire inside of me that warmed me to the very marrow of my bones. And then reality came crashing down. His status, Anna's feelings, the betrayal I felt that my dearest friend would do this and ruin everything. And, even more shaming, my Kennedy pride and the indignation aroused by the notion that he would dare lay his lips on mine.

My hand whipped back of its own accord and the sting of my palm against his cheek caused tears to prick at my eyelids.

"How dare you, you boorish oaf!" I hissed, an almighty yell contained in the confines of a whisper.

Fletcher fell silent, flummoxed, and I allowed myself a moment of grim satisfaction. But then, the familiar light flared in his eyes. He smiled, as though it was quite worth the consequence.

"Clara, surely you must know how fond I am of you?"

"Don't," I warned, holding up my hand to ward off his words. "Don't you say another word."

"I must speak my heart." He reached for my hands, trapping them within his own warm palms, sending trickles of delight up and over my skin.

"Don't." I whispered, shaking my head from side to side, but there was no stopping the words he had finally summoned the courage to utter.

"I love you, Clara." Not a trace of his usual devilry remained in his clear, open eyes as he squeezed my hands even tighter. "I am in love with you."

I felt the anger rising, unrelenting in my chest. Six little words which ruined everything, and still he wasn't finished.

"I have tried to hold my tongue but I would be betraying my own heart if I didn't tell you this."

"You... you," I searched for the right words but it was my father's which burst from my still tingling lips. "You street rat!"

He flinched at that, the words having far more impact than my palm against his cheek had. Snatching my hands free, I stumbled to my feet, drawing myself up to my full height, as unimpressive as it was. Mustering all of my spoilt upbringing, I gazed down at him disdainfully.

"I am a Kennedy!"

Fletcher's own temper rose as he stood, dwarfing me with his tall frame.

"And I am the orphaned son of a coal miner," he retorted angrily. "I suppose that makes me good for nothing but to shine your pretty shoes."

"Exactly! If my father ever learned..."

"Your father is a tyrant!"

I had no breath to form a response, sucked as it was from my lungs. Fletcher, devil that he was, used my speechlessness in his favour and tried to woo me once more.

"Run away with me, Clara. I know that your father would never approve of me, but I cannot believe you would let him stand in your way. I'm a hard worker, I could provide for you... come with me. We will be married and happy, so long as we are together."

"Have you taken leave of your senses?" I asked, the blood draining from my face. "I couldn't possibly! He would find us – he would find me!" Fletcher could not know the power of the Guild, but I did. There was nowhere on earth they wouldn't find us.

"I know you, Clara," Fletcher said then, head downcast, his eyes hooded beneath the peak of his newsboy cap. "You deserve more than this. You are different to them." He gestured through the trees in the direction of the house, encompassing the occupants in one sweep of his arm. Encompassing Anna. "At least, I like to think so," he added, but I barely heard because having thought of Anna I could now think of nothing else.

"Fletcher," I said, my voice breaking. "Anna... my sister is in love with you." I had never meant to break her confidence, but I needed to say something to get him to stop.

"Your sister is a fanciful girl with romantic ideals." The words were softly spoken, but any slight to Anna brought my blood to a boil.

"How dare you! My sister is warm and kind and deserving of someone far better than you!"

"Then let her find someone better than me!" he yelled. "I don't want her! It is you I lo..."

"No!" This time my hand was gentle, pressing against his lips in an effort to still him. Still, the feel of those lips against my palm made me dizzy. The thought of those lips on mine was encompassing, overwhelmed only by the fear that I would lose his friendship if I allowed this to continue. "Please, Fletcher. Don't say it. I beg this of you. If you care for me at all, then swear you will never speak of this again. I cannot lose my sister and I cannot lose you. Don't make me choose."

ELIZABETH HAS FALLEN SILENT, so still that I feel the urge to shake her, to elicit a reaction. When she finally realises I am not going to continue she picks up my mug and gives me a small smile.

"You did choose, though, didn't you? You chose Anna."

"I couldn't hurt her."

"So, instead, you denied your own feelings. That was very noble of you, Clarke, but a very foolish decision."

"I know that now."

"I still don't understand why Fletcher would court Anna when he was so obviously in love with you. Even if you did reject him," Aunt Elizabeth muses.

"He did it because I asked him to."

"What? Oh, Clarke, why would you do that?"

"I did it because the Guild came for her and I thought she would die of a broken heart. I needed him to bring her back to me. We hadn't spoken since that day at the orchard, but he agreed to help me."

"And she thought he loved her." Aunt Elizabeth's eyes close, her face pinched with sadness. "Oh Lord, girl, a right mess you made for yourself."

Aunt Elizabeth seems to sense that I need a minute and she busies herself making me another cup of coffee. When she's done, she sets it before me with a small plate piled high with chocolate chip cookies. Absentmindedly I pick one up and dunk it in my coffee.

"You blame yourself," Elizabeth says gently. "You shouldn't."

"Who else do I blame? Give me an option and I'll be happy to go along with it."

"Okay," she announces briskly "How about the Guild?"

"The Guild?"

"Yes, why not? After all, the Guild decided that Anna would be the next Clock Keeper, even though she clearly didn't want the job. I've always disagreed with the nomination system. I think the Guild should allow volunteers to serve in the Hall, rather than drawing names out of a hat."

"They don't draw names...."

"I know that," she snaps, "but my point is that the appointed Clock Keepers don't have a choice. It's a recipe for disaster. Drink up," she adds, indicating my rapidly cooling coffee.

"Now," she continues when I've taken an ample swig. "Let's get back on track. So, Anna was selected...?"

I nod, grateful for the reprieve, although I have no doubt she will bring up the topic of my relationship with Fletcher again when she feels I'm ready.

"They came on Christmas Eve, 1915. Anna and I were so frightened in the months leading up to the re-election, but somehow I convinced myself it wouldn't be a Kennedy. Ridiculous, really, considering it was our family's turn. Your mother wasn't born yet, so it came down to Anna or me."

"Did Fletcher know?"

"No," I shook my head violently. "Neither of us ever betrayed the Guild or broke Tempus law. For all our animosity we always believed in the Guild and what it stood for." I set my cup aside in disgust. "Do you know what the worst thing was? I was relieved when they said it was her and not me. I was thankful that my sister would bear the burden."

"That's natural, Clarke. Anyone would feel the same."

"She cried for days, refusing to come out of her room. I kept checking on her – fearful that she would try to flee, but I should have known better. The Kennedys serve the Guild, pure and simple. Eventually, in desperation, I called on Fletcher to get her out of bed. Father had informed the townspeople that Anna was unwell to excuse her absence while he went ahead and made preparations for our journey west. Fletcher hadn't been to see me once since our argument, not even when he heard of Anna's illness."

"Perhaps he was afraid that your father might discover your relationship?"

I can't help but smile at that.

"Fletcher Kincaid wasn't afraid of anything."

"So, you travelled to Arizona?" Elizabeth prompts, and again, I'm relieved to be back in safer territory. As exhausting as it is, reliving our past, Elizabeth is right – there might be some clue in all of this to Fletcher's whereabouts.

"Yes, to Flagstaff. Almost eighteen hundred miles by carriage and horseback. The journey took over a month but we still arrived in plenty of time for Anna to begin her duties by mid-February." I remember saying goodbye to Anna, how she'd clung to me, my dress wet through with her tears. My next words are spoken in a hushed whisper.

"I never saw her again."

By the 5th of April 1916 my sister was dead by her own hand.

Aunt Elizabeth waits for me to compose myself but I can feel my self-control slipping.

"I'm sorry, I need a break," I say, the strain raising my voice to a new pitch.

She glances at her wristwatch and gives a start.

"Heavens, look at the time! You need to rest, go on and get some sleep. We'll continue in the morning."

I don't argue. Dog-tired, I lurch up the stairs and collapse face down on my bed. The last thing I hear before sleep takes me is the sound of Henry Abbott's scream which morphs into the wailing cry of a baby boy named Cody Johnson.

EIGHT
ANOTHER TRIP TO CHARLESTON

GETTING out of bed the following morning isn't easy. I slept fitfully, haunted by dreams of Anna, Fletcher and the weight of my own immortality. I am an abomination, a crime against nature and the laws which govern our species, laws which the Tempus Guild upholds. My father, rest his bitter soul, died forty-four long years after my sister, but he never spoke to me again after he discovered what I had become. First Anna had shamed our family, and then I had become a monster, cursed and unworthy of his affections.

After years of separation, I had finally visited him on his deathbed, desperate to make amends and hopeful that, in his final hours, he might forgive me. Unfortunately, I overestimated my father's capacity for compassion. What actually happened was quite the opposite.

1960, *Charleston, West Virginia*

. . .

I APPROACHED the house with a hollow feeling in my gut. I hadn't been back to my childhood home in twenty-four years but the house remained unchanged. It looked exactly as it had the day we left it for Arizona, forty-four years previously. The orchard was in full bloom, the tree boughs heavy with the weight of fruit. I had forgotten about apple season, but the sight of spoiled fruit littering the ground indicated that the Kennedy orchard was no longer being tended. The sweet cidery smell made my stomach churn.

I couldn't bring myself to walk through the front door. I no longer belonged in this house. I was no longer welcome, and so, like a common servant or a criminal, I went around back. The top of the stable door was open and I heard low voices coming from inside the kitchen as I approached. I steeled myself, stepping up to the door and swinging the lower half open.

Two faces stared at me with conflicting emotions, one pale, one dark. I recognised Elizabeth immediately, although she was older than the last time I'd seen her. At twenty-four, she was already considered a spinster.

"Clara?" her eyes were shrewd as she took in my appearance. She had seen me frequently as a child, unbeknownst to my father or hers, but this was the first time she was seeing me through the eyes of someone who had surpassed me in age.

"Hello Elizabeth," I spoke in hushed tones, still uncertain of my reception. Unlike Elizabeth, whose face reflected only mild curiosity and a hint of devilry, the black woman standing beside her was staring at me with a look of abject horror. When she finally found her tongue, she let loose a string of guttural prayer and crossed herself.

"Oh, Bettie, don't be ridiculous," Elizabeth chided. "Now you be a good girl and finish Master Kennedy's lunch."

The girl nodded, eager to get away from me.

"She's a strange one," Elizabeth mused, leading me through the kitchen and into the hall at the foot of the stairs. "But there's not many who will put up with your father so I'm happy to have her. Now," she turned to look at me properly and seemed to become distracted. "It's unreal," she breathed after a lengthy silence. "You haven't changed a bit."

"My hair's shorter," I pointed out, tugging at the ends which fell just below my ears. I had lopped off my waist-length braid only a few days ago in a fit of irritation and had regretted it ever since.

"It'll grow back," Elizabeth said, with that uncanny intuition of hers and then, getting straight to the point. "You're here to see your father, I assume?"

I nodded nervously, my eyes lifting to the ceiling as if I could see him through the plaster.

"I thought you might come," Elizabeth sighed, "but I must warn you, Clara, he's not likely to appreciate your effort.

"How is he?"

"Fading fast. I doubt he'll live through the week. He's deteriorated rapidly over the past few months and he's stopped eating, although we prepare all his favourite food."

"How long have you been caring for him?"

"About a year now. My father sent me to help when he started needing assistance to get around."

"I'm sorry."

"What for?"

"It should be me. It's not your responsibility."

"That's very noble of you, Clara but we both know he wouldn't have tolerated you living under his roof." She was not being unkind, simply honest, but I was surprised how much it hurt to hear. I would've thought that, after all these years, I might have stopped caring how my father perceived me.

"Well, I suppose we'd better get this over with," Elizabeth said briskly. "You can bring his food up with me. Just give me a minute. It's probably better if you wait here."

She disappeared into the kitchen and returned with a plate of mashed potatoes and a few slithers of cold meat.

"Are you sure you want to do this?"

No! my head had screamed, but I had forced a nod and followed her up the stairs.

The last time I had seen my father he had been forty-five years old, a strapping man with a healthy belly and a hint of grey in his copper hair. The shell of that man lay in the bed before me. His hair, or the tufts that remained, were colourless and wispy, and his once handsome face had collapsed, his eyes sunken into a gaunt creasing of flesh and all-too-prominent bone. At eighty-nine, he looked like a living corpse and I wondered if, perhaps, he had died sometime this morning without Elizabeth being aware of it. The sight of me, however, galvanised him into action. The milky eyes recognised me immediately and he started thrashing in the bed.

"Get her out of my house!" he roared, in a voice that didn't belong to a frail old man. "Demon!" he added, spittle flying from his lips.

Elizabeth was unperturbed.

"You cut that out!" she snapped, setting the tray on the table beside his bed. "Clara has come to see you and you aren't in any position to argue so you may as well just put up with it for a few minutes. Then you can get back to dying."

I marvelled at her courage while my father's eyes bulged at her insolence.

"How dare you?" he gasped, temporarily distracted. "You are an embarrassment to this family. Couldn't even find yourself a husband, you worthless girl!"

"Neither could Clara," she pointed out, turning to give me a secret smile. "Well, I'll leave you two alone, then."

She left without another word and I fought the urge to run after her. Taking a deep breath, I moved toward the foot of his bed. The sheets had fallen from his chest, displaying a concave hollow and folds of empty skin.

"I won't stay long," I murmured. He didn't reply; his lips puckered in disapproval and he refused to look at me. As I stepped closer his arm shot out and he snatched up the pocket watch from the table beside him, gripping it tightly in his hand as if he feared I might wrest it from his grasp.

"You still have that," I mused. Again, no response was forthcoming. A breeze lifted the drapes and the cidery smell hit me anew, a smell that was as nostalgic as it was nauseating.

"I always wondered why you came back here," I said, speaking more to myself than to him. "I thought you might stay in Arizona to be closer to the Guild." It made sense to me, given that Tempus had always been the most important thing in his life. From the shadow that passed briefly over his face I got the sense that perhaps the Guild had no longer needed the services of an old man who had nothing left to offer, but I held my tongue, not wanting to upset him.

"How have you been?" I asked, and then, in a moment of pure weakness, my shoulders slumped and I fell into an old habit. "Are you really not going to talk to me, Papa?"

The word was a catalyst for the wave of rage that boiled out of him. A vitriol of hurtful words cascaded over me, hurled from his bloodless lips in a tirade of hatefulness. He called me devil, demon, every possible version of the word, and each falling sound was like a physical blow, until I found myself retreating from him, trying to escape the avalanche of pain that rained down on me.

His outburst was so emotional that the pocket watch fell from his shaking hand. It landed on the square of carpet beside his bed intended to protect his chilblained feet. My father had treasured that watch for most of his adult life – a gift from his own father, intended to be passed down the generations. Automatically I stepped forward to retrieve it for him, not noticing how he had gone completely still.

Scooping it up, I realised that this was the very first time I had held it. The heavy 18 karat gold casing was cold and unfriendly as I opened it, exposing the fine porcelain dial - a mark of the most delicate workmanship. I had never noticed the seven rubies set inside the cover, but I knew my father must have had them put there at some point. Seven jewels for seven families. My father's obsession with Tempus, marked in fine artwork.

A rasping sound drew my attention back to the bed. My father's rheumy eyes regarded me with suspicion and disappointment, but the watch held his gaze far longer than my traitorous face. He seemed unable to speak after the effort of his tirade, but if he could have, I knew what he would have said. He wanted it back. It had been intended for his children, but I was no longer worthy of that title. He would take it to the grave.

"It really means that much to you?" I asked sadly. "More than me? More than Anna? I may be cursed, but I'm still your child, Papa. I didn't ask for any of this."

He drew in a wheezy lungful of air.

"You are not my child. I have no children."

I felt the wetness of shameful tears on my cheek. One made it's escape over my chin and splashed onto the watch I was holding. A small crack in the glass caught my eye. The carpet hadn't cushioned the fall as adequately as I'd believed. I wiped at it futilely with my sleeve. My father's breathing, laboured already, began to rasp in a faster rhythm and, not wanting to cause him any further physical pain, I wordlessly handed back the pocket watch. That was the last time I'd ever see him or the watch. He had been buried in the Tempus cemetery and had left the houses in Charleston and Flagstaff, as well as all of his other earthly possessions, to the Guild.

THE SOUND of Elizabeth preparing breakfast downstairs brings me back to the warmth of my temporary bedroom. Shaking off the shame of my father's parting words, I braid my hair and pin it on top of my head and then I take a shower, washing the sleep from my eyes, which feel dry and scratchy.

"Lord, girl, will you ever take any pride in your appearance?" Aunt Elizabeth groans the second I step into the kitchen. It is unusually bright inside, the sunlight making me wince. The rumbling sound of the dryer is accompanied by the lavender scent of fabric softener.

"Curtain day?" I ask, grinning, and the last of my sadness

vanishes. Every six months Aunt Elizabeth teeters on one of the kitchen chairs and hauls down masses of fabric which she insists on washing by hand. I have lived with her on and off for the past five decades and this routine has never changed. I once offered to take the curtains in for dry cleaning and she almost toppled off the chair.

"Why on earth would I pay for something I can do myself?" she had asked.

"I'll pay," I replied easily.

"You mean some unsuspecting housewife will pay," she had snorted, making it plain what she thought of my thieving ways, and I hadn't brought up the subject again.

"How are you feeling?" she asks me now.

"Tired."

"You look it." She observes me for a moment and then turns to switch on the coffee machine. "I'm sure it wasn't easy, reliving what happened. For what it's worth, I'm proud of you Clarke."

"Proud of me? Whatever for?"

"For finally telling me the truth."

"It was my fault. Everything that happened was my fault. I brought this upon us all."

"No, child," Elizabeth shakes her head gently from side to side, her expression open and earnest. "It wasn't your fault." She takes a seat across from me, our positions so identical to last night you would think we'd never moved. "Let me guess. You think that if you hadn't pushed Fletcher away and asked him to care for Anna while she was ill, she would never have fallen so in love with him and she would never have tried to destroy his clock. Am I right so far?" I nod and she looks pleased with herself. "That's a little arrogant, don't you think?"

"What?"

"Your theory has a few glaring holes, I'm afraid. Firstly, you seem to forget that your sister was a Kennedy too. Now I may not have known her, but I do know that Kennedy women are, in general, stubborn and strong-willed. What makes you think Anna would've done any different if you hadn't refused Fletcher?"

"Because he wouldn't have given her the time of day before I refused him, and he certainly had no intention of visiting her when she was ill. I let Anna believe he cared for her – made her believe they had something special."

"Ah, see, now you're giving Fletcher too much credit."

"I'm not following."

"That's because you're as pig-headed as she so obviously was. *Anna* made her choice, Clarke. For whatever rhyme or reason she decided to stop Fletcher's death. Not you. Not him. Anna. I know you'd like to lay the blame on your own shoulders, but this time there's just no twisting the truth, kiddo. You do your sister a disservice."

"Anna wouldn't have wanted this."

"How do you know what Anna wanted? It seems to me she knew exactly what she was doing. She made Fletcher immortal and then killed herself. Why would she do that? I'll tell you why," she continues, as I open my mouth to answer, "because Anna knew exactly what she was doing. And she knew how wrong it was. She knew he'd never forgive her."

"And did she know that Fletcher's revenge would be taken out on me?" I snap. "Do you think that my clever, devious, plotting sister knew that he would take out his rage on me – that perhaps she thought I deserved it?" The words flow out of me like lava, caustic and cutting. I can't help myself – the familiar urge to protect Anna's memory rising inside of me.

"Drink your coffee," Elizabeth replies, refusing to rise to my bait.

It takes me only the span of a single mug of steaming caffeine to decide on my next course of action.

"I'm going back to Charleston," I announce, setting my mug in the sink.

"Again?" Elizabeth asks. Every few years I head back to my hometown, to where it all began, hoping to find some clue, something I have missed that will lead me to Fletcher.

"Yes," I nod. My decision made, I bound back upstairs. I retrieve the envelope Truman gave me and snatch up the first passport that falls into my lap.

I have had more names than I can count over the past century. The Guild provides me with a never-ending stream of fake documentation. Within Tempus, there is a definite split between those who believe I am the only hope the Guild has to find Fletcher and restore order, and those who believe I should've been locked away years ago. I can always tell which group the compiler of my documentation belongs to. From those who despise me, I've been issued names such as Lilith Damon, Ebony Nox, and, my personal favourite because the compiler must have given it a lot of thought, Evelyn Side. I open the passport and smile at the name that only Truman could have come up with. Hope Foreman. He must have pulled a lot of strings to get that one approved. I root around in the bottom of the bag for my cell phone which is flashing a red battery. I plug it into the charger and dial the Tempus private line allocated for my sole use.

"Clara?" a detached female voice answers on the first ring.

"I need the first flight out to Charleston," I say, "book it under the name Hope Foreman."

"I'll email you the details," she replies smoothly and the line disconnects.

NINE
AN UNKNOWN FAMILIAR FACE

I SPEND the last week of February prowling the streets of Charleston, West Virginia and questioning the locals for any news of Fletcher. I have the latest Tempus identikit, which is the closest resemblance to Fletcher we could come up with, but which could never capture the fire in his eyes or the low velvet of his voice. I avoid looking at it myself, but no matter how many times I hold it up in front of me, I am rewarded with nothing but shaking heads and negative grunts. No one has seen him. For all I know, Fletcher has never returned to this town and is lying on a beach in the Caribbean right now, drinking *Pina Coladas* and enchanting the local female populace. Still, I persevere, visiting bars and bistros, hotels and diners, and losing hope with every negative response.

At the end of each soul-destroying day I find myself in the orchard behind the house. The ground is hard, the earth cracked beneath my feet, and the trees are bare, winter having taken its toll. West Virginia is about as Appalachia as it gets. I sit on the cold ground, my feet tucked under me and relive the secret meetings Fletcher and I had in this very spot. All is quiet, but I can almost swear I hear the haunting wail of a harmonica.

I spend my nights tossing and turning in my childhood bed. The Guild retained the Kennedy Estate, but it is more like a museum than a home – perfectly preserved in the exact state it was in the day we left, over a hundred years ago. The same state it was in the day my father died, forty-six years ago. I have stayed here a few times in the past years, my search for Fletcher bringing me back, but the house is still as unwelcoming as it was that day. The nights are icy and the scent of snow hangs heavily in the air.

My only company is the two-minute-long conversation I have with the nightly pizza-delivery man, who, thanks to the frigid cold, doesn't linger. With no other ideas, I stay longer than I intended and February becomes March. The anniversary of my sister's death and Fletcher's rebirth is hurtling toward me and Cody Johnson's clock is ticking. I've never felt more helpless than I do now.

By the end of the second week I've turned every nook and cranny in this town upside down when I realise I've been avoiding Anna's bedroom. I never enter my father's, a habit from my youth, but I had spent many a night creeping down the hall to Anna's room after a bad dream. Anna would barely shift in her sleep as I crawled in beside her and curled myself into the hollow of her back.

I make myself a steaming mug of cocoa and climb the wide staircase, trailing my left hand along the bannister. A thin layer of dust comes away on my fingers and I wipe it on my jeans, which are so old and discoloured it hardly shows.

The door to Anna's bedroom is closed. I closed it the night I arrived and it's been sealed shut ever since. I push it open with a low creak. Anna's bedroom, like mine, reflects the Edwardian era of our childhood. The room, as floral and feminine as Anna had been, is sparsely furnished. The baroque chair at her dresser is upholstered in a pale peach damask, which brings out the faded Sweet Peas in the wallpaper. The dresser is empty, all of Anna's belongings having travelled with us to Arizona, but, in her wardrobe, I find a few discarded dresses and a lonely white glove, frayed at the wrist. Anna wouldn't wear anything spoiled, but I can guess that this glove's partner was the very one Anna had dropped in the dirt and which Fletcher had returned to me. I hadn't passed it on to Anna because I couldn't explain why or how I had gotten it from him. I carry the glove with me to the window, skirting around the bed. From here, I can see the front lawn, the gravel path to the white picket gate and the street beyond. A streetlight flickers, distracting me for a moment, but when I look back down I see them coming for us.

1915, *Charleston, West Virginia*

"IT'S THE GUILD," Anna was wringing her fingers so tightly that they had gone as white as her blood-drained face.

"Stop that," I prised her hands apart, holding them in my own as we watched the two immaculately dressed men approach the front door. We couldn't see their faces, obscured as they were by the brims of their top hats, but we knew who they were. And, if we had harboured any doubt, the fond warmth of our father's greeting from below confirmed it. Our father respected the council of Tempus alone among men.

"It's Christmas Eve," Anna lamented. "How can they do this on Christmas Eve? Have they no respect?"

"The new Clock Keeper's term begins in just a few months," I say automatically, "I suppose there's no time to waste, especially since the journey to Arizona will take weeks."

"Hush, Clara! Let us pray that we are wrong and that neither of us has been chosen."

I nodded, praying fervently alongside her while the low drone of male voices drifted up the stairs.

It took only five minutes before the sound of father's heavy footfalls reached us, accompanied by the tick of his cane against the heavy wooden block flooring. A heavy rapping on Anna's door followed and my heart stuttered in my chest.

"Come in," I managed to croak. Anna seemed incapable of speech, her eyes wide with fear, her lips pressed tightly together to keep her from bursting into sobs. The door opened and father regarded us both, no hint of sadness in his steely gaze. I watched as his mouth opened, forming the word that would decide our fates.

"Anna." Brusque, firm, unapologetic.

Relief washed over me, so strong that my knees buckled beneath me and I hit the floor with a painful thud. Anna, however, gave a cry of pitiful despair and fainted clean away, collapsing in on herself like one of our ragdolls.

"Pull your sister together," father hissed, his voice a whip crack through the ominous silence. "You will both present yourselves downstairs in five minutes. There are members of the Guild present who wish to congratulate her."

And that was all he had had to say on the matter.

I TURN AWAY from the window, the memories coming together in a tumultuous wave. As I perch on the edge of her bed, I see Anna as she lay, pale and frightened, in the days that followed the announcement. Congratulations had poured in and father had read each letter as if it was a gift from the Sovereign himself, while Anna had refused to eat, refused to speak, her already tiny frame wasting away while I watched, powerless to stop it. I went from hoping Fletcher would never see her like this to praying that he would come, if his presence was able to rouse her from the dark pit of her depression. Father barely noticed, so intent was he on planning our imminent journey to Arizona.

In the end, it was my own desperation that made me seek Fletcher out. I had precious few weeks left to spend with Anna and I couldn't even reach her. Fletcher and I hadn't spoken a word to each other since the day I rejected him, but I would have made a deal with the devil himself if it would have roused Anna from her trance...

. . .

I FOLLOWED the sound of the harmonica, barely conscious of the curious glances of the townspeople. A few called out to me, trying to discern the reason a young lady of my status would be walking the streets unchaperoned, but I paid them no heed. There was nothing father could do to me now that would hurt more than losing Anna.

I found him in a small tavern surrounded by the men he worked with, if their blackened faces were any indication. As I entered, the room fell into a stunned silence. Fletcher's eyes widened at the sight of me, the lilting melody cut off abruptly. He was on his feet in an instant, stowing the harmonica in his pocket as he shouldered his way through the room, leaving behind a tankard of ale that had probably cost him a full day's wage. He didn't stop when he reached my side, his hand gripping my elbow and dragging me alongside him as we emerged back onto the street.

"Clara!" he sounded angrier than I'd ever heard him. "What the hell are you doing here?" I'd never heard him curse before and certainly never at me directly. I don't know who was more surprised.

Conscious of our exposed position, Fletcher ushered me down an alleyway, out of sight of prying eyes. He scanned my face, as if searching for something.

"Are you hurt?"

"No," I shook my head, trying to still my trembling hands. "I'm fine."

"Then why are you here?" I saw it then, the tiniest cinder of hope spark in his eyes. It pained me to see it – to know that, deep down, a part of him still hoped that perhaps I would run away with him, that I would choose him.

Instead, I uttered the words that would drive the wedge even further between us.

"My sister," I croaked, wondering if it were possible to feel any more wretched, "my sister needs you."

I never told Anna that I had summoned him. Instead, when he

crept into her room she believed he had come of his own accord, out of concern for her. He had played the part well, barely glancing in my direction as he removed his cap and straightened his unruly dark hair.

"Hello, Clara," he had said, greeting me as if I was a stranger, before turning his attention to my sister.

"HELLO CLARA." The voice from the past was louder, part memory, part reality, and before I knew it for sure, I was on my feet, daggers drawn. Fletcher stood in the doorway, looking exactly as he had in my memory, except that the ragged dress shirt and frayed trousers had been replaced by an expensive jacket and tie and his face bore no trace of the empathy it had that day. Now, it was a mask of hatred.

TEN
THE NIGHT FLETCHER DIED

"YOU CAN PUT THOSE AWAY," Fletcher gestures at my daggers before pushing off the doorframe and stepping into the room.

"I'd prefer to hold on to them." I keep my eyes on him, but my mind is a tumultuous wreck. After all these years of searching Fletcher is here and I have no idea what I'm going to do.

"As you wish." He pulls back his coat, a casual gesture which reveals the slim blades at his hips. I notice every detail about him, from the expensive cut of his clothing to the intricate cubic diamond cufflinks adorning his sleeves. A five o'clock shadow darkens his jaw, and, despite his nonchalant attitude, his mouth is a grim line.

"What are you doing here, Fletcher?"

"Word has it you've been looking for me."

"Everyone's been looking for you," I correct.

"And by everyone, obviously you mean everyone at Tempus. I doubt anyone else would care about my whereabouts."

I don't rise to the bait, but, as he moves toward Anna's dresser, I adjust my stance slightly, keeping my body in line with his, prepared to defend myself if he attacks.

"You're so twitchy," Fletcher grins disarmingly, but my only response is to tighten my grip on the daggers, the smooth steel comforting against my palms. "Look, Clara," he pauses deliberately before adding, "oh, wait, it's Clarke now, isn't it?" My stomach contracts at the mention of my new name. I know nothing about Fletcher but he is obviously well-informed. His next words are even more alarming. "I do prefer Clarke to Hope Foreman – that's a bit presumptuous, don't you think? After all, you only really represent hope for the Guild, not all mankind."

I refuse to rise.

"Okay, Fletcher, I get it - you're up to date and well-informed. Now why don't you stop showing off and get to the point of why you're here?"

"Fine, but could you put the daggers away? I only came here to talk and I prefer to do it without you waving those blades around. You might hurt yourself."

I hesitate for about a second and then I spin the daggers gracefully in my palms before returning them to my belt.

"That's better." Fletcher drapes himself over the baroque chair. "Please, sit," he waves his hand airily toward the bed as if he owns the place. I back up to the bed, my eyes never leaving him as I perch on the edge of the mattress. Fletcher rolls his eyes. "Well, I can see there's no getting you to relax so we may as well get this over with."

"Get what over with?"

"You tell me. You're the one who's been hunting me down like a common criminal."

"Are you saying you don't deserve to face justice for what you've done?"

"For what *I've* done? In case you've forgotten, Clarke, your sister did this to me."

"And in case *you've* forgotten, my sister paid for that crime with her life."

"Your sister was a coward." He says it so matter-of-factly, with so little compassion, that my anger spikes.

"Don't you dare speak about Anna like that!"

"I'll speak about Anna any God-damned way I choose. She condemned me to an eternity of misery."

"You dress pretty well for someone in so much pain."

Fletcher's jaw drops and I experience a surge of triumph that I've shocked him, but he recovers quickly, the emotionless mask slipping back into place.

"You've changed," he muses.

"It's been a hundred years, Fletcher, I'm sure we've both changed. Although it's nice to see you at least remember some small part of who you used to be." I raise my eyes to the newsboy cap on his head, such a startling contrast to the rest of his business-like clothing.

"They're making a comeback," he drawls, indifferent, but I sense that he's lying. My comment bothers him more than he's willing to let on. "And you've certainly taken a new fashion direction." He gestures at my nondescript jean and hoodie.

"Pretty dresses draw unnecessary attention."

For just a second his gaze softens.

"You've never needed pretty dresses to draw attention, Clara." He says it almost without thinking, but the moment the words are out of his lips they curve into a wicked smile. "Although you might want to think about taking a shower every once in a while. You could pass for a coal miner's daughter."

"Beats the alternative," I say.

"Ah, yes. You never were very enthusiastic about your dad. I was sorry to hear about his passing."

"No, you weren't."

"No," he agrees, "I wasn't."

"My father was an asshole. His death was hardly something to grieve over."

"And yet you went to see him just before he died."

He smiles at my involuntary intake of breath.

"You see, Clarke. You may not have been able to find me, but I have always known where you are. I have watched you for a century... well, almost."

The blatant reminder of the centenary anniversary is a low blow, even for Fletcher.

"Why are you doing this?"

"Doing what?"

"This - all of it. You say you've been watching me, so why not show yourself before now. You've spent a hundred years lurking in the shadows. What are you waiting for?"

"The right moment."

"The right moment for what?"

"Ah, now that would be telling."

Against my better judgement I close my eyes. My head is pounding and I'm already growing weary of his games. I find myself missing the old Fletcher – the one who was kind and direct and didn't speak in riddles or look at me like I was something to despise rather than someone to be cherished.

"Do you remember old man Radley?" Fletcher asks suddenly and I haul my eyelids up to look at him. "You stole his watch, do you remember?"

"I didn't steal it. He dropped it in the dirt." I admit, no longer feeling any need to impress him with the lie.

Fletcher chuckles.

"He didn't drop it. I took it from his pocket and planted it not three feet in front of your nose."

"More of your games?"

"Not at all. You felt the need to prove yourself, I simply provided the means."

"Yeah, well now I've got something else to prove."

"That you can bring me in? That you can deliver me to Tempus like a lamb to the slaughter?" The tension is back, mounting in the air and crackling between us.

"You can't, Clara. You must know that by now."

"Don't call me that."

"Clarke." He rolls the name off his tongue in drawn out contempt.

We both fall silent and the seconds stretch into minutes. My hands itch to reach for my daggers but there are still things I need to know.

"Ask me," Fletcher urges after a time, as if he's reading my thoughts.

"What did you do with my clock?"

"You'll know soon enough, but that's not the question you should be asking right now."

"How did you do it?"

I can tell immediately that this is the right question. Fletcher settles back in the chair, crossing one leg over the other.

"You remember how I died?"

I nod. It's all I can do. Despite everything he's done since then, the night that Fletcher died was one of the most excruciating nights of my life.

1916, *Flagstaff, Arizona*

ANNA HAD BEEN GONE two weeks and her absence was a dark void that couldn't be filled. I missed her every single minute of every single day. Even sleep couldn't deliver me from the hell I was living in without her and I dreamed of her constantly. Arizona was a dry, inescapable landscape of loneliness. Father had deposited me in Flagstaff along with a small bevy of servants, but he spent most of his time down in Phoenix to be closer to Guild headquarters. When he was home, he spent his every waking moment primping and preening that our family was so honourably serving Tempus, neglecting the daughter he seemed to have forgotten and becoming caught up in his own self-importance. Anna's sacrifice was a personal triumph, one that elevated his status within the Guild. He didn't even miss her. Left to my own devices, I alone mourned her, longing for the life we had had back in Charleston, and I let my resentment and hatred of the Guild grow stronger as each day dawned without her. I wanted to strike out at the people who had taken her from me, to punish them, but what could a mere scrap of a girl do against an organisation like Tempus?

The answer came to me one afternoon as I waited for father to emerge from his office. I had been summoned to Phoenix to attend the grand unveiling of a new wing of the Guild's headquarters, one that had been under construction for months, long before we arrived. One would think that the week in Phoenix might have distracted me from my melancholy, but it only served as another reminder that I was now utterly alone. At least at home I had had Hattie and the other servants to fuss over me. Here, I had no one to talk to and no one who cared.

The Grand Master at the time was a Washington, and his arrival was a ceremonious affair. I found myself standing very near to him as members of the Guild gathered around the site of the unveiling. Lack of food had made me weak, and I stumbled, collapsing against him. My father yelled at me, his furious face beet red with embarrassment. The Grand Master was kind enough to enquire after my wellbeing before pressing me into my father's biting grasp, but those few seconds were all I had needed. I left the ceremony with a solid gold button pulled from his sleeve.

And so began a personal siege on Tempus. Many members of the founding families resided in Flagstaff and, without my father's presence to temper my bravery, I fleeced them all. No member of the Guild was safe as I honed my skills, stockpiling a veritable fortune beneath a floorboard pried loose in my new bedroom. Three weeks later my luck ran out. I was attending the market when a firm hand gripped my own, withdrawing it from the pocket of a passing merchant. I did not know the man, only that he was a Cleveland – one of the founding families. His face contorted in a bellow of rage and he flung me from him. I landed in the dirt, the dust clouding my eyes and making them water.

"Thief!" the man roared, taking a step toward me. I curled myself into a ball, preparing myself for a beating that never came. Instead, a pair of strong hands lifted me to my feet.

"Run!" I heard Fletcher's voice in my ear as he dragged me through the throng, giving me no time to catch my breath as we fled the scene of the crime.

Gasping for breath we finally took shelter in a small alleyway on the opposite end of town.

"Are you trying to get yourself whipped?" Fletcher rounded on me in genuine fury. I shrank away from him, my so recent encounter with naked male anger arousing genuine fear in me. Then, before I could formulate a reply, Fletcher crushed me to him, his strong arms drawing me to his chest, his heart beating frantically beneath my ear.

"God, Clara, you could've been seriously hurt!"

I let the feel of his warm, solid presence soothe me and relaxed against him as both of our hearts settled into a familiar rhythm. I hadn't seen Fletcher since we had left Charleston, since I had asked him to reach Anna and bring her back to me, only to lose them both a short time later. I hadn't even said goodbye to him when we had left, not knowing how to bridge the distance that had grown between us since my denial of his proposal.

"What are you doing here?" I asked when I finally found my voice. He released me, staring down at me from under his newsboy cap.

"I followed you," he admitted, a light flush warming his cheeks.

"From the house?"

He laughed at that. "From Charleston, you twit."

"Fletcher that was weeks ago! How did you manage it?"

"It doesn't matter."

"Why didn't you tell me you were here?" The thought that he had been here all along, that my loneliness might not have been so awful, brought tears to my eyes.

The sight of my tears was too much for him to bear.

"Clara, I'm sorry! I didn't know how you'd react, or if you even wanted me here."

"It's not that," I sniffed. "It's Anna... she's gone. She's gone and I'm so alone."

"Gone? Gone where?"

His eyes searched my face for an answer but I couldn't tell him. No matter how angry I was at the Guild, I understood the brevity of our task.

"Father sent her away," I lied. "To a finishing school in Europe."

"Oh, Clara." he pulled me to him again and I gave way to the sobs I had been holding back since Anna left. Fletcher let me cry until my tears ran dry and then he held me at arm's length so he could look into my eyes.

"You're not alone, do you hear me? I'm here now. I'll take care of you."

He led me back to the house.

"You know where I live?" I asked, finally noticing where we were.

"I know everything," he replied mysteriously.

I smiled up at him. "I'll make my way from here."

"Your father's still not open to your friendship with a street rat?" His voice was teasing, but a glimmer of the unspoken hurt shone through. I wondered if he'd bring it up again, but he didn't.

"Some people never change," I said softly.

He looked at me for a long moment.

"And some people do," he murmured. His hand reached for mine and I felt the softness of leather brush my palm. I glanced down to find a brushed brown wallet in my hand. Engraved along the front was the name Edward Cleveland.

"I assume that's what you were after?" Fletcher asked. His tone was still teasing, but he was cautious of my reaction.

"You got it," I breathed, gazing up at him in wide-eyed wonder.

"You have a lot to learn, my little thief."

Fletcher began teaching me in earnest after that. He taught me how to feint, how to distract, how to play on a target's compassion. Nothing made a man so vulnerable to my sleight of hand as dropping a basket of apples in his path and batting my eyes coquettishly at him.

We worked relentlessly, my father's prolonged absences affording us plenty of opportunity to spend time together without fear of being caught. Fletcher drilled various methods of thievery into my brain until I could recite them in my sleep. My stash under the floorboards overflowed into a secret compartment in my dresser, and then onto a high shelf in my wardrobe.

"You need to give back," he told me one Saturday morning. We had found a new secret meeting place, one that, while not as pretty as the orchard back home, afforded us the same privacy. The small pond at the edge of our property was overgrown with nettles and bugweed, keeping passers-by at bay, but we had taken to wearing thick socks and had stowed an old blanket amid the branches of a weeping willow at the water's edge.

"Give back?" I asked, flummoxed.

"Yes. You can't keep all that wealth for yourself. It's not as if you need it," he added pointedly, picking at the Parisian lace of my sleeve.

"What do I do with it, then?" The thought of relieving myself of some of the evidence I was hoarding was appealing.

"You can give it to those who need it," he replied simply.

And so we started to disperse the wealth we had amassed, slipping wads of notes under needy doorways and depositing jewels in hiding spots around town, where only the poorest of people would find them.

Anna had been gone almost seven weeks and, while I still felt that a part of me was missing, Fletcher had eased the pain in my heart. I could function, so long as I had a purpose and he was part of my life. Arizona afforded us a freedom we had never had in West Virginia. The people here didn't know me yet and it was easier to disappear – to blend in with the crowd and go unnoticed.

"What time will your father be home this evening?" Fletcher asked. We were at the pond, and his playful tone alerted me to the fact that he was up to something. I swatted a gnat dancing around my face and eyed the bag at his feet.

"He'll be home early. The Grand Master is visiting relatives in town and father has been invited to dine with them this evening. I'm to accompany him," I add forlornly.

"Will you be expected to go, being so sickly?"

"But I'm not sickly at all."

"Are you sure?" He placed a warm hand against my brow, a concerned look coming over him. "You feel quite feverish to me. And you look awful," he added, running an admiring eye over my face.

"Now that you mention it, I do feel quite faint." I clutched my chest in mock alarm.

"Good girl." He approved.

"What's in the bag?"

"Your disguise."

Despite my determined rebellion at the Guild, sneaking out of my father's house in a pair of dungarees and a newsboy cap that smelled faintly of smoke and coal dust invoked pure terror in me. No men's shoes would fit my size 4 feet, so Fletcher had traded half a day's wage for a pair of leather loafers which were so comfortable my feet promptly protested going anywhere, preferring to simply relax and enjoy the uncharacteristic comfort.

"You men are so lucky," I told Fletcher when I met him at the bottom of the garden. "I'd like to see you wear heels for a day and see how you fare!"

"Did you prop up your pillows?" Fletcher asked, ignoring my griping. He had waited as close to the house as he dared without fear of discovery, but still released a sigh of relief when I was finally under his protection.

"I did. A perfect Clara-shaped lump now resides beneath my blankets should anyone decide to check on me."

"Do you think anyone will?"

"No. I instructed Hattie that I was retiring for the evening and I didn't want to be disturbed." Hattie was one of the servants who had travelled with us from Charleston and one of the few servants I liked in my father's household.

Fletcher relaxed then, finally taking note of my appearance. The chuckle that rose in his chest took an age to burst from his lips before he grabbed my hand, swinging me wide to get a good look at me.

"Why, Clara, you make a delightful street urchin!"

I gave a dainty pirouette and ended in a curtsey.

"Why thank you, Mister Kincaid."

"Shall we?" he asked, offering his hand. I slipped my arm through his and felt the familiar lump in his pocket.

"Will you play?" I asked. He considered this for a moment, his arm warm against my own.

"Perhaps later," he promised.

Of course, he never got to play that night. Fletcher died at 8.27 p.m. before we had even reached our destination – a fireside jubilee at which, unbeknown to either of us, he would have given me my second kiss, and this time, I would not have refused him. We had thought that sticking to the shadows of the back alleys would protect us from discovery and my father's wrath, but not once had we considered the danger lurking there. They had come out of nowhere - a band of filthy, desperate men. One had grabbed me, holding me back with biting, blackened hands, while the others subdued Fletcher.

"IT HAPPENED SO QUICKLY," I whisper, breaking the tense silence. "I thought they might leave us alone once they got what they wanted."

The men had been after Fletcher's wallet, meagre as its contents were, but my feminine yelp of fear had alerted them to my true identity. The newsboy cap had been whipped from my head, revealing the heavy braid that tumbled down over my shoulder, eliciting looks of evil delight. My heart had plummeted into my stomach, but when Fletcher saw the blackened hand stroke my cheek, he retaliated, struggling wildly, yelling at them to leave me alone. And that's when it happened. A knife, plunged deep into his belly and the shocked understanding dawning on his face. His yelling, however, had done what his struggles could not and the men had fled the scene, leaving us alone.

"You watched me die," Fletcher murmurs, here, in the safety of Anna's old bedroom and I raise my eyes to his, staring at him through the veil of my memory.

"I did," I say. "And it almost destroyed me."

1916, *Flagstaff, Arizona*

"FLETCHER!" I sobbed, my head on his chest, my shoulders heaving. His heart had stopped a few minutes ago, the blood pooling on the ground around us a warm, wet nightmare that soaked the knees of my borrowed trousers. My hands were covered in it - the smell of metal heavy on the air, assaulting my senses as I gasped in huge lungfuls.

"Fletcher!" a deeper voice and I turned to find a skinny, pock-faced youth crouching beside me.

"What happened?" he asked, his eyes finding mine. Shock flared in the dark orbs, his brow rising as he took me for a woman.

"They stabbed him!" I sobbed again, tears flowing freely down my cheeks. The youth leaned over and put his ear to Fletcher's mouth, then placed it against his chest, listening intently for breath or heartbeat. I knew he would find neither. Fletcher had died minutes ago, while I sat beside him, helpless.

More people arrived, cries of recognition filling the air, and my ears rung with the wails of his friends – those who had known him for so brief a time and yet had grown to love him, as only those who knew Fletcher could. I backed away slowly, disappearing into the crowd, my eyes never leaving his face. Through it all I was mortified to find that my mind still functioned – urging me to get home, to get cleaned up and destroy any evidence that I had been out here tonight. The fear of my father still resided in my broken heart.

I almost missed it. The crowd was thickening, jostling me around, but it parted suddenly and, through the space, I saw Fletcher's eyes open. A collective cry of relief rose up around me, but I didn't hear it. The blood thundered in my head, drowning out all else. Fletcher's eyes flickered to mine as if he knew exactly where I was standing - as if there was no one and nothing between us. A question, pained and fearful, shone in those eyes; but I had watched him die. I knew he shouldn't be awake. And I knew there was only one person in the world who could raise the dead.

"Clara," Fletcher's voice was a whisper of breath on the wind, but I heard his plea as loudly as if he was shouting in my ear. My lips formed an apology, my heart contracting violently at what I was about to do, but I tore my gaze from his and I turned and fled, my loafered feet barely touching the ground as fear lent them wings.

Fletcher caught me in the garden only a few feet short of freedom. The light from the porch spilled over the grass just out of reach as his hand seized my arm with the inhuman strength of adrenalin and yanked me around to face him.

"Clara!" his voice was deeper, more dangerous, as though he had touched the darkness of death and brought some of it back with him. I shuddered under his touch – tried to hide it – failed. He released me as if I'd burned him, his eyes widening in fear and understanding.

"Stay away from me, Fletcher!"

"What... what's happening to me?" he scrabbled at his shirt, hitching it out of his trousers and exposing the ruby stain of blood smeared across a gaping wound that was devoid of any fresh blood.

"It will heal," I whispered, catching myself only a second before my fingers brushed against his stomach.

"I died." He couldn't seem to catch his breath and his hair was streaked scarlet with the vestige of blood run through with his hands.

"I died, Clara. I was dead. I could see myself, lying there – I could see you weeping by my side. And then... And then something happened. It feels different. I feel different." His panic-stricken face paled still further, although it was hard to believe that was possible. "I'm not supposed to be here!"

I swallowed the hysteria rising in my throat and tried to run from him but he caught me easily.

"I can't help you, Fletcher!"

"You can't leave me. Please. I... I'm afraid, Clara. I don't want to be alone." His words cut me deeply, but I was afraid too, afraid of him – of what he had become and what it might mean.

"What am I?" he asked, as if he had pulled the very notion from my mind.

"You... you're something that shouldn't exist." I bit down on my tongue to keep from crying out as his fingers reached for me once more, but this time I was too quick for him. Unhindered by my usual attire, I fled, the soft cotton of my imposter shirt slipping between his fingers. I lost both loafers to the night, but neither stick nor stone could hinder my terrified escape. My name on his lips, a curse of righteous anger and confusion, followed me through the pool of light.

I didn't slow as I burst through the front door of our home, slamming it behind me, as if the solid wood might keep the demon at bay.

"Papa!" I cried, shoving aside a serving boy and darting through the house. "Papa!"

He emerged from his office a second before I reached it and we collided in the doorway.

"Clara!" he glared down at me, his face turning thunderous as he took in my imposter's clothing. And then he noticed the blood, registered how I was clinging to his arm like a lifeline, the only thing holding me up and his expression changed to one of panic. "Clara, what is it? What's happened?"

"Anna," I croaked, my voice hoarse and pathetic. "She's done something terrible!"

ELEVEN
DREAMS OF DEATH

"SO YOU *DO* REMEMBER," Fletcher murmurs, bringing me back to the painful reality of Anna's bedroom. He is watching me, intently, his eyes gun-metal beneath the peak of his cap, and once more I get the eerie sensation that he can read my mind.

"Of course I remember, Fletcher. I was there wasn't I?"

"Yes. You were there. And yet you left me, alone, confused and petrified, rather than betray your precious Guild."

"I never wanted that! Do you think leaving you was easy for me? You just don't get it – you've never understood how the Guild works. The founding families swore an oath. I couldn't break it. I wouldn't break it."

"Is that your excuse for fleeing like a coward?"

"I needed to see my sister! I had to know if she was all right!" I roar, the sound reverberating around the room in a howling rage.

Fletcher's smile is pure malice.

"And how did that turn out for you?" His words are knives, cutting through the flesh and bone of time itself. They throw me backwards into the most painful memory of all.

. . .

1916, *The Hall of Clocks, Arizona*

MY SISTER'S body was cold by the time we arrived. It had taken us a few hours to reach the canyon. I had never been to the Hall of Clocks before, but my father had stashed me in a carriage and had hurtled into the night like a man possessed. It was the only time I had ever seen him show any emotion other than arrogance or irritation and it chilled my bones. I had been surprised that he hadn't stopped and informed the Grand Master, but I think he was still praying that I was wrong, and hoping that there would be no need for any investigation other than why I had been out of the house without his consent. For the first time in my life I was on the same page as he was, and we were praying for the same result. I would take any punishment for my disobedience, if only Anna was all right.

He led me through the maze of hallways and down the ancient ladder, surprisingly agile for a man of his size, but neither of us spoke. I had told him that I'd watched a dead man come back to life. He hadn't asked me who, or where I had been, but I knew I would be interrogated later.

The Hall was breath-taking, but I barely noticed. I only had eyes for the small figure in the antechamber. The entire city buried within the canyon could have burst into flame and I wouldn't have cared in that moment, because Anna was slumped on the ground, her chest a blossom of red against the backdrop of dusty cream Parisian silk. Her hair, left loose, cascaded wildly around her shoulders and she had lost even more weight since the last time I saw her. Black shadows beneath her eyes only emphasised the deathly chalk of her skin.

My father's eyes swept the scene, a curse bursting from his lips. Anna had killed herself, of that there was no doubt. Her small hands still clasped the dagger protruding from her left breast. But I sensed it wasn't my sister's senseless death that had caused my father's emotional outburst. Instead, his eyes were fixed on a clock that lay at her feet. An identical dagger had been rammed into its centre, although the wooden surface was far harder than Anna's flesh and it hadn't penetrated as deeply, gouging only a tiny hole through the disc. Despite my mounting hysteria, I squinted at it, trying to make out the golden words below the blade.

"What has she done?" my father murmured, clutching his head in his hands before rounding on Anna's frail corpse. "What have you done!" he roared, the words echoing around the antechamber and into the Hall of Clocks.

"Father!" I got to my feet, staring him down, the tears streaming my cheeks in an endless flow. I couldn't comprehend how unmoved he appeared to be, how angry at a dead child.

His lips moved, a repetitive mumbling that I couldn't make out at first, until I followed the line of his sight. He was reading the words written on the clock. A name: Fletcher Robert Kincaid followed by two lines of numbers. 03-27-1893-10.12 and 04-05-1916-20.47. The second number made sense – it was eight forty-seven pm, the 5th April 2016 - today's date. The date and time of Fletcher's death. The first line would represent his birth.

The sight of his name and the confirmation of his death was my undoing. With a bellow of rage, I wrenched the dagger free before my father could stop me, hurling it away. It skittered across the stone floor, coming to rest beneath an ornate desk, atop which lay an open book and a flickering candle.

"Why would she do this?" My father was ashen and a sheen of perspiration shone on his brow.

"She loved him," I croaked, another sob welling in my chest. His bewildered expression gave me a deep satisfaction and I laughed, taunting him with how little he knew of his own children.

"She loved him!" I shrieked. "Your precious daughter loved a commoner and you didn't even see it! You see nothing! You knew nothing of Anna and you know nothing of me!"

"You hold your tongue, girl!"

"I shan't! Anna is dead because you didn't take the time to know her! To love her! This is your fault! It's all your fault!"

His backhand came out of nowhere. One minute I was hurling accusations in his face and the next I was flying through the air, my arms wind-milling uselessly at my sides. I landed in a heap alongside Anna's body, her blood mingling with Fletcher's in the fabric of my clothing, my face not inches from the damaged clock.

I don't know if I would have retaliated. I'll never know for certain, because, in that moment, the clock began to change. The golden letters slowly faded, leaving no trace that they had ever existed and a new name began to appear, faint at first, and growing steadily clearer. Viktor Anton Ivanov, 04-05-1916-23.31, 01-10-1964-11.34.

I knew what the clocks meant. Obviously I did. Every member of the seven founding families knew that the clocks represented life and death. But when Fletcher's clock changed, only I knew that he was still alive.

"What was the name?" My father's frantic voice cut through my own stunned bewilderment. "The name, it vanished! It's imperative we find him. You said she loved him, you must know who he is - what was the name, Clara?"

Without any consideration of the consequences, unaware of the path it would set me on, I replied.

"Fletcher," I croaked. "It was Fletcher Kincaid."

"YOU SHOULD HAVE HELPED ME," Fletcher hisses now. I don't know when he got to his feet or when he drew the knives at his waist, but I pull mine from their sheaths, facing him in the cold, draughty room. The same matching daggers I had pulled from my sister's corpse, from Fletcher's clock, that awful night. I will never know where Anna got them, but they have been my constant companion ever since. The atmosphere in the room has changed, the conversational tone is no more. Fletcher's eyes are as sharp as his blades, his mouth the ugly echo of a smirk.

"I came to you – confused and disoriented and you lied to my face."

"I had no choice!" I stand my ground. "The Guild isn't something you turn your back on. Right or wrong, we protect time for a reason."

"I died!" his voice staccatos through clenched teeth, his jaw twitching with the effort of keeping his composure. "I died and was reborn and you had the answers I needed. But you refused to help me! I did more for you than the Guild ever did, you ungrateful bitch!"

"Where is my clock, Fletcher?" I can sense the seconds slipping away – the time for discussion drawing swiftly to an end.

"Go to hell, Clara. I'm sure your sister's waiting for you there."

And just like that, with those awful words, the fragile peace is shattered. I lunge for him, my daggers whistling through the air as I slash out with both hands. He retaliates, dodging my blows. His knives are longer than my own, tapering to precise and lethal points. A low hiss is my only warning before a sharp pain slices across my cheek, dangerously close to my eye.

Fletcher and I face off, watching each other's every movement. I resist the urge to lift my fingers to my cheek, feeling the slow oozing of blood from the cut he left there – superficial at best, but he's made his point. I wait for an opening, for the chance to strike out again, but his body is an unflinching coil, tensed for any form of attack.

"This is pointless, you know?" he remarks conversationally, his tone light, even if his stance is not. "We can't be killed."

"I don't need to kill you."

"Only to contain me?" he muses. "Incapacitate me so you can hand me over to the Guild?"

"You've always been smarter than you look."

"As I recall there was a time you liked the way I looked."

I ignore the implication in his words and focus on his hands, the veins standing out against the smooth tan of his skin.

"And as I recall there was a time when you were an honourable man. Why are you so dead set against accepting the Guild's help?"

"I prefer to make your life a misery."

The breath escapes my lungs in a sigh.

"Why do you hate me so much, Fletcher? Surely the punishment you dealt me is enough."

"Enough? Your sister condemned me to an eternity of loneliness and pain. I begged you to tell me what was going on and you refused. Instead, you ran off into the night and left me!"

"And yet you found out exactly what you needed to know without my help."

"I make no apologies for following you. I needed information and I got it."

"How long did you hide in the Hall of Clocks, Fletcher? I know you came back to see me when I took Anna's place, but you'd already stolen my clock by then. How long did it take you to figure it all out?"

"I was there long before you replaced your sister," he retorts. "I followed you that very night – you and your father fleeing to the canyon. I almost got lost, you know, in the labyrinth – I assume that's the Guild's sorcery to ensure no one finds the Hall? Thankfully, I had you to lead me in."

"You... you saw Anna? You saw her body?"

"Yes. And I saw your reaction to my clock. I learned it all from you."

"Then why are you so angry?" I yell. "You were hardly in the dark!"

"Because you didn't tell me - you had no intention of telling me! I was your friend, Clara, you owed me that much at least." He pauses, as if considering whether to tell me something. "I heard you, you know. You could've given him any name, but you handed mine over without the slightest hesitation. You betrayed me when I needed you most." He shrugs, trying to feign nonchalance. "I thought it only fair you suffer the same fate." He flips the knife in his right hand, the glint of steel flashing with each rotation and I stiffen, sensing his next move.

"How long did you stay?" I repeat the question. I know that he was there when Anna died, and again when he confronted me, but I want details. There might be a clue in his actions that will lead me to my clock.

Fletcher's smile is malevolent.

"I never left."

His words leave me momentarily speechless.

"That's not... that's not possible."

"I'm afraid it is," he sneers, as the full implication of his words hits me. "That's right, Clara. I smuggled your clock out from right under your nose. I entered the hall with you and your father and I only emerged ten days later, after I had made you just like me. The night I told you I had taken it, your clock was still inside the Hall."

A strangled sound erupts from my chest as I realise I could've stopped him. I could've stopped him from taking it, but I let him walk right out of the Hall.

"I didn't know," I whisper.

"Of course you didn't. You know nothing unless I want you to, but I know everything. I was there when you found Anna's body, I was there when you were brought in to take her place." He catches sight of my ashen face and his grin widens. "I saw your tears, I heard you sobbing yourself to sleep. It was all very dramatic."

"And all the while you were searching the Hall for my clock." I hiss in disgust. "So that you could destroy me."

He shrugs, unaffected.

"How did you find your way out?"

"Quite easily. I guess once you've been inside you fall under the Sovereign's protection."

"And then you sent word to my father that you had made me just like you." I had hoped to hide my immortality from the Guild, but, of course, Fletcher could not allow that. He wanted me to suffer the same fate as him, in every way possible, and so he had sent a letter to my father, telling him what I had become. I remember the look of disgust on my father's face as the Grand Master himself cut through my hand and, hours later, his revulsion that the wound had healed itself.

"Yes. I delivered the letter myself. I believe you lost your job over that – how unfortunate. After all, ten years would hardly have been a sacrifice for someone who's going to live forever."

"God dammit, Fletcher! What Anna did to you was wrong. Nobody knows that better than me, but the Guild might be able to help us. To end this, once and for all. Why won't you let us help you?"

"The Guild cannot help us. There's no undoing what your sister did." The words spike as his anger mounts again, and, without warning, the knife streaks from his hand. I dodge aside, but not fast enough, and the blade pierces the muscle of my right arm. It isn't deep, but I curse in frustration and pain.

"Son of a bitch!" I yank the knife out and hurl it aside, as Fletcher's throaty chuckle pricks at my pride.

"Do you know I dream of death, Clarke? I dream of an end to this existence and it's only been a hundred years. What will we be like in a hundred more – in a thousand more? When the world finally tears itself apart, will we alone remain in the ashes of mankind?"

"It won't come to that. The Guild..."

"The Guild want me for a prisoner and nothing more! There is nothing they can learn from me that they can't learn from you. We are the same, Clarke – if they want a lab rat, I say you go first."

I use his momentary distraction against him and catapult forward, knocking aside his arm as it comes up to protect him. With my other hand, I drive my dagger upward, aiming for his chest. There is an infinitesimal second during which I believe I've succeeded, but then the air is driven from my chest and I am flying backward, Fletcher's perfectly formed fist still clenched in mid-air. I land painfully beside the bed, stars bursting in my vision as my head cracks painfully against the wooden block floor. Through the humming in my head I hear the desolate clatter of my daggers sliding away.

He is on me in an instant, his bare hands around my throat.

"Trained by the Guild all these years and this is the best you can do?" he hisses, his breath hot on my face. My empty hands scrabble against his wrists, but he barely notices. Instead, I bring my leg up and twist my torso, shifting his weight off me. It's all I need. His grunt of surprise becomes a howl as I drive the palm of my hand up, and, a second later, the blood from his nose spatters onto my chest. Automatically he claps his hands to his face and I scramble out from under him, landing a well-aimed kick to his torso. I scan the ground, finally locating one of his own discarded knives and I dive for it. A hand seizes my ankle, pulling me backwards and I kick out at him, rewarded by a satisfying thud of flesh. The hand releases me, but my relief is short-lived. Fletcher hurls himself onto my back, his body weight halting my progress. I twist savagely below him until we are nose to bleeding-nose.

"Stop it!" Fletcher hisses, a mixture of blood and spit flecking my face. I close my eyes under the intensity of his own. "Stop it," he says again, but this time he is talking to himself and I feel his body relaxing over mine. When I open my eyes again he seems to have regained some of his composure. Suddenly, he leaps to his feet – a graceful movement – and offers me his hand. My chest is heaving and I eye it wearily, but the knife is too far away and he is right. This is pointless. We can't kill each other, and, despite my years of combat training, I won't subdue him easily. His grip is firm as I place my hand in his and he hauls me to my feet.

I slump onto the edge of the bed, rubbing my bruised chest. I've waited for this moment for so long but all I feel now is a sense of overwhelming weariness.

"Why are you here, Fletcher? Just tell me."

His answer, when it comes, is nothing I would have expected.

"Because it's time you entered the game, Clarke."

"What game?"

"The game we've been playing for decades."

"I'm not playing any game."

He gets to his feet, straightening his sleeves and I watch in silence as he retrieves his knives, stowing them away and pulling his jacket over them.

"Where are you going?" I ask, panicked. This might be my only chance to finally bring him in, but my daggers are nowhere in sight.

"I'm leaving," he says, "but don't worry, you'll see me again soon. As soon as you figure it out, you'll know where to find me."

"Figure what out?"

He grins, gazing down at me as he pulls the newsboy cap low over his eyes.

"You can keep the cufflinks," he winks. Of course he noticed I'd taken them. "And here's something else to remember me by." He tosses something at my feet and it makes a solid clunk, but I know better than to take my eyes off him.

"Come and find me, Clarke." He throws down the challenge before disappearing from the room.

The second he is out of the door I leap to my feet, scouring the room for my daggers, but by the time I find them, he is gone. And, lying on the rug at my feet, is my father's pocket watch.

TWELVE
A LINCOLN GIFTS A KENNEDY

"HOW DOES he expect you to find him?" Aunt Elizabeth asks, her intelligent eyes narrowed. We are sitting at the kitchen table, emotionally exhausted after I have relayed everything that happened in Charleston. I caught the first bus out of Flagstaff the morning after Fletcher's visit, but I have come home to Aunt Elizabeth's and I haven't made contact with the Guild, although I can't for the life of me explain why.

"I have no idea." I turn the pocket watch over and over in my hand, my fingers tracing the dent in the casing. It looks exactly the same as I remember it, including the deeply gouged scratch on the glass.

"How do you think he got hold of it?" Aunt Elizabeth asks, her face a scowl of fearful disapproval.

"He didn't rob my father's grave," I reassure her, sensing where her dark thoughts are headed. "I suspect he was telling the truth about following me all these years. He probably took it from my father's dying hand shortly after the last time I saw him."

She crosses herself, an uncharacteristic gesture from one so unflappable.

"Think, Clarke," she instructs. "He told you to come and find him. Which means that, somehow, you're supposed to figure out where he is. He must have left you a clue."

"He didn't. He didn't mention anything about where he's been." I scratch irritably at the gauze bandage on my arm. The wound beneath it hurts, but it will heal. One thing I've learned about being immortal – we can be hurt and we can feel pain just like everyone else – we just don't die. The immunity that prevents us from becoming ill doesn't extend to physical injury. You stick a knife in me, I'm going to bleed; I just won't bleed out, no matter how many litres of blood I lose. I always recover.

"He had nice clothes, you said?" Aunt Elizabeth asks. "Expensive clothes?"

"Yes." I stop fiddling with the bandage. "And the cufflinks were definitely not within your average budget. Jimmy valued them at around $35,000.00."

Her lips pull tight in the way they always do when I mention my pawn broker's name.

"And I bet he only gave you a fraction of that," she says primly.

"He gave me enough."

"I can't believe you sold them. How do you know they weren't supposed to lead you to Fletcher?"

"The only place they'd lead me is Jacob & Co."

I am opening and closing the cover of my father's watch, the clicking sound driving Elizabeth to distraction.

"Stop that!" She bats at my hand and the watch drops innocently onto the table before us.

"I hate this thing," I say, but I don't pick it up again.

"It was your father's most prized possession." Elizabeth reminds me, as if that is reason enough for my loathing of the harmless object. Elizabeth is well aware that I care little for my father's memory. "Why do you think Fletcher stole it?"

"Because he's Fletcher," I growl, getting to my feet and moving over to the window. "He probably did it just so he could throw it in my face a hundred years later."

"That seems a little petty."

"It's Fletcher," I remind her. "His sole mission in life is to cause me pain and suffering."

"But he knew how you felt about your father."

"So?"

"So he knew this wouldn't hurt you. If he had wanted to cause you pain he would've given you something of Anna's."

Automatically, my fingers go to the daggers at my hips, brushing the silver handles. The familiar feel of the grooved etchings steadies me. Elizabeth watches, empathy shining in her eyes. I took these daggers from Fletcher's clock and Anna's chest, respectively. They are the very same ones my sister used to kill herself and to destroy Fletcher's clock. I've been carrying them for almost a hundred years, a constant reminder of the gravity of the burden I bear.

"Clarke?" Elizabeth's voice is gentle, bringing me back to the breezy kitchen.

"I'm fine," I say, turning back and scooping up the watch.

"Oh, I doubt that," she says breezily, "it's just that your phone is ringing."

"What?" I ask, squinting at the fine, delicate print on the back of the pocket watch.

"Your phone?" Aunt Elizabeth's voice is an unanswered question. "Clarke?"

I feel a shiver run up and down my spine, slowly at first, and then the hairs on the back of my neck prickle as understanding dawns.

"Look at this!" I shove the watch under her nose and she takes an involuntary step back.

"What am I looking at?" She squints at the battered casing, seeing nothing. "I don't have my glasses on." Her unhurried movements as she turns to search for them is infuriating.

"The manufacturer's stamp," I say, slightly breathless, "it reads P.L, 1863."

"And? Aha!" she exclaims, finally locating her glasses on top of her head and putting them on. She looks at me questioningly over the rims.

"Do you know why my father loved this damn watch so much?" My mind is racing, already ten steps ahead and trying to figure out what it means, but I need to bring Elizabeth up to speed. "It belonged to Abraham Lincoln."

"*The* Abraham Lincoln? Grand Master of the Guild?"

I smile at her. "And President of the United States, yes. But that's not the point. The point is that the watch belonged to him before he gifted it to my grandfather who served on his council at the time."

"Who, in turn, gifted it to your father?" Elizabeth is enjoying this guessing game now.

"No," I shake my head. Grandpa Kennedy gave it to Jeremiah, actually, when he was inducted as Grand Master."

"So why didn't Jeremiah pass it down to his sons?" Elizabeth muses. "To my dad, or uncle William?"

"He gave it to my father in his dying hour in an effort to make amends."

"Amends?"

"When Anna committed her crime, the whole family paid the price. Jeremiah was asked to step down as Grand Master and my father was ousted from the council. They fell out - Jeremiah blamed my father for his monumental fall from grace. They didn't speak again until Jeremiah was in his final hours."

"And that's when he gave the watch to your dad?"

"Yes."

"Right!" Elizabeth punches the air beside her and then a frown creases her already lined forehead. "And the point of all of this would be?"

"Sorry, I got distracted. The point is that this is a Waltham pocket watch. It belonged to Abraham Lincoln, but was made for him by the American Watch Company in 1863."

Aunt Elizabeth has the look of a woman who is trying desperately to look enlightened when, in truth, she's drawing nothing but a complete blank.

"The American Watch company," I repeat, brushing the engraving with my thumb. "So who the hell is P.L?"

I am still racking my brain when my phone starts to ring again.

"Hello?"

"Clarke." Truman's voice, panicked and breathless with relief. "It's about time."

Truman, I only missed one call about a minute ago."

"Yeah, right, sorry. It's urgent. Harrison needs you at the Hall of Clocks."

"Right now?" I'm still in my pyjamas.

"Yesterday."

It's not long before I'm heading downriver, the sun beating down on my bare arms.

The dinghy's engine whines as I try to make it go faster than it's capable of going. Eventually the nose bumps against the stone and I start to climb, wincing as my injured arm protests every inch of the way. My mood doesn't improve as I make my way through the labyrinth of hallways and it's certainly no better as I descend the final ravine.

"Whatever this is, it better be good," I announce as I enter the antechamber. Neither Vincent nor Harrison, who stands beside him looking thunderous, responds. Harrison looks grey, and not in his usual grizzly way, but rather as if he's aged ten years overnight. The lines on his brow could be etched in stone and his mouth is pulled so tight his lips have all but disappeared.

"Vincent?" I turn to the Clock Keeper, who looks only marginally less grim. Vincent shakes his head, a twitch that is barely noticeable.

"Clarke," Harrison breaks the silence, his gravelly voice hoarse with strain. "There's something you need to see."

Without any further explanation he moves across the room toward the wooden screen that hides Fletcher's clock from sight. My panic mounts as I follow, my thoughts immediately turning to the child, Cody Johnson, whose name is on that clock. Has something happened? Did I read it incorrectly? No, I couldn't have. I have months – plenty of time before baby Cody's time is up. As we get closer, I can almost imagine I hear the dial whirring, encompassing 360 degrees in the space of only eight months. A short life - a cruel one.

"Harrison?" I say as he starts to pull the screen forward. He ignores me. "Harris—"

The name dies a swift death on my lips, replaced by a gasp of shock. My knees threaten to buckle beneath me, but I remain standing through sheer force of will. Beside Fletcher's clock, hung perfectly, as though it has been there all along, is a second clock. A clock bearing my name and a date of death thirty-four years ago.

THIRTEEN
THE KEY TO THE CLOCK

"THIS ISN'T POSSIBLE." They are the first words I'm capable of uttering. "It can't be real."

"It is," Harrison's voice is gentle, the softest tone he's ever taken with me. "I've examined it extensively. It's yours."

"But Fletcher destroyed my clock. He had to have or how am I still here? How is my name still on this clock?"

"Because he didn't destroy it," Harrison gestures again at the perfect wooden disc. "He found a way to freeze time. For you, anyway."

Now that he's mentioned it, I wonder why I didn't notice it immediately. My clock is in perfect condition, the smooth surface unmarred, the golden writing clear and concise. The clock is identical to every other clock hanging in the Hall of Clocks, except for one glaring omission. It has no dial.

"Fletcher removed it," Harrison murmurs unnecessarily, as though he fears I might be inclined to blame someone else.

The mention of Fletcher sparks an anger within me.

"How the hell did he get in here?" I round on Vincent. "How did my clock end up on this wall?"

"I have no idea. I woke up and it was there. The screen had been moved or I wouldn't have known."

"That screen makes one hell of a noise, Vincent. Are you telling me you slept through that, from only a few feet away?" The Clock Keeper's sleeping quarters are in a small room off the antechamber and I point toward the doorway in disbelief.

"Yes." He lifts his chin defiantly. "That's exactly what I'm telling you. Unless you think I let Fletcher Kincaid waltz in here and handed him a hook?"

"We know that Fletcher's been here before," Harrison interrupts brusquely, "when he stole your clock in the first place." He glares at me, warning me to back down. "How he got it back is worrying, but that's not the most pressing issue at hand. To be honest, I'm glad he did. I'd rather that clock be here where it belongs, and, besides, now we know how he did it."

His words draw my eyes back to the clock. It looks naked, almost vulnerable, without the shifting golden dial. I force my feet forward and place my palm over the smooth wood. It's warm under my hand, pulsing with life - *my* life – and it dawns on me how fragile that is, despite my immortality.

"How did we not know this could happen?"

The question is rhetorical, but Vincent answers me anyway, so immediately it's as if the response is programmed inside of him. Which, obviously, it is. All members of the Guild take the oath.

"We don't interfere with time. It's our most sacred law."

I am so sick to death of the Guild's laws, but I refrain from saying so.

"You're telling me that in the entire existence of mankind no one in the Guild ever yanked off a dial to see what would happen?" I snap.

"That would be a crime against the Sovereign himself. We are here to watch over time, not to interfere with it. No Clock Keeper would ever consider it..." he trails off uncomfortably and I grit my teeth.

"Except Anna," I say, giving voice to what we are all thinking. "Anna destroyed Fletcher's clock."

"If only she'd done this instead," Harrison sighs, gesturing at my clock.

"What?" Vincent and I speak as one.

"Think about it, Clarke. Fletcher's clock is destroyed. Yours isn't. There's a way to reverse what happened to you."

I fall into stunned silence as the full impact of his words washes over me. The dial. If we could find it – if we could put it back...

"I'll die," I whisper, my feet moving of their own accord, pulling me further away from the clock as if they might be able to outrun death itself.

"Yes," Harrison grunts and I am at least comforted to see that the thought makes him uncomfortable. "In theory. We can only assume that if that dial is put back it will try to follow the course of action it was destined to. You would age and die within seconds."

"Of course, it *is* just a theory," Vincent is quick to add. "In reality, we have absolutely no idea what would happen."

I appreciate that he is trying to soften the blow, but in my heart, I know that Harrison is right. For so long I have cursed my immortality – my life stretching before me on an endless horizon – but now, suddenly, I'm afraid of the alternative.

"What do we do now?" I ask Harrison, all business, masking my fear.

"Fletcher has that dial."

"So we still have to find him," Vincent offers, but he doesn't sound as thrilled by the prospect as he once was. I exhale deeply, mentally facing the consequences of my actions, and I pull my father's watch from my pocket.

"I have something that might help," I say, preparing myself for the awkward conversation coming.

Harrison leaves first, his shoulders stooped, and I wonder how he even managed the treacherous climb into the Hall. I am about to follow him, fear for his safety overriding my dislike of him as a man, when Vincent halts me with his words.

"You would've died an old lady," he says quietly. I look to him for an explanation and he gives me a nostalgic smile. "I looked at it. I hated doing it, but I needed to know what it was before I contacted the Guild. You would've been eighty-four."

"I'm a hundred and eighteen, now."

"You look pretty damn good for your age." A moment passes between us, neither of us knowing exactly what to say. He will be gone soon and I don't know if I'll be back before then. Vincent takes a deep breath, as if coming to a decision.

"Pismo Beach," he says.

"What?"

"Pismo Beach. That's where I'm headed when I get out of here. After ten years of being cooped up in the dark, I can almost smell the surf." He meets my curious gaze and his eyes send a silent message.

"If you ever need me, that's where you'll find me."

I throw my arms around him and squeeze as hard as I can.

"You deserve it, Vincent. Be happy." I let him go and his face is flushed with embarrassment. "And make sure you get your retirement package," I add, trying to lighten the mood.

"Oh, don't you worry," he says, "I've already put in my list of demands. I'm going to be drowning in all the candy I can eat."

FOURTEEN
A RIDDLE IN PLAIN SIGHT

"WHOEVER ALTERED the inscription knew exactly what he was doing," Truman whistles through his teeth, the magnifying glass making his eyes look enormous as he glances up at me.

I bite my tongue to keep from snapping that he's said that at least ten times in the past month, but it's not Truman's fault that we aren't getting anywhere. I suspect this is a riddle that only I am meant to solve, and only when Fletcher deigns to let me.

"Are you sure this is Abe's?" Truman asks sceptically. "I thought the Lincoln watch was in the custody of the Smithsonian?"

"We control the Smithsonian," I remind him. "And no, the watch they have is a fake. Lincoln's great-grandson donated a replica back in the fifties to appease public curiosity."

"I probably could've found that in our records," he admits sheepishly before going back to examining the engraving. A moment later he continues where he left off.

"The change is virtually undetectable. If you hadn't pointed it out I would never have picked it up."

"You've spent a month examining every inch of that watch and that's all you've got?" I say, momentarily losing my fragile grip on my frustration. He pouts and I relent.

"Are you sure he didn't just sand away the original inscription?"

"No," Truman shakes his head and the magnifying glass clipped to his headband falls back into place. "You'd see the damage immediately. More likely he had the casing melted down and reset, then banged it up a bit so no one would notice. There can't be many moulds like this one lying around this century. It might be a lead."

"In that case, I suggest you get onto it, Truman." Harrison's deep voice growls from the doorway. We hadn't even heard it open. For a large man, Harrison is incredibly stealthy on his feet. "We've wasted enough time already."

For once I am in wholehearted agreement with the Grand Master. Every day that goes by brings me closer to Cody Johnson's death. It's been weeks since my clock reappeared in the Hall and we have made absolutely no progress.

"Clara," Harrison says, as Truman starts typing frantically beside me. "A word in my office? You too, Truman," he adds, and Truman obliges immediately, bringing his laptop with him.

Harrison waits until the door is closed behind us before he weighs in. The same argument we've had almost daily since I showed him the watch.

"This investigation is getting us nowhere," he says, and then, eying me closely, "are you sure you haven't seen him?"

"Harrison, if I'd seen him I would tell you."

"And yet you didn't inform us when you saw him in Charleston."

"I did. The day after I got back."

"When you offered up your father's watch," he muses, "after Fletcher returned your clock and you realised you had something to gain."

"Are you questioning my loyalty?"

"It's hard not to," he admits. "Fletcher was in Charleston – that's the closest we've ever been to catching him. You know we have a strong Guild presence in West Virginia - you should've informed me the very same night. I could've sent a team to search the area and assist you."

"That wouldn't have helped. He'd have been long gone by the time your team arrived. I'm telling you the watch is the key - we need to focus on the inscription. That's the way to find him."

He can't help having one final dig.

"We wouldn't need to investigate the inscription at all if you had done your job and brought Fletcher in."

"I've *told* you, I tried. He got away."

"You've spent decades training with some of the best fighters in the world."

"Yeah, well I guess Fletcher's are even better than ours. By all means, though, Harrison," I gesture pointedly at his rotund frame, "if you feel you can do better, be my guest."

"Don't forget who you're talking to, Clara," he warns menacingly.

"It's Clarke," I sigh, the fight draining out of me. "And yes, I failed to bring Fletcher in, but I'm going to find him. And soon."

Truman's fingers cease their relentless tapping. His big eyes peer at me over the screen and I fight the urge to snap at him for his lack of tact.

"How do you know that?" Truman asks.

"Because he wants me to." It's the first time I've admitted it.

"He wants you to find him? How do you know this?"

"Because he told me."

"That wasn't in your report!" Harrison snatches up a stack of papers and starts flipping through them ferociously. "What else did he say?"

"It's hard to recall." I am being petulant, but I'm tired and frustrated. I have been over this with Harrison so many times I'm sick of talking about it. Or so I tell myself. In truth, I've been out of sorts all day. Today is April 5th. The one-hundred-year anniversary of Anna's death - of Fletcher's death – and it's a date I've been dreading, knowing that it will bring up all the pain of that night again.

Harrison's leathery hands hit the desk with such force that Truman's fingers are buoyed back into action.

"Dammit Clarke, stop being so God-damned difficult! I know it's the anniversary, but this is important! Fletcher may have said something that could help us bring him in. Isn't that what we all want?"

Harrison and his predecessors have asked me this question so many times that my internal response is almost automated. *Of course it is. We share a common enemy, a common goal.* But, for the first time ever, something in me protests, and it has nothing to do with my newfound fear of my own death. Something about seeing Fletcher again has changed the way I have come to think of him. All these years I have built him up as a monster in my mind, but, having seen him in the flesh made me realise that there is a part of him that is still Fletcher. It is a small rebellion, one that takes place deep down inside of me, but it takes me completely by surprise. Fortunately, Harrison doesn't seem to notice my hesitation. He sets the papers back down on his desk, visibly pulling himself together, taking my silence for agreement.

"Let's go back to what we know," he says and, feeling guilty, I nod my consent.

"He's amassed a fair deal of wealth?"

"Yes. He definitely has money."

"What else?"

"He still wears the newsboy cap."

"The what?"

"I think we call it a flat cap now," Truman offers helpfully. "It's a rounded cap with a small stiff brim in the front..."

"I know what a flat cap is, thank you Truman," Harrison barks. "What I don't understand is why that's important?"

"I don't know," I reply, "I just thought it was worth mentioning."

The phone on Harrison's desk rings, and Truman gives me an apologetic grin as Harrison bends over the desk to answer it. He is silent for a moment and then his face seems to drain of what little colour it has.

"Get a trace running immediately," he orders. "Immediately!" And then, catching my eye, "Wait five seconds and put him through." He holds out the handset, looking as though it might combust in his hand. "It's for you. It's him. He says he'll only speak to you. We need at least thirty seconds," he adds meaningfully before he falls absolutely silent and the phone is in my hand.

I hold the receiver up to my ear.

"Hello."

"Hello Clarke," Fletcher sounds positively jovial. I snatch my father's pocket watch from Truman's hand and watch the second-hand ticking. It seems to be moving in slow motion.

"I'm disappointed," Fletcher says. "It's been a month. I thought you would've found me by now."

"I'm working on it," I say.

"I'm sure you are. You and Harrison and even young Truman. Between you and me, I think he fancies you, the way he follows you around."

I feel again the frustration that he seems to always be one step ahead of us. How has he seen Truman and I together? How does he even know his name, for that matter?

"You returned my clock," I say. Twelve more seconds.

"I did. I hope you appreciate the effort."

"I would, if it wasn't missing one very important component." Seven seconds.

"Yes, your dial. I thought you might notice."

"Where is it, Fletcher?" Two seconds.

"It's right in front of you." I know before I even hear the click that he's hung up. I stare at the pocket watch, not sure if we got the trace, but then Truman shakes his head and Harrison's curse ricochets around the room.

As Harrison bursts into frenetic energy, snatching up the phone and barking into the receiver, and Truman shakes his head, getting to his feet and pacing the floor, I slump into the same chair I sat in almost two months ago after I'd killed Henry Abbott. The door opens and people file in, rushing to follow Harrison's instructions. A sheet of paper floats off his desk and I watch it until it lands at my feet, my mind strangely blank, shutting out the sounds of the chaos around me. *I'm disappointed.* Something is flitting just beyond my reach, something important. Fletcher made this call for a reason. He knew I'd be here. He was trying to tell me something, I just need to figure out what it is. *I thought you would've have found me by now.* Truman's fingers are drumming his keyboard so quickly that the individual taps blur into a steady drone and I focus on the sound, blocking out everything else. *I think he fancies you, the way he follows you around.* I lift my eyes and fix my gaze on the window. *It's right in front of you.*

It hits me between the eyes with a clarity that is as dazzling as it is chilling. Only Fletcher could be that arrogant. I rise, moving like a ghost through the bodies crammed into Harrison's office. By the time I reach the window, I am one hundred percent certain and a wry smile pulls at my lips. There's something to be said for the irony of an immortal making his fortune from humanity's fear of death.

"Clarke?" Harrison has finally noticed me. The room falls silent, as though every person inside it is holding their breath. I turn away from the window to face him.

"When did *Perpetual Life* buy that building?"

"What?"

"The building across the street. The insurance giant. When did they buy the building?"

"The seventies, early eighties maybe? How am I to know?"

"He's been watching us for decades," I say, shaking my head at how easy it must have been for Fletcher. How he discovered where the Guild's headquarters were situated is anyone's guess, but he positioned himself perfectly to monitor all of its comings and goings.

I hold up my father's watch.

"P.L.," I say, seeing understanding dawning on a few faces. "*Perpetual Life.* Fletcher made his fortune selling life insurance. He's been rubbing our noses in it for decades and we never picked it up."

Harrison follows the line of my gaze to gape at the skyscraper opposite.

"Son-of-a-bitch!" he breathes. "He's been hiding in plain sight."

"That's impossible," Truman insists. "We would've known – someone would've seen him..."

"Who?" I ask, opening my arms to encompass everyone in the room. "No one alive today knows exactly what he looks like." I turn back to the window, lowering my voice. "No one but me."

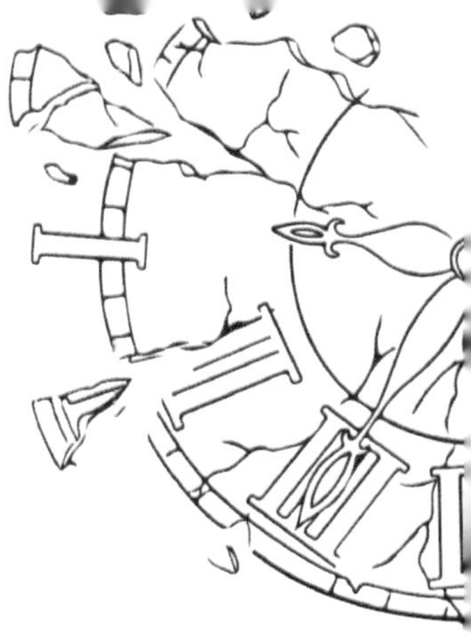

FIFTEEN
A NARROW ESCAPE

THE GUILD, for all its history and culture, has adapted beautifully to a modern, technological world. Within minutes of Fletcher ending the call, Harrison has assembled a small but highly effective team to infiltrate the *Perpetual Life* building. They move in unison, dressed in state of the art black suits, and each of the seven men carries a high-tech sniper's rifle with a scope that could no doubt pick Fletcher off from half a mile away in the middle of a Katy Perry concert.

I watch with conflicting emotions as Harrison starts to formulate a plan which involves both roof and road access and a thorough sweep of the building, but my mind is revolting against his idea just as soon as he voices it.

Truman is frantically searching the Guild's database, and, no doubt, a few others that he shouldn't theoretically have access to.

"Company records list one Edward Fletcher as the CEO of *Perpetual Life*," he announces to the room at large. My stomach flips. Edward was my father's name.

"It must be him," Harrison grunts approvingly. "I want all of you ready to go in three minutes. We'll have to..."

"Harrison," I interrupt, and, to my, and the team's astonishment, he stops speaking immediately, giving me his full attention. "I have to go in alone," I say, not mincing my words. I probably have about six point four seconds before he dismisses my idea as insane, so I need to make them count. "He'll expect this," I gesture at the assembled team with a sweep of my arm, "and he'll have made provisions to evade capture. You won't catch him. It's me he wants to see – he's practically invited me in. If we have any chance of this working, it has to be me."

"Clarke..."

"Besides," I continue, not letting him shoot me down just yet. "What if I'm wrong about *Perpetual Life*? Do you really want to bring attention to the Guild? If we storm over there, putting guns on the streets, there's no going back, and no matter how much PR you throw at it, it's going to bring a whole lot of unwanted attention down on you. For all we know that could be his plan – remember the newspaper article? He did it for no other reason than to bring heat to bear on Tempus. We can't take that risk again unless we're absolutely sure he's in there."

"So what would you have me do?" Harrison asks, displaying extraordinary self-control.

"Send me in first – alone. I can identify Fletcher and send you a signal as soon as I've confirmed it's him. I assume we have some tech that'll do that?" I add, turning to Truman.

"A simple transmitter will do," he says, as if the matter is already resolved.

"Clarke," Harrison glares at Truman as if to remind him who's in charge. "He'll know you're a decoy."

"So?" I shrug. "It's not as if he can kill me. He'll let me in, though, of that I'm certain." And I am. Fletcher making contact in Charleston, giving me my father's watch, returning my clock – it's all part of an elaborate plan and this is his final move.

"What if he escapes?"

"There's more chance of that happening if they rush in there," I say, casting an apologetic look at the soldier nearest me. "At least this way I can keep him contained long enough for them to get inside."

"He beat you before."

I wince at the brutal reminder of my failure in Charleston.

"He caught me unaware."

"You think you can beat him?"

"I don't know," I admit, "but I can promise you I won't let him out of that building until the team arrives."

Harrison holds my gaze longer than is necessary but I don't lower my eyes. Finally, he nods.

"You better get going, then. Truman?"

"I'm on it."

As he rushes from the room Harrison calls for the attention of the soldier standing nearest me.

"Jefferson, she'll need a weapon – a gun – something small that can be concealed."

"I don't want a gun," I insist, waving away the revolver he holds out and lifting my shirt to reveal the daggers at my hips.

"Those aren't going to be much use if he has a gun." Jefferson's derision is so comically mortal that I laugh.

"Why don't you try and use it against me and see how far it gets you," I smile wickedly. "I will take this, though," I whip the black cap off his head and pull it over my own, threading my braid through the back. Truman stumbles back into the room, knocking over a chair as he does and Harrison raises his eyes heavenward.

"Here," Truman shoves a small, compact device into my hand. A single red light flashes at the base. "Press this," he gestures at an almost undetectable button at the top, "to call in the cavalry."

I pretend to measure its weight in my hand for a moment, but in truth, I'm inspecting the device. It's heavier than it looks, but other than the button and the light, there are no obvious signs of surveillance tech. They won't be listening in and, for some reason, this comforts me.

I walk across the street in full view of the *Perpetual Life* building.

To the people milling around, I must make a fine sight, turning slowly, 360 degrees, with my hands held high. I can feel the eyes of Harrison and the Guild on my back and something darker - an intense scrutiny - from ahead. Still, I keep my face impassive as I walk through the revolving glass doors and into the cool, inviting lobby.

"Hello," I greet the desk man warmly. He gives me a professional smile.

"How can I help you today, Ma'am?"

"I'm here to see Mister Fletcher."

"Do you have an appointment?"

"As a matter of a fact, I do. Could you tell him that Clarke Kennedy is here to see him."

Before he can respond, the switchboard on his desk lights up and he snatches up the receiver. He listens intently for a second, as though hearing the word of God himself, and then he mutters a quick "Yes Sir" before replacing the handset.

"Mr Fletcher has asked that you come straight up." He gives me a far friendlier smile than before. "Take the elevator up to the tenth floor."

"Thank you." I walk through the security sensor and it lights up like a carnival ride. A beefy security guard steps toward me with a baton in his hand, his eyes roaming the length of my body for concealed weapons.

"She's not to be searched!" the deskman calls urgently. The man is taken aback, but he steps aside and lets me pass.

When the elevator stops on the tenth floor, I take an automatic step forward, but the doors remain firmly shut. A second of panic surges through me - what if I've walked into a trap – and then the doors slide open innocently, as if they had intended to do so all along.

"Hello Clarke." Fletcher is standing in the shadows to my left, his face lit eerily by the green glow emanating from the keypad beside him. He must have punched in a code to open the doors.

I don't say anything, distracted by my gloomy surroundings. The tenth floor is a shrine to Fletcher's history – a mish-mash of old and new, of antique wood and aluminium, culture and modern technology meeting in glorious vulgarity. Every interior wall has been torn down, creating a veritable hall that encompasses the entire floor. Light spills through the windows, while the globes in the ceiling remain dark.

The walls are a riot of haphazardly placed paintings and clocks of all shapes and sizes. On the wide mahogany desk beside the window nearest me is an assortment of pens and quills, and a glossy black laptop neighbours an old, dented typewriter. If I didn't know Fletcher's history, it would seem that insanity is reflected in every object.

"All this time," I breathe, a hushed whisper. "All this time and you've been right here."

"Not technically," he says. "To be fair, I only bought this building forty odd years ago."

"You've made a fortune out of life insurance." I don't know what makes me say it, but something about the fact that he has become so wealthy – so powerful – irks me. I have a sudden longing for the man I knew – the humble street rat who didn't care about money, so long as he had a warm bowl of stew and his music for company.

"There's a certain beauty in it, isn't there? I figured if I could live forever, why not trade in life? At least this way I get to die vicariously through my clients."

"You're insane."

"I'm eccentric. There's a difference."

"No, there's not. Eccentric is just a word to describe crazy people who happen to have money."

Fletcher laughs as if this concept is new to him.

"What am I doing here, Fletcher?"

The laughter dies on his lips. He glances at an ornate bronzed calendar on the far wall.

"You know what today is."

I stare at the date, the significance of it bringing a lump to my throat.

"Of course I know."

"One hundred years," he murmurs. His face goes blank, as though he is recalling each and every one of those years, but he offers nothing further.

I turn way from his intensity and my eyes light on a framed painting cast in shadow. It's the orchard, I realise, recognising the white picket fence running alongside a row of apple trees. It's the orchard at the Kennedy estate in Charleston where Fletcher and I used to spend our afternoons in secret. For some reason it pains me to look at it and I turn away from the painting, only to find another on the opposite wall. This one is of the pond in Flagstaff, complete with nettles and bugweed, and the beautiful willow tree which had made it magical.

Fletcher is watching me, gauging my reaction.

"Why do you have these here?" I ask. My breathing is becoming shallow, my head swimming. Fletcher is an anomaly; one I can't figure out. His hatred of my family is obvious, he has condemned me to a lifetime of loneliness, and yet he keeps these reminders of our past – reminders of a time when we were as close as two young people can be without crossing the line between being friends and lovers.

"I commissioned them to commiserate the ten-year anniversary." Something about his smile gives me pause for thought and I step closer to the landscape of the orchard.

"Monet?" I breathe, running my hand over the frame and squinting at the cramped signature. "Claude Monet?"

"He painted them just months before he died. Of course, he wasn't thrilled with having to abandon his perpetual documenting of the French countryside and his health was failing, but he owed me a favour. Besides, I'd kept him in Bolivar cigars for years."

"Monet died of lung cancer," I point out.

"Yeah," he grins unabashedly, "I always felt a bit bad about that."

"You lived in France?"

"For a while."

I am about to ask him about it when I pull myself up short. I'm not here to take a trip down memory lane. Fletcher is my enemy, not my friend. If he senses the change in me, he doesn't show it. Instead, he pulls the harmonica from his pocket and plays a haunting tune. It makes the hairs on the back of my neck stand on end. It's the same tune he was playing the night I last saw him. The night he stole my clock and made me immortal.

1916, *The Hall of Clocks, Arizona*

I STOOD IN THE ANTECHAMBER, staring, without seeing, out into the Hall where a sea of clocks stretched out before me. I had pleaded with my father, in this very spot, but it had been of no use.

"You have to take your sister's place." He had been harsh, unyielding.

"Papa, please, I've just lost Anna, I can't lose you too! It will drive me mad being on my own. I can't do it..."

"You can and you will, Clara! It is your duty and an honour to serve Tempus." He never mentioned Anna's name. It was as if, in his mind, she had never existed.

That had been ten days ago, the day after my sister died and I hadn't seen a soul since. Other than the weekly food delivery, which consisted of a lowly Guild member ferrying in a couple of boxes of sustenance and supplies, leaving them just outside of the antechamber doorway and departing as quickly as she or he had come, the life of the Clock Keeper was one of isolation. It was considered too great a temptation for anyone else to visit the Hall.

I swayed slightly on the spot, recalled I hadn't eaten, and dug unenthusiastically through the boxes. Armed with a fistful of dried meat and a single candle, I collapsed onto the small cot in the bed chamber and stared up at the ceiling. Shadows danced in the flickering candlelight. Heaving a sigh, I dropped the dried meat onto the small table beside the bed and pulled the covers over me, curling in on myself until I was nothing more than a tightly wound ball of pain and misery.

I slept, eventually, though my slumber was fitful and fraught with nightmares. I missed Anna so deeply that her absence filtered into my dreams. I missed Fletcher, too, and, knowing that the Guild was hunting him fanned a burning guilt deep in my core. If I had been braver I would've warned him – I should've warned him - to flee, to hide, to never stop looking over his shoulder. The Guild would help him, but secretly, I'd rather he be free than dead. Because that was their intention – to set right Anna's wrongs. Fletcher shouldn't be alive, and, as soon as they figured out how, the Guild would send him to his grave.

When I woke, the candle had long burned out, reduced to a cold, hard nub of wax. Blinking the sleep from my eyes it took a few moments to put my finger on the reason for my unease. The candle had gone out but I could still see. I should be shrouded in blackness, but a faint light filtered into the bedchamber, enough for me to see the outline of the door frame. My door was open, when I clearly recalled closing it.

My heart was beating somewhere near my throat as I tiptoed out of the room. I didn't have to go very far. As soon as I rounded the doorway, the source of the light became clear. A fresh candle burned merrily on my desk, and, in my chair, sat Fletcher. I watched, entranced, as he raised the harmonica to his lips and played a haunting melody, one so different to his usual ditties that it made me afraid. It ended on a long, lingering note, drawn out as if from his very soul.

When he was done he slipped the harmonica back into his pocket.

"Hello Clara," he said. I couldn't make out his eyes, hooded as they were by the newsboy cap, but his lips were tight, lacking their usual smiling softness. A muscle in his jaw twitched in harmony with the light flickering across his face.

"Fletcher." My lips were dry and my voice cracked under the strain.

He spread his arms, encompassing our surroundings.

"As you can see I've learned your secret."

"I'm sorry." A simple, underwhelming admission.

"For what?" Fletcher stood, rounding the desk and coming toward me. My legs backed up of their own accord, but there was nowhere for me to run, trapped as I was between him and the exit.

"Why are you sorry, Clara?" he continued, and now he was towering over me. With the feeble light now behind him I could barely make out his features.

"I died and came back to life. Your sister didn't only destroy me, she turned me into a demon. And, instead of helping me, you abandoned me and kept your precious secrets. So I'll ask you again, Clara. What exactly are you sorry for?"

"For all of it. But especially for what Anna did to you."

"She cursed me."

"Yes." To deny it would go against every belief I held sacrosanct.

"Well," Fletcher proceeded, sounding a little less intimidating, "at least I don't have to suffer alone."

I opened my mouth. Closed it. Tried to make sense of his words as a frozen hand swept down my spine. I suddenly wondered just how long he had been here – how long I had slept – and what he had been doing while I did.

"What have you done?" I managed eventually.

The curve of that terrible smile.

"Nothing that you don't deserve."

"Fletcher!" my heart stuttered, sped up, stalled. I could feel gooseflesh rising on my skin, my intuition hurling the answer at me before he could explain.

"What have you done?" I gasped, more insistent.

"You know what I've done. You should be thanking me. I saw you pleading with your father – I know how miserable you've been down here, alone. I've set you free, Clara."

"No," I shook my head frantically, my loosely-knotted braid whipping free. "No, Fletcher, please tell me you haven't...?"

"Come with me," he interrupted, holding out his arm. Like a moth to the flame I was drawn to the horror he was about to show me, and I slipped my arm through his. We walked through the Hall of Clocks in silence, moving deeper into the labyrinth, the single candle he held aloft providing the only light. I kept my eyes on the stone floor in front of me, studiously avoiding looking at the names on the clocks around us, but Fletcher turned his head this way and that, curious and unrepentant.

"It took me a while to find it," he mused, as we rounded a corner, and I fought the urge to ask him how long he had been down here with me.

"Here." He stopped abruptly and released my arm. I dragged my eyes up to find a bare patch of earthen wall amidst the chaos of clocks. Such a small empty space, it seemed remarkably insignificant, but for the fact that I knew, deep down, whose clock should have been here. Mine.

"Why?" A whisper of breath, pregnant with pain.

Fletcher laughed, the sound as dry and guttural as the dust around us.

"Because now, like me, you can spend eternity alone. You will share my curse and my isolation. Loneliness will be your constant companion."

"We were friends," I sobbed, searching his face for any sign of the man I had known before. "I didn't do this to you."

"Anna may have wielded the blade, but you are responsible. You denied my affections so that Anna wouldn't be hurt, and you made me show her affection when she was ill, which led her to believe I felt the same way for her as she did for me. Her feelings for me would have been fleeting if you'd just told the truth."

I tried to shy away from him, burned by the venom in his voice, but he gripped my arm once more, forcing me to stay, to hear the awful words.

"You betrayed not only me, but your own heart, Clara. You are responsible, and now, you will know vengeance."

His hatred was my undoing and my knees buckled beneath me. Fletcher, unmoved by my tears, set the candle on the ground beside me and melted into the shadows as though the darkness had swallowed him whole.

IT WAS YEARS AGO, but thinking about it I can still feel the gravel pressing painfully into my knees. I focus on his office, on the here and now. Fletcher is still playing the mournful tune and, in a fit of temper, I knock the harmonica from his hand, silencing both the music and the memory.

"You didn't wait long to let Tempus know what you'd done," I say. "They came for me the next day - the Grand Master himself confirmed I was immortal. My father never spoke to me again."

"Then I guess you should be thanking me."

"Enough!" I yell. "I'm sick of your games!"

"But we're only just beginning."

I blink away tears of frustration, knowing that by letting him get to me I am only falling deeper into his twisted web.

"You have the dial," I say.

"Yes."

"Where is it?"

He grins at that, stooping to retrieve the harmonica.

"Now why on earth would I tell you that?"

"Because I'm begging. I'm tired, Fletcher. I'm tired of your games and I'm tired of cleaning up Anna's mess. Do you know that your clock is still working? New names appear on it, except that those people don't die."

"You make sure they do," he corrects, and it doesn't even surprise me that he knows about what I've been doing. "I thought you handled Henry Abbott's death especially efficiently," he adds.

I feel my temper fray.

"Do you know who replaced Henry Abbott?" I snap. "A child, Fletcher. A baby. One who is supposed to die only a few months from now."

"That's unfortunate." He sounds unmoved, but the skin around his eyes pulls tight and he scratches his hair beneath the cap.

"I can't do this anymore."

"You're going to have to. You're in this with me for the long haul, remember. I live forever, you live forever. My curse is your curse."

Something occurs to me then, a seed that Harrison planted bursting into bloom.

"Deep down you don't mean that."

Fletcher gives me a quizzical look.

"Oh, really? And how do you figure that?"

"You didn't destroy my clock. You could have - you've had a hundred years to do it - but you didn't. If you really wanted me to suffer for eternity you wouldn't have left me a way out."

It is only when I speak the words out loud that I truly believe them, but ever since Fletcher returned my clock something had changed within me. I had started to see him as something other than a monster – an enemy. He hadn't condemned me as Anna had done him. And therein lay his salvation. Despite his anger and his hatred there was still compassion inside him. He was redeemable.

"Give me back the dial, Fletcher," I murmur, and then, without knowing why, I lift my hand to his cheek and rest it there. "Let me go."

Time seems to slow down. I hear his shocked intake of breath and, for just a second, the briefest instant, I am transported back in time, faced with a different future, a different life. In this version, I do not deny my feelings. I do not fear my father's wrath or my sister's jealousy. In this version, I take a different path. *Yes, Fletcher, I love you. Yes, I will run away with you. Because you have my heart. I choose you.* And then he shoves me away from him, slapping my hand aside and the spell is broken.

"Very clever, Clarke," he drawls, assuming all his previous condescension. "You almost had me going for a second. It was a valiant effort, but I will never give you that dial."

"Why? Because you're so terrified of being alone? Come with me, Fletcher, please. Let the Guild try to fix this. Let us die, finally – we've lived long enough!"

"Do you honestly believe the Guild can make me mortal again?" he challenges. I urge my mouth to speak the words but the lie dies on my tongue before it even has a chance to materialise.

"No." I shake my head, my heart heavy.

"Well then I guess we live to play another game."

"No," I say again, and this time, the sadness that washes over me is overwhelming. He senses it as he always does and the knives appear in his hands.

"I'm sorry, Fletcher." I try to blink away the pain, but I feel the wetness on my cheeks. "but you've left me no choice."

I don't reach for my own daggers. Instead, my hand is curled around the transmitter in my pocket and I withdraw it slowly. Fletcher doesn't look surprised to see it.

"Still," he sighs, as if he has been waiting for this moment. "After all this time, you still choose them."

It floods my senses, an emotional assault, as I realise, finally, what his game means. It's been a test – all of it. I had betrayed him once and Fetcher wanted to know if I would do it again. I realise this a nanosecond too late, knowing I have failed, because my finger has pressed the button and the red light has turned green.

SIXTEEN
BLOOD ON MY HANDS

ONE SINGLE DECISION can change not only the course of your own life, but the lives of those around you. Anna had proved this. She had made a decision to pull Fletcher back from death, but that action had set in a motion a sequence of events that affected the lives of so many people, my own included. Anna had gone against the Guild with dire consequences. I could only hope that my own defiance wouldn't have the same effect.

"We have to go," I tell Fletcher, tossing the transmitter aside. "We only have about ten minutes before they storm this building so I hope you have a way out of here."

When he doesn't move, I seize his face in both of my hands, forcing him to look at me. "Fletcher! We have to go now!"

The stunned look is replaced by one of fierce determination, and, without saying a word, he snatches my hand and hauls me toward the elevator. He jabs at the keypad and the doors emit a low hiss as they open.

"Where are we going?" I ask, once we begin our descent.

"The basement."

"They'll come through the lobby and from the roof."

"We'll be long gone by then."

The doors open into a stark parking area. Fletcher breaks into a run and I follow him to a ridiculously flashy two-door coupé parked in one of the bays. There are no more than five cars in the entire lot.

"All yours?" I ask, as I yank open the passenger door.

He shrugs. "Life insurance is lucrative."

The powerful V10 engine roars to life and then surges forward like a beast escaping captivity as Fletcher tramps on the gas. A key-card swipe later and we pass beneath a boom-gate and emerge onto the street at the back of the building. I swivel in my seat, scanning the area, but I see nothing that raises any alarms. Not even four minutes have passed since I pressed the transmitter button.

"What kind of car is this?" I ask, my white-knuckled hand gripping the seat as Fletcher weaves the coupé recklessly in and out of traffic.

"An Audi R8."

We round a corner at breakneck pace and I prepare for a flip, but the low car grips the road like a long-lost lover, holding a perfect line.

"How much does it cost?" I ask through clenched teeth.

"You don't want to know."

Fletcher is enjoying himself. His hands are light on the steering wheel, the Audi responding to his slightest touch. He doesn't slow down even when we are miles away from the Tempus building, and my muscles begin to ache in protest at being bunched up for so long. I force myself to relax and take in our surroundings.

"Where are we going?"

"My place."

"Fletcher, now that they know who you are, the Guild will already be investigating your property and holdings. They'll come for us within an hour."

"Which is exactly why this house isn't listed in my name. I've eluded the Guild for a century, Clarke, you might want to give me some credit."

It still feels risky, but I keep my thoughts to myself and simply hold on for dear life as we streak through the streets, leaving the city behind.

The house is a sprawling estate nestled in the Foothills, with a sweeping drive, barricaded by two tall wrought-iron gates and flanked by marble pillars. A sleepy-looking man emerges from the small guardhouse on the left, but he becomes fully alert when he catches sight of Fletcher's face through the window.

"We weren't expecting you, Sir," he stammers apologetically.

"That's because I didn't call ahead, Luke," Fletcher says. "It's not a problem, but if anyone comes to see me, don't let them in, okay. And buzz me immediately."

Luke nods before disappearing back into the guardhouse.

"He's not going to keep the Guild out," I say.

"I'm not worried about the Guild," Fletcher grins. "There's a new divorcée across the valley who shows up unannounced every time she sees my car coming in."

I try desperately not to smile as the gates open and the Audi growls menacingly all the way up the drive.

The house is just as ostentatious as I expect it to be.

"Why didn't you just buy yourself a palace?" I grumble as we walk toward the front door, which is a full frosted-glass plate.

"I actually do own a small castle in Ireland. Why, don't you like it?" He gestures at the grand staircase, the antique piano in the hall, polished to within an inch of its life. Without thinking, I reply.

"I think I preferred the street rat."

Fletcher drops his arms. All the boyish charm vanishes as the darkness seeps back into his face.

"You rejected the street rat, remember?"

He stalks through a door to the left and I follow him into an enormous kitchen. Everything in this house is white – white marble, white tiles, white drapes. It makes it seem even bigger, but it's clinical, detached, as if Fletcher couldn't be bothered to stamp anything with his own colourful character.

"Tell me something, Clarke," he says, pouring a glass of water. He doesn't offer me one. "If I had been the son of a nobleman, would you have accepted me as a suitor? I'm just curious," he adds, sliding the glass toward me.

"Fletcher, this isn't the time to..."

"No," he agrees before I finish, "I guess you're right. It's not. This isn't about the past. It's about right now."

The glass is halfway to my lips when he pulls the gun from behind him. A flash of steel, and I freeze, so taken aback that I forget to be afraid. Slowly, I set the glass down on the Caesar Stone counter, trying to comprehend how we went from light teasing to this in such a short space of time. It strikes me again that Fletcher might be mentally unstable.

"Are you going to shoot me, Fletcher?"

It makes no sense. I'm immortal. A bullet can't kill me, although I have no doubt it'll hurt like hell.

"No." The barrel of the gun swivels and twists the skin beneath it as Fletcher presses it hard against his temple.

"What are you doing?" I whisper.

He gives me a smile of such sorrow that my heart constricts painfully in my chest.

"You chose me." Three little words with more emotion behind them than I could believe possible. "You chose me today over the Guild."

"I did." I nod slowly, my voice soothing, as if speaking to a child. "We can figure this out, Fletcher. You and me, together."

"I wanted so badly to hate you, to hold on to the past, to Anna's sins."

"But?" I take a tentative step to the left but he stiffens, the muzzle of the gun pressing so hard into the hollow of his skull that the edge disappears in a spiral of skin.

"But I can't. I needed you to choose them again, Clara, so that I could hate you for another hundred years."

"Why?" I ask as we face each other over the counter.

"Because hating you is the only thing keeping me from giving you what you want."

There is only one thing in the world I want from him, but I ask anyway.

"My dial?"

He nods. Takes a deep, steadying breath.

"Fletcher, please. Why are you doing this?"

He laughs then – a mournful, crazy, helpless sound.

"Because I love you, Clarke. I've always loved you. And I know I should give it back and let you go, but I don't want to be alone."

I squeeze my eyes shut, feeling his pain as if it is my own. I still don't understand what his intentions are – shooting himself won't end his life – but I suspect that something else will happen. Something terrible. I feel the sting of hot tears welling in my eyes and I blink them away, too afraid to take my eyes off him. His face is haunted, a conflicted myriad of love and hate, past and present, life and death.

"Please don't," I croak, but he doesn't hear me. In the second I open my mouth Fletcher pulls the trigger and I shut my eyes against the gruesome sight, feeling the flecks of his blood land softly on my skin.

PART 2

SEVENTEEN
SCARS BOTH OLD AND NEW

I STAND dumbstruck for at least ten minutes, unable to get my legs to move around the broad counter. The red spray is so vivid against the stark white, but my mind refuses to believe what just happened. I don't want to see Fletcher's body. I don't want to face the gruesome wound or the thick warm blood which I can already see creeping past the left side of the counter, as if it has all day to get to where it needs to be. No one comes to investigate the source of the gunshot, which was so loud I could still hear it echoing in my head. In a home such as this one there is, no doubt, a small troop of servants, but either they haven't heard, or, more likely, Fletcher has instructed them not to respond. There is a strong possibility that everyone in this house knows exactly what just happened. Was prepared for it, even. Everyone except me.

Ears still ringing, I thump my head with the palm of my hand, trying to kick-start my brain, which seems to have taken a momentary leave of absence.

"What were you thinking?" I murmur. I can smell the blood now, the awful, iron-tinged stench that is gathering momentum. *Pull yourself together, Clarke,* I tell myself. *He's not dead.* I take a tentative step around the counter. *He's not dead, he's not dead, he's not...* my silent mantra cannot stop the bile rising in my throat and my chest heaves. I turn away from Fletcher's body, vomiting spectacularly across the white caesar stone.

I rinse my mouth with the water in the glass and then I give myself a stern talking to. Fletcher will wake up. Maybe not today – in fact, I have no idea how long it will take to recover from an injury of this magnitude – but he will wake up. Right now, I need to get him somewhere safe. I cannot bear the thought of the Guild finding him. If he woke up alone and in custody, I would never get to say the things I needed to say. Fletcher had said his piece before pulling the trigger without affording me the opportunity to do the same.

"Selfish bastard," I snap, letting my anger give me strength. "And I'm not getting my shoes dirty," I add, moving to the side of the counter where his feet are protruding. I grab his ankles just above his expensive Italian shoes and pull him away from the pool of blood, averting my eyes from his head, where his dark hair is mopping a scarlet streak on the floor.

"And I am not cleaning this up," I continue. Talking, even if only to myself, is the only way I'm able to stay sane. "It serves you right for having such a stuffing white house."

"Miss Clara?"

I give a Tarzan yell of fright and promptly drop Fletcher's legs. A grey-haired woman, as wide as she is tall, is standing in the doorway of the kitchen, wringing her hands. I clutch my hand to my heart and she immediately starts to apologise.

"I didn't mean to startle you," she pants, wincing at the sight of the blood, "but you are Miss Clara?"

"Yes."

"I'm Martha, Mr Fletcher's housekeeper."

I don't respond, because 'it's nice to meet you' doesn't feel quite right under the circumstances.

"You'll be needing to clean him up, I'm guessing?" Martha continues, her eyes shimmering with tears. "His bedroom is upstairs. I can help you take him there. I'll sort this out," she adds with steely resolve as I glance helplessly around the kitchen.

"You knew he was going to do this?"

She nods.

"And you know he's not dead?"

Another nod.

"I've served Mister Fletcher for thirty-two years," she offers in explanation. Rubbing her hands briskly, she steps inside the kitchen. I realise Fletcher's top half is going to be a lot heavier than his bottom half, and, while Martha might be tougher than she looks, she is still well into her sixties. I move aside, gesturing at his feet and I back up until I reach his head. Already, the blood seems to be slowing. Fletcher's hair is slick with it, but when I lift him, only a few fresh drops fleck the tiles below.

Together we wrestle his lifeless form up the stairs, stopping every few minutes so Martha can catch her breath. I don't ask why she doesn't call for someone else to help – the guard at the gate, for example – because I assume that she has good reason. She seems calm enough and moves with single-minded purpose. When we finally reach Fletcher's bedroom there are dark circles in the pits of her sleeves and her hair is damp with sweat, but she soldiers on until he is laid out on his bed.

I know I'll have to assess the wound at some point, but I need a minute before I do. I turn away from the gruesome sight of him and my breath catches in my throat. Hanging above the fireplace directly opposite his four-poster is a life-size painting which makes it abundantly clear how Martha knew who I was.

"It's a great likeness," she whispers, coming to stand beside me. "Although he was right. You are far more lovely in the flesh."

I cannot formulate a response as I collapse heavily on the edge of Fletcher's bed. I perch there for a minute, feeling as though I've entered the twilight zone.

"I'll just leave you here for a minute, Miss Clara, while I sort out the kitchen," Martha says. Out of the corner of my eye I see her bustle out of the room. I should offer to help but I can't bring myself to do it and a few minutes later I hear the faint sounds of her cleaning downstairs.

Fletcher is still drenched in blood, but I can't tear my eyes from the painting. I have no idea how the artist captured me so perfectly, given that Fletcher had no photographs of me. How many canvases had come before this one? How much time had Fletcher spent with the artist, ensuring they got it right? All this time we had been enemies and yet he had this picture hanging in his bedroom. It dominated the wall. He must have looked at it every day. It was exquisite – a work of perfection, but what struck me the most – what drew me to it – was the fact that I wasn't depicted as a monster. If anything, just the opposite – I looked positively angelic. I was standing in a library of sorts – shelves of books were visible in the foreground, and, in the background, towering behind me stood a beautiful grandfather clock. The oaken colouring offset the milky fairness of my skin and my eyes were wide, my lips parted in a soft smile. My hair looked like spun gold, and the simple white dress I was wearing seemed to glow, creating an ethereal imagery. I looked how I must have before Anna died – a young girl with an air of innocence. There was no hint of rage or revenge here – only the memory of a man who so obviously cared.

The sun has dipped low on the horizon by the time I finally convince myself to move. Despite my endless inner monologue, I still cannot make sense of any of this, but the fact remains that I have decisions to make. I need to get Fletcher somewhere safe, somewhere he can recover without fear of the Guild finding us. I know he said we would be safe here, but my gut isn't in agreement and that means we need to go. First, though, I need to get a good look at his injury.

I leave the main light off and switch on the bedside lamp instead, angling the lampshade so that the light is focused on Fletcher's face. Blood has poured into his eyes, which are closed, and covers the entire right side of his face, as if a suicidal face painter went to town on it. Gingerly, I press my fingers against his temple, confirming that the wound has definitely stopped bleeding. Moving my hand around the back of his head, I find an exit wound, also not bleeding. It's as if the flesh has simply decided to send the blood away from the area, bypassing the injured area, until the wound can heal itself.

"You're an asshole," I tell a still unconscious Fletcher and then I heave a sigh and start to unbutton his shirt. I catch my breath at the sight of the ugly ridged scar on his abdomen. My fingers move across it of their own accord, tracing the line of the wound. This is where they stabbed him that night. This is how he should have died. I pull my hand away, brushing a solitary tear from the corner of my eye and start to pull the sleeves of the shirt down. Once he's naked from the waist up, I head into the *en-suite* bathroom and fill the basin with warm water. I soak the hand towel which I use to slowly clean Fletcher's face, hair and torso. It takes about ten trips before I don't have to refill the basin each time I return and the water starts to lighten to a pale pink.

Fletcher is relatively blood free by the time Martha returns, and together, we change the sheets on the bed, rolling him from one side to the other like a hospital patient.

"We should cover the wounds up," Martha says when we're done. "To minimise the risk of infection."

The wound in Fletcher's temple already looks smaller, a puckered black hole, and I wonder at the remarkable healing process, but she's right. I'd rather be safe than sorry.

"Are you sure he's going to be okay?" Martha asks as I bandage Fletcher's head a few minutes later with the gauze she has provided.

"He'll be fine."

"But... his brain...?" she lets the question linger there, unable to continue.

"Let's just say if he had a brain, I'd probably be a lot more worried," I tease, keeping my voice light, and I'm rewarded with a twinkle-eyed smile.

"You've taken this very well," I say, wishing there was a more tactful way to bring the subject up. I'm curious to know exactly how much Martha knows, but it's not an easy topic to discuss.

Martha, however, seems completely at ease as she replies.

"It's like I said – I've worked for Mister Fletcher for thirty-two years. In all that time, he's never changed – never aged even a day." She looks down at him fondly.

"When I first came to work here, my son, Henry, was only a boy. Mister Fletcher used to buy him the most extravagant gifts, every birthday and Christmas, like clockwork. He never forgot a single one. Henry's got a boy of his own, now – only a few years younger than Mister Fletcher, and he gets the same treatment. Lord that boy's eyes light up when he sees me coming home on special occasions. Spoilt rotten, I say, but Mister Fletcher insists."

"It doesn't bother you?" I ask. "The fact that he... that Fletcher's so different?"

"Why would it? He's a good man. That's all I need to know. He's taken care of me and my family."

"And you've never asked him about it? About why he doesn't age – why he can't die?"

"Lord, no! It's none of my business."

She smiles wryly at me then.

"Your painting's been hanging on that wall since I first set foot in this house. You're the same, you and him."

I nod, feeling suddenly and inexplicably shy.

"I don't know what happened between you young folk, Miss Clara, but I can tell you that you need to fix it. Mister Fletcher wouldn't do this unless he was desperate." Her eyes fix on the bandage around Fletcher's head and she gives a little sniff.

"Do you know why he did it?" I ask.

She regards me carefully for a few seconds, as though trying to decide if telling me would be a betrayal.

"I don't," she admits eventually, and my shoulders slump until I hear her next words. "But sometimes at night he'd take out that gun and hold it in his lap. It scared me half to death. That's when he told me not to worry – that if ever he used it he would come back."

She gives a shaky sigh.

"I asked him why he would bother, then, if it wouldn't kill him."

"And what did he say?" I ask between the space of her next breath.

"That he'd done things he wasn't proud of. Things he'd rather forget. I think he felt he deserved to be punished."

EIGHTEEN
THE POINT OF NO RETURN

THIS LOOKED *like a lot more fun when Fletcher was driving*, I think to myself the following morning, easing my foot down. For the second time the Audi stops abruptly and I smack my nose on the steering wheel. I've never been a confident driver and I can't seem to master the brakes, which, no matter how gently I press the pedal, respond as though an elephant is driving. The car also has a horrible habit of switching itself off at every stop which sets my nerves on edge.

I've left the still comatose Fletcher in Martha's capable hands while I scout my options. The luxury coupé is hardly ideal for blending in, and the start-stop jerking motion is making me feel nauseous so I abandon it a few miles out of town and jog the rest of the way, which is how I find myself hanging, like an orangutan, outside Aunt Elizabeth's kitchen window, crammed between the branches of a Jacaranda tree. It's not long before my thigh muscles begin to cramp in protest, but I stay put, watching the house for any sign of movement.

Thankfully I don't have to wait long. Aunt Elizabeth emerges onto the porch after just a few minutes, a steaming mug held aloft in her soft, white hands.

"You shouldn't be here," she murmurs through a breath of air over the cup. Steam billows from the hot tea and I automatically turn to scan the yard, searching for the person she's talking to. "I'm talking to you, Clarke," she says, looking anywhere but in my direction. The woman is uncanny. "Don't speak," she adds quickly, turning to lean against the porch rail, so that she is facing the house. Her words are harder to make out and I have to strain to hear her.

"They're watching the house. It's not safe for you here. At least you had the wits to sneak up." A hint of pride in her voice. "Harrison has already been here looking for you. I don't know what's going on but I assume you have a good reason for protecting Fletcher and I'm not about to turn in my own flesh and blood." By her furious tone I know, without a shadow of a doubt, that these are the exact words she must have told Harrison and I fight the urge to leap down and hug her. "I'm going back inside," she says, "I suggest you get as far from here as you can. Be careful, Clarke."

I watch her go back into the house, wishing for all the world that there was some way to communicate with her, to tell her how much I appreciate her and everything she's done for me; to explain why I betrayed the Guild and why I'm going against everything I believe in to keep Fletcher safe. But then I realise that I don't even know the answer to that last part, and so, instead, I climb down, and, keeping my head low, I disappear like the wraith that I am.

I take a cab back to the place where I left Fletcher's car. The cabbie waves as he drives away, one fare richer and one cell phone poorer. I lift the phone to my ear as I get back into the annoying Audi and dial my private line to the Guild. The woman who answers on the first ring sounds frantic and she quickly patches me through to Harrison, who is obviously not in the building.

"Clara!" he thunders as soon as the line connects. "What in the hell do you think you're doing?"

I'm a little offended that he hasn't even considered the fact that perhaps Fletcher overpowered me and has been holding me against my will, but Harrison doesn't give me the chance to voice my objection. "You tell me where you are right now!"

"No."

"No?" he sputters, and I can picture his red face, apoplectic with rage.

"No," I repeat firmly. "Harrison I have to do this on my own. I have an idea and I need time to test my theory."

"Have you lost your mind? You don't get to have ideas! That's why there's a council – the Guild is bigger than just one person."

"I know that. But it only takes one person to change the course of history."

He pauses, falling silent as he tries to decipher my words.

"You think you can reverse Fletcher's immortality?"

I hear it in his voice. I had never been sure, but the hope I hear now confirms that the Guild truly has no idea how to help Fletcher. I refuse to do the same thing they have – lie and claim to have all the answers - so I answer truthfully.

"Maybe."

"Then let us help you. Bring Fletcher in and we can..."

"It won't work," I cut him off. "I'm asking you to trust me, Harrison. The Guild has no idea how to fix this. I might, but I need time. I need the one thing that Tempus has sole control over." I take a deep breath. "And I need access to the Hall."

I can practically hear his ego battling his common sense and it takes a while for him to answer.

"How much time are you talking about?"

I think of Fletcher, lying unconscious in his bed.

"I can't tell you that yet."

"What can you tell me?"

"Not much," I admit. "This is all very hypothetical, but I promise you I wouldn't ask if I didn't think I could do it. So, will you help me?"

"I..." he trails off, unconvinced.

"The Guild has made absolutely no progress in a hundred years,"

I say boldly. "What's a few more weeks? You can either help me, or hinder me, but whatever you choose I am going to do this. It'll just be a lot easier with your help."

"I can't give you any guarantees."

"Yes, Harrison. You can."

He sighs. Grunts. Sighs again.

"I can probably buy you a few weeks."

"I'll take it." I punch the end call button and start the Audi's engine. As I pull out onto the street I allow myself a tight smile. Whether Harrison will keep his word or not, it's good to know that there's a chance I may be able to get back into the Hall of Clocks when I need to. Still, I'm certainly not going to publicise my location. If the Guild is still hunting me I'm going to make it as difficult as I can for them to track me down. I press my foot down harder on the accelerator and toss the phone out of the window.

There's been no change in Fletcher's condition by the time I return to the house, but Martha is happy to report that he's 'looking better'. Taking in his grey pallor and the slight drool on his chin, I tend to disagree, but I keep my thoughts to myself.

"I need you to pack a bag," I tell Martha, "I'm getting him out of here. It's not safe," I add, as her hands flutter nervously. "There are people looking for him. I have to get him somewhere far from here, please understand." She gives a watery-eyed nod and springs into action.

While she lovingly packs a few necessities into a black Gucci duffle, I wander through Fletcher's wardrobe, trying to decide what to dress him in. The cotton drawstring pyjama bottoms he's currently wearing over his two-day-old underwear are hardly ideal travel attire.

I can't help but smile as I gaze upon a shelf full of newsboy caps. I pick one at random - a dark grey wool-blend - and then find a pair of soft jeans and a black long-sleeved T-shirt.

"Where would I find...?" I begin, but Martha has beaten me to it and she hands me a pair of perfectly pressed boxer briefs. "Thanks," I take them from her and try to maintain an air of indifference. Which fools her only for the time it takes me to stride back into the bedroom and come to a mortified halt beside the bed.

"I can do it, Miss Clara," she announces.

"You won't be able to lift him," I reply. It's not as though I haven't seen a naked man before. Actually, it's exactly that. I've never seen a naked man before. Spending all my time searching for Fletcher hasn't left me much time for anything else, least of all dating.

Between Martha and I we manage to dress Fletcher. A combination of embarrassment and dexterity means that I don't actually see much, although I'm pretty sure Martha got an eyeful when she leaned in to pull up his boxers.

"Right!" I dust my hands in relief when it's over. "You've packed the bag?"

"Yes," she nods, sliding a pair of sneakers onto Fletcher's feet. "And I've thrown in a few of his smaller shirts for you, just in case. And," she looks embarrassed, "a few other items that have been left behind by various lady friends over the years."

I don't know which one of us is more uncomfortable.

"That's very kind of you, Martha," I say carefully and she relaxes.

"There's one other thing." She moves back to the wardrobe and disappears into its depths. When she emerges she is holding a simple, brown envelope.

"Mister Fletcher would want you to have this," she says, shoving it into my hand.

With the intuition of a true thief, I deduce that it's filled with money. I open it and peer inside, taking in the thick wad of hundred dollar bills. Fletcher must trust Martha a lot to leave this lying around. Then again, this small fortune is probably pocket change to him.

It takes us the better part of an hour to get Fletcher into the car. Martha props him up with pillows while I bemoan the fact that there's no back seat.

"There are other cars at the office," Martha offers helpfully, but I shake my head. We can't go back there even if Harrison has given me his word.

"Where will you go?" she asks, when the duffle bag is stowed safely in the miniscule trunk in the nose of the car. The back, I've learned, is completely taken up by the mid-mounted engine.

"Some place safe," I say. I cannot risk telling her where, in case the Guild ever finds and questions her. "You should lock up the house and go too. Fletcher will find you when this is over."

She gazes tearfully back at the house and then fans at her face.

"Take care of him, Miss Clara."

"I will, Martha. I promise."

NINETEEN
AN UNLIKELY DESTINATION

THE ONLY GOOD thing about Pismo Beach is that there is a veritable smorgasbord of motels willing to take cash for a room and, at an extra charge, they do not demand to see proof of identification. Unfortunately, I suspect that even the wad of notes in Fletcher's envelope isn't going to buy the silence of witnesses to the sight of an unconscious man being carried inside said motels, so instead, after a nine-hour long drive to get here, I find myself driving aimlessly around the streets of the seaside city.

Fletcher hasn't so much as moved, trapped in his death-like state, and I am loath to leave him unattended in the car, so eventually, I break one of my own rules and pull into a service station to boost a phone. I usually avoid small, low-traffic areas which make it more difficult to go unnoticed, but it's late and I'm in a hurry.

I mull around in the convenience store, keeping a watchful eye on the car. I can see the fluorescent lights outside reflected in the dark tint of the Audi's windows as I page casually through a magazine. I dismiss two customers wearing board-shorts before my victim walks through the doors. A young man, probably in his early twenties, wearing jeans and, better yet, a button-up shirt, bounds into the store. The tell-tale bulge of his breast pocket is all I need to see, and, less than a minute later, I allow him to bump conveniently into me.

"Sorry!" he apologises as I rock on my feet. I shoot out a hand to steady myself, spot the camera overhead and then draw it back, smiling shyly up at him.

"I'm so clumsy!" I giggle nervously, and then I take a step backward, wincing a little as I put weight on my foot.

"You okay?"

"Yeah, I'm fine. I'm Laura, by the way," I hold out my hand and he takes it with a delighted grin.

"Steven. Do you live around here or are you on vacation?"

"Vacation," I bob my head like the overzealous eighteen-year-old he thinks I am. "I'm here with my parents. And you?"

"I'm a local. I actually live just around the corner."

"That's cool. I wouldn't mind living here permanently."

"Pismo has its charms," he admits, leaning casually against the magazine rack, which teeters dangerously on its feet. I giggle again and then pull out my mobile.

"Oh shoot!" I look dejectedly at the black screen.

"What's wrong?"

"My phone's dead." I hold it under his nose and shake it in frustration. "And I can't remember which chips my brother asked me to get."

"Here," he announces helpfully, pulling his mobile from his pocket, "use my phone."

"Oh wow, are you sure?"

"Yeah, absolutely."

"Thanks!" I touch his arm briefly and he nods. We both stand there for a second while I wait for him to walk away. When he doesn't, I turn around and pretend to punch in a number. Steven takes the cue and starts moving, heading toward the bakery section. *Took you long enough*, I think irritably. Discreetly, I place my finger on the pad of my phone and the screen lights up. I find the number

I'm looking for and punch it into Steven's phone, smiling at him over the shelving while the call connects.

"Hello?"

I turn back to face the magazines.

"Vincent, it's me."

"Clarke?" his voice is filled with disbelief.

"Yeah. I can't talk right now." I cast a cursory glance over my shoulder at Steven who is moving back toward me with a loaf of bread in his hands. "I'm at the service station on Shell Beach road."

"You're in Pismo Beach?" His disbelief has become full-blown incredulity.

"Yes." Steven rounds the corner of the aisle I'm standing in. "Cheetos, I should've known," I say brightly. "I'll see you in a bit." I end the call and delete the number from the call register before Steven can see.

"All sorted?" he asks.

"Yes, Cheetos. And a bottle of Cola," I add, handing back the phone.

"You know, if you're going to be in town a while, I'd be happy to show you around."

"Ah, that's so sweet of you. I'd love that. My boyfriend's useless with directions and so far all he's done is try to convince me to play volleyball. My hand-eye co-ordination is terrible." That last line wasn't really necessary but I was enjoying his discomfort. At the mention of a boyfriend, Steven is already backpedalling.

"Let me put my number in your phone," I offer, holding out my hand.

"Sure," he agrees, with far less enthusiasm. I punch in a series of random digits and save it under L for Laura.

"Well, I'd better be going," he says when I hand it back. "It was nice bumping into you."

He pays for his bread and then leaves the store. I wave, rolling my eyes the second his back is turned.

Vincent either drives like a maniac or lives nearby, because, within fifteen minutes, he pulls into the service station.

"You're really here," he announces the second I appear at his door.

"I'm really here," I say, feeling guilty already. He must notice the expression on my face because his eyes narrow suspiciously.

"I bought you these," I say, holding out a packet of chocolate bars.

Vincent ignores my peace offering.

"What exactly are you doing here, Clarke?"

I lean past him, dumping the candy on his seat. "I need your help."

"Oh hell no!" Vincent barks the second he lays eyes on Fletcher in the passenger seat of the Audi. I slam the door and turn to face him.

"I know it looks bad, but I swear, I can explain."

"That's Fletcher Kincaid in there, you do know that, right?"

"Yes."

"Then you can't explain!"

"But..."

"No," he holds up his hands, "there's no but, Clarke! Why haven't you taken him to the Guild?"

"It's a long story."

"Well then call me from the road, I'd love to hear it."

"Vincent I wouldn't be here if I had anywhere else to go."

"I know you wouldn't!" He's angry now. "You made it perfectly clear that we wouldn't be seeing much of one another after I left the Hall of Clocks."

"And you made it perfectly clear that, despite me being an awful friend, if ever I needed you I should come here. Pismo Beach, remember?"

"If you needed a night off," he clarifies, "or help with an anomaly, or just somewhere to get away. Not to bring the most wanted fugitive in Tempus seeking sanctuary! You are aware that the Guild knows where I live?"

"Yes, but they would never think to look for us here. No one at Tempus knows we're friends." I was taking a leaf from Fletcher's book and hiding in plain sight – within the very organisation I was hiding from.

Exasperated, Vincent pulls at his hair.

"I've just got my life back! I've barely been out of the Hall a week, Clarke. All I want to do is lie on the beach drinking cosmopolitans and watching west-coast girls in bikinis. I don't think that's too much to ask, given that I spent the last ten years of my life underground."

"You can still do that," I insist. "You won't even notice we're there. And it'll only be for a couple of days," I add, noticing that we've attracted the attention of the cashier who has come outside to watch us. "Please, Vincent," I lower my voice. "At least let's have this conversation somewhere a little more private"

He follows the line of my gaze. One thing about members of the Guild, we stay away from prying eyes.

"Follow me," he says abruptly and marches back toward his car.

It's obvious, as we cruise through an upmarket residential area that the Guild makes good on its word. Vincent's house is one of the nicest on the street. He doesn't speak a word to me as we haul Fletcher inside and deposit him in one of the spare rooms, but the second we enter the living room, he points at an armchair.

"Sit," he instructs, taking a seat on the sofa opposite me. "Explain."

It takes me a while to get through it all, but I try not to leave anything out. I owe him this much – the truth, or most of it. I don't tell him what I've got planned, but I do tell him about our history and that I still want Fletcher to hand over the dial of my clock.

"Of course you do." He seems to have calmed down, but I've never seen him this thoughtful.

"All this time, Clarke. Why didn't you ever say anything? How does nobody know that you and Fletcher...?"

"We never were," I correct. "We were friends, that's it."

Vincent gives me a knowing smile, but, rather than ease my conscience that he's no longer furious with me, it sets me on edge.

"You're going to deny it?" he asks wryly.

"Deny what?"

"That you're in love with Fletcher."

"That's ridiculous – I don't even know him anymore."

"Maybe, maybe not. It sounds to me like the Fletcher you knew isn't as far gone as you thought."

I groan and cover my face with my hands.

"This was all so much simpler when I hated him."

"I don't think you ever hated him. Not really."

"The man cursed me to an eternity of misery."

"No, your sister did that to *him.*" Vincent, like most of the Guild, has no issue with brutal honesty where Anna is concerned. "Fletcher, on the other hand, simply gave you more time. It can be undone."

"That's the plan."

"You're really going to restart your clock? If you get the dial, I mean?"

"I don't want to live forever. And I have to do it before November 6th."

"Cody Johnson?" At the mention of the baby whose name is currently on Fletcher's clock I nod grimly.

"I can't do it, Vincent. If I can't figure out how to undo what Anna did before then, I'd rather die."

"You'd leave Fletcher alone? To face infinity on his own?"

"Why is he my responsibility?" I practically yell. "My sister did this, not me! I've been punished for a crime she committed! Does nobody see how cruel that is – how unfair?"

Vincent doesn't respond to my emotional outburst. His eyes are fixed on something beyond me, something that drains the blood from his face. I have a split second to register the danger and then I throw myself forward, out of range of Fletcher's furious grasp. One look at his face tells me that Fletcher is not himself and that he's a danger to both of us.

"Run!" I yell, shoving Vincent toward the back door. He hesitates for a minute, torn between his own inability to defend himself and fear for my safety. I reach for my daggers and then remember that my belt is still in the car. I'd taken it off at the service station and stashed it in the glove compartment. Being with Fletcher has made me drop my guard.

"Where am I?"

His eyes are glazed, black in the dim light. He must have ripped the gauze from his head and the small circular hole is raw and angry on his temple. He stares at me, his hands shaking so badly that he balls them into fists at his sides.

"Fletcher," I say, keeping my voice as calm as I can. "Calm down." At the sound of my voice he shudders, shaking his head from side to side as if trying to clear it. The front of his black shirt is wet with what looks like vomit. I brace myself, prepared for anything, but, as we stand facing one another, his eyes start to clear. The trembling subsides, slowly – infinitely slowly – and a flash of recognition crosses his face.

"Clara?" he says. His voice is thick, slurred, as if he hasn't fully regained the use of his tongue. I am about to answer when his eyes roll back in his head and he falls forward. I move, faster than I thought possible, and catch his shoulders, slowing his fall and laying him gently across the table.

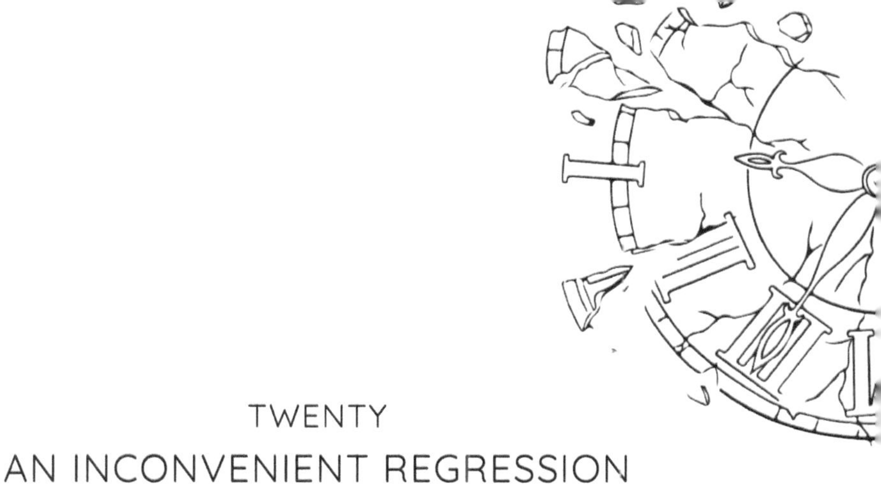

TWENTY
AN INCONVENIENT REGRESSION

VINCENT and I take turns watching over Fletcher but he doesn't wake again. My eyes are scratchy and burning by the time I hear the birds waking, and I press my thumb and forefinger into the bridge of my nose in an effort to drive away the headache creeping up the back of my neck and pounding inside the base of my skull.

Fletcher is laid out on the sofa, a tartan blanket draped over him. I had removed the puke-stained shirt and wiped his mouth, but other than that I hadn't ventured near him. Instead, I study his face, soft in repose, his lips slightly parted, the long lashes sweeping the dark hollows beneath his eyes.

1913, *Charleston, West Virginia*

"I KNOW you're not really sleeping," I said teasingly, shoving at Fletcher's shoulder. He grinned, peering at me through slitted eyes. It was autumn in Charleston and leaves floated serenely across the pond, catching in the rushes and dancing away in delight. Anna had gone to the market and father was busy with Guild business, leaving me the whole day to do as I pleased.

"Do you have to go?" Fletcher lamented, pushing himself into a seated position.

"In a while." The sun was making its descent in the sky with lazy abandon and father would be home shortly after nightfall.

"Perhaps you could confide in Anna," Fletcher mused, as though reading my thoughts. "About our friendship. That way we could still spend time together..."

"No!" I shook my head violently, copper ringlets bouncing gaily about, as if this was something to be celebrated. "Anna cannot know." My sister had a fiery temper and I feared that, in a fit of spite, she might tell father of my secret meetings and his wrath would be fearsome indeed.

"I would prefer it if we kept our friendship a secret. Besides," I added, trying to soften the blow. "there may come a time when I have something over Anna – something she would want me to keep secret." I paused dramatically, but the giddiness overcame me almost instantly.

"I think she has a crush on someone!" I blurted out. "I plan to follow her and find out who has captured her heart!"

I giggled girlishly at the fact that my sister might be falling in love, but Fletcher didn't share my merriment. Instead, he looked uncomfortable, a small frown creasing his forehead and he did not push the matter further.

As if he wanted to distract me, he pulled the harmonica from his pocket, playing a low, mournful tune. His eyes held mine, warm and teasing, and I sighed, leaning back on my arms to enjoy the last few moments of our visit.

"Clara." His voice was a melody on its own, deeper than the instrument, but just as soothing. I opened my eyes to find him still staring.

"Yes?" My heart thumped in my chest. He had never looked at

me like that – so intently, as if he was seeing something for the first time.

"There is something I must tell you."

I held my breath, my stomach curling itself into a tight ball.

"What is it?"

Fletcher opened his mouth and I braced myself for what was to come, but it never did. He seemed to pull himself up, his hand, which had been reaching for me, dropped to the ground, and his face underwent a subtle change until the teasing smile was once again firmly in place and his eyes twinkled with merriment.

"There is a beetle on your collar," he said, and then launched into peals of deep laughter as I leapt to my feet, shrieking and brushing at my blouse.

"HERE," Vincent taps my shoulder and I jump.

"Easy!" he says, handing me a cup of black coffee. I accept it gratefully, curling my legs beneath me on the armchair.

"What do you think?" Vincent asks, indicating Fletcher, who is still sleeping.

"I don't know. I mean, we're immortal, but he basically tried to blow his brains out. He's healing, but who knows what kind of long-term damage it might've caused."

"What's the worst you've ever been injured?"

I consider the question.

"I fractured my spine in the early forties. I fell two storeys."

"Ouch."

"I was out for twenty-four hours. Some good Samaritan took me to the hospital before the Guild could come and get me. The doctors who attended me said I'd never walk again."

"They must've thought you a medical miracle when you did."

"They never had the chance to see it. Tempus had me moved into their private care until I healed. It took me weeks to walk again."

"Well if you sustained an injury that bad and made a full recovery, there's no reason to think he won't either."

As if in agreement, Fletcher groans. I'm at his side in an instant, but Vincent, who is still cautious, stays out of arm's reach, peering at him over my shoulder. Fletcher's forehead is hot to the touch, but his colour is better.

"Fletcher?"

He groans again.

"Fletcher, can you hear me? Squeeze my hand if you can hear me."

I feel the faintest pressure on my fingers.

"You're going to be okay," I say, dizzy with relief. "Can you open your eyes for me?"

After what feels like forever, his dark lashes flutter and I find myself staring into the warm gaze I remember from Charleston.

"Clara?" His voice is faint but clear. "Where am I?"

I heave a sigh of relief. His speech is perfect, with none of the slurring I heard last night.

"You're safe," I say. He blinks rapidly a few times and then focuses on me.

"I knew you'd come back," he smiles. "I knew you wouldn't leave me there." His hand goes to his abdomen; to the place I know his scar to be.

"Leave you where, Fletcher?" Goose-flesh is rising rapidly on my arms.

"On the street," he sighs. "You ran away, but I knew you'd come back." I hold my breath, waiting for him to elaborate, but after a few minutes his gentle snores rend the air.

"That can't be good," Vincent murmurs as I back away from Fletcher.

Wild-eyed, I turn to face him.

"He's talking about something that happened a hundred years ago. Oh God, Vincent, he's gone back to when it first happened. To the night Anna made him immortal."

I don't need to explain why this affects me so badly. If Fletcher doesn't remember the past hundred years he won't remember stealing the dial from my clock. He won't remember where he put it.

"Do you think he knew this would happen?" Vincent asks. "I mean, the man did shoot himself in the head. He must have had a reason."

Martha's words come back to haunt me.

He said that he'd done things he wasn't proud of. Things he'd rather forget. Except she had it wrong. Fletcher didn't want to forget the things he had done as a punishment. He wanted to forget where he'd hidden my dial so he wouldn't have to make the choice to give it back.

"He must have suspected," I tell Vincent, my anger growing. "He never intended to give me that dial because he thought I would always choose the Guild over him. When I didn't..." I shake my head. "When I didn't, I think he realised he couldn't keep it from me out of spite, so he chose another way. Damn it!"

"Calm down," Vincent urges. My breathing is accelerating, coming in short sharp gasps and my face is clammy. "You said yourself that it took a while for you to recover from your injury. Maybe he just needs a little time."

"Time!" A hysterical gasp of laughter escapes me. "Time is the one thing I don't have right now!"

When Fletcher wakes again I've pulled myself together. Going to pieces won't help me in our current situation. Vincent has left the house for the time being – we both decided his presence would only be more confusing for Fletcher and he's going to spend the night in a motel, paid for in crisp hundred dollar notes.

I force Fletcher to drink a cup of tea loaded with sugar and then hand-feed him half a ham sandwich. By the time he's done, he looks almost like his old self. I don't explain where we are, save to tell him this house belongs to a friend, but I can tell by the way he's scrutinising the modern furniture that he'll be wanting a full explanation.

"I died," he says eventually, swallowing the last bite of crust and I nod.

"I felt myself dying," he continues, his eyes never leaving my face. "And then I wasn't dead, and I saw your face and I knew you understood what had happened."

"Do *you* know what happened?" I prompt. He shakes his head.

"Anna, she... she knew what was going to happen. She knew you were going to die and she tried to stop it. She brought you back."

"Anna? How could Anna do that?"

"What I'm about to tell you isn't going to be easy for you to believe, but I want you to hear me out, okay? Can you do that?"

He lifts a hand to cup my cheek, his night-sky eyes boring into my face. "You've changed."

I take his hand and lay it in my lap. "We both have."

Defiantly, throwing a hypothetical middle finger at the Guild, I tell him about the Hall of Clocks. I tell him about Anna being chosen as the Clock Keeper and about her stabbing his clock. When I get to the part about her suicide I have to brush away the tears and I feel Fletcher's hand tighten convulsively on my own. He doesn't interrupt or react, and then I bring him back to waking up on the street and his hand goes automatically to his stomach. He rubs at the scar, staring down at it for a long tense moment.

"When was this?" he asks eventually.

"It was a long time ago."

"How long?"

"It's been a hundred years, Fletcher."

His eyes widen in disbelief, his mind trying to deny what he's hearing, but then he takes in my clothing, the furniture, the long-since healed scar and he slumps back onto the sofa cushions.

"I know it's a lot to take in."

"Why don't I remember?"

I choose my words carefully, knowing we're venturing into dangerous territory.

"You suffered a head injury." His hand goes to his temple and I wince as it moves over the crusted bullet wound. "It's affected your memory."

"Will it come back?"

"I don't know."

He nods grimly, takes another long moment to process and then his head whips toward me.

"None of this explains how you're here."

"That's a whole different story and one that's going to be a lot harder to explain. Why don't we get you cleaned up first?"

He seems to sense that I need a moment to gather my thoughts, and, being Fletcher, he lets me take it. I point him in the direction of the bathroom, show him how to operate the modern mixer taps and hand him a fluffy white towel I find in the linen cupboard. Then, I raid Vincent's liquor cabinet, pour myself a healthy shot of whiskey and take a seat on the sofa as I try to figure out the kindest way to tell my best friend that he ruined my life.

TWENTY-ONE
ONLY PURITY REMAINS

FLETCHER DOESN'T WALK BACK into the living room. He erupts into it with the fury of a man who has just remembered the most painful moment of his life, which, as it turns out, he has.

"You abandoned me!" he roars, his eyes wild and darting – the eyes of a madman with no control over his emotions. Unprepared for the violence of his attack, I don't react quickly enough, only barely managing to stumble to my feet before his hand clamps around my throat. We grapple for a moment, my fingers scrabbling pathetically at his hand, trying to pry it away from my throat, my body gasping for air.

"Did you think I wouldn't remember?" he hisses, spittle flying into my face. "I saw you leave, Clara! You knew what had happened to me and you left me on the street!"

Something is happening to him – his injury has done something inside his head and his utter loss of control is being exacerbated by the pain of his memories returning. It's like he's going through all the emotions of the past in such a short space of time that he can't control them, can't control himself. Stars burst in my vision and desperately I kick out at him, my foot connecting with something hard, although whether his shin or the table, I can't be sure.

Mercifully his hands release my throat and I suck in a lungful of much-needed air but my relief is short-lived. Fletcher shifts his weight, grabs hold of my shoulders and slams me into the wall, leaving a red blossom of blood on the tranquil grey paint. My nose is bleeding badly and I taste the blood in my mouth as it gushes over my lips. I can't think of any other way to defend myself, so I drop to the floor, making myself boneless, as a child does when having a tantrum, leaving him nothing to hold on to. I slither through his grasping hands and the second I hit the floor I tuck my body and roll, before getting to my feet on the other side of him.

"Fletcher, calm down!" I yell, dodging another attack.

"You left me!" he roars, "I had to find out the truth for myself – what your sister did to me!"

"That was a long time ago! Fletcher there's something wrong with you, you've suffered an injury and it's made you forget everything that's happened since..."

I cry out as his hand slaps my cheek, hard enough to send me reeling.

"An injury?" He laughs scornfully, "An injury, Clara? Is that what you call it? I died!"

"That-was-a-long-time-ago!"

I kick out at him, catching him in the chest and his arms windmill as he tries to keep his footing, but I use his temporary imbalance against him and bring my elbow up into his face. He goes down in a flail of limbs, cracking his head magnificently against the coffee table as he does.

I ponder for a second on how much more damage his brain can possibly take and then I step over him.

"Fletcher, I'm here because I want to help you. Please, let's talk about this." I stick out my hand and he eyes it hatefully. "We're friends now," I add, figuring this isn't the time to point out that this is a very new *status quo*, but something in my tone must convince him, because he grips my hand firmly and I help him to his feet.

Half an hour later we have gotten nowhere but at least we're functioning under the relative peace of a temporary ceasefire.

"I'm sorry, Clara – Clarke - but I just don't remember." Fletcher peers balefully at me from under the frozen bag of peas I'm holding against his head. It has taken a while for him to get used to my new name.

"It's okay, it'll come back," I insist, dumping the peas on the coffee table. I'm exhausted through to the bone and I slump back on the sofa, my eyelids sagging under the weight of Fletcher's amnesia. He remembers following me and father to the Hall of Clocks and the conversation we had, but he cannot remember anything past that point. It strikes me that this might be a second chance – an opportunity for me to do right by Fletcher – as I should have done all those years ago. The man facing me today was, by all accounts, the one I would've helped had I defied the Guild a hundred years ago.

"I really shot myself in the head?"

"You really shot yourself in the head," I mumble, my eyelids drooping even further. "You made a damn fine mess, too."

"What do I do, now? In this time, I mean."

"You're a very successful businessman. You have a lot of money."

He shifts his seat, a small smile lifting the corners of his lips.

"That's ironic."

I shoot him a look of slit-eyed curiosity.

"Ironic how?"

"Well, if I'd been wealthy back in 1916 your father would have welcomed me as your suitor."

"You never needed my father's approval, Fletcher." It is meant as an insult to my father's memory, but it comes out softer than I anticipate. Fletcher, to my surprise, takes my hand.

"I did," he murmurs softly, his thumb making gentle circles on my palm. "More than you know."

Uncomfortable, I remove my hand on the pretence of rubbing at my face. Fletcher doesn't miss the not so subtle withdrawal and his expression darkens.

"So, how do we find this clock of yours?"

"We have the clock. You gave it back. It's the dial we're after."

"Okay, the dial. How do we find it?" He is brisk and business-like.

"You're the only person who knows where it is," I point out. "We need to get your memory back."

I suspect that, in time, all his memories will return. Each one will be a trauma for him to relive until we get back to the present.

"So far your memories seem to be coming back in chronological order."

"So, what can I expect next?" The question is loaded, but I feign ignorance, hoping to avoid an awkward moment. Typically, Fletcher takes the bull by the horns.

"Did we ever... you and me, I mean. Was there ever anything between us?"

"No," I reply, my voice as small as the answer itself. "We were only ever friends – then enemies – and now we're friends again."

"Oh." His disappointment is palpable, but he says nothing further.

"Fletcher," I begin, wanting to explain, but he stops me with a single look.

"Don't," he says. "You don't need to tell me why. I think it's fairly obvious."

The meaning of his words sinks in slowly, my baffled brain taking a while to process his interpretation.

"Oh, Fletcher, no!" I say, without thinking. Without considering the impact of my own admission. "It's not because I didn't lo-" I catch myself, "care for you. I did. I still do."

"Then why? All these years, with your father long in the grave and nothing to stop you, why didn't you act on your feelings?"

"Because of my loyalty to the Guild, because I believed you hated me, because I haven't seen you in a hundred years," I rub savagely at my crumpled face. "There are so many reasons and so much history between us, I don't even know where to start."

The frown between his eyes slowly softens, a look of unexpected joy filling the dark blue pools.

"We can't change the past so how about we start in the present. How do you feel about me *now*, Clarke?"

It's just too simple. For years I denied my feelings for Fletcher because I feared my father's wrath, my sister's heartbreak, the Guild's judgement. Now there is nothing standing in my way, nothing to prohibit me from voicing the truth, a truth I buried so many years ago and held close to my heart for over a century. A truth that defies every logical fibre of my being, but which has transcended time and space. Fletcher and I became immortal enemies, but long before that we were mortal, and so much more than that. I had walked away from him once. I wouldn't do it again.

Raising my hands, I place them on either side of his face, feeling the stubble on his jaw, the quickening of his pulse against my palms as they cradle his neck. I take a deep breath in and when I release it, it takes with it the pain and the anger I have used to dull my true feelings, leaving nothing but purity behind. I smile shyly, watching as understanding dawns on his face.

"I love you, Fletcher," I say simply.

Waiting a century to consummate a relationship is ill-advised. I learn this the hard way, as, in a tangle of limbs and flesh, Fletcher and I only just make it to the bedroom. Fletcher's memory may currently be trapped in 1917, but his body has come a long way since then, and his desire is uninhibited. If he is shocked at the wanton sexuality of the modern woman, he adapts beautifully, holding my hips in his strong hands as I buck above him, his eyes devouring every inch of my body. The pain is fleeting – a tiny pinprick in the fabric of my feelings – and then it is gone, and a slow building inside of me takes over. Fletcher rolls me over in one swift movement and covers my body with his own, the two of us melding into one as he drives me closer to the brink.

Afterward, Fletcher's hands stroke my hair, my back, my arms, everywhere he can reach, as if he is a blind man and my body his braille. As his arms tighten around me, my eyes close. I feel safer than I ever have. It feels right and beautiful, and I catch a glimpse of the life we could have had if only I had been brave enough to admit my feelings back then: A mortal life, filled with children and laughter. I might have lost my father and Anna, but I would've had Fletcher and, deep down, I know now that it would have been enough.

I open my eyes to find him staring at me.

"This was your first time," he murmurs.

Unable to speak, I nod, my cheek rubbing against the soft cotton of my pillow. To my surprise, he smiles, as if the thought pleases him immeasurably. I want to ask him why this makes him so happy, but my body feels heavy – sluggish and unresponsive and infinitely relaxed.

"Sleep, Clarke," Fletcher whispers, lifting his head to kiss my eyelids. His lips are warm and dry, feather light across my skin, and I obey, letting my body and mind relax against him until a dreamless sleep carries me away.

TWENTY-TWO
WHEN THE MIGHTY FALL

I AM ALONE in the bed when I wake. My fingers reach for Fletcher's pillow as I lift my head to scan the room, but it's empty. I pull one of the over-sized T-shirts Martha packed over my head and pad through to the bathroom to freshen up. Catching sight of my ridiculous grin in the mirror overhead, I can't stifle a hysterical bubble of laughter.

Sadly, my euphoria doesn't last long. I find Fletcher in the living room, white and shaking.

"Fletcher?" I take a tentative step toward him, fighting the urge to rush to his side, but the look on his face keeps me at bay.

"What is it?" I ask, "what did you remember?"

"We fought," he hisses. "You tried to kill me and I put a knife through your arm."

"That was only a few weeks ago," I breathe a sigh of relief. "Does that mean you've remembered everything else?"

"No!" he barks, frustrated. "That's all I have." His face scrunches up with the effort of trying to remember and then he opens his eyes to glare at me. "Why? Why were we trying to kill each other?"

"Technically we weren't trying to kill each other. We can't die, so there's not really any chance of..."

"Why, Clarke?" he roars, wiping the amused smile from my face.

"Because we were enemies," I say more gently. "I told you this last night."

"I can't believe I would do that to you. What kind of a man have I become?"

I cross the room to sit beside him, forcing myself into his tortured solitude.

"We both did awful things, Fletcher. I've spent the last hundred years trying to hunt you down to deliver you to the Guild. What my sister did to you was unforgiveable, and when I turned my back on you... well, let's just say I don't blame you for hating me."

"I could never hate you."

"You'd be surprised," I tease, and then, seeing his expression, I add quickly, "besides, I deserved it."

He is about to respond when I hear the front door opening. I yank the T-shirt down over my knees, horrified. I'm not wearing any underwear. By the time Vincent rounds the corner, my face is flaming. Fletcher gets to his feet, but I quickly ease his fears.

"It's okay," I say, placing my hand on his waist. "This is Vincent. He's a friend."

Vincent's gaze moves from Fletcher's defensive stance to my hand on his waist, to the length of my bare legs. His eyebrows disappear into his hairline and he gives me a questioning look.

"I didn't expect you back today," I say feebly.

"Neither did I," he admits, coming into the room. He looks washed out, his lips tight and determined. I know the look of a man on the verge of giving bad news and I get to my feet, the short T-shirt forgotten.

"What is it?"

Vincent steadies himself. Looks at me. Looks at Fletcher. His words, when they come, are the last thing I expect.

"Jonathan Harrison is dead."

It takes a while for the words to sink in.

Despite my sometime aversion to the Grand Master and our decades of disagreement, my chest pinches painfully. I sway on the spot and Fletcher's arm shoots out automatically to steady me.

"What happened?" I manage, my voice sandpapery.

"He had a heart attack last night. Apparently he's been unwell for some time but he kept it to himself."

I recall how ill Harrison had been looking recently and I feel a stab of guilt, knowing how much I must have added to his stress these past few months. Despite our mutual disapproval, Harrison was not a bad man and he had trusted me, to a degree. I sit down heavily on the sofa allowing myself a moment to grieve. Vincent, however, wastes no time.

"You need to get out of here Clarke."

I raise my eyes to his face, my brows knitting together in confusion. Then it dawns on me that there's only one reason Vincent would be concerned about my being here – if the Guild were looking for me.

"Who replaced him?" I ask. "Who's the new Grand Master?"

His grimace is apologetic. "Andrew Lincoln."

"But isn't the new Clock Keeper a Lincoln?"

Vincent nods. "Sienna Lincoln replaced me in the Hall of Clocks."

"That's not possible," I shake my head, "no founding family has ever held both positions. It's too much power for one bloodline."

"Tell that to Tempus." Vincent's lip curls in distaste. "From what I hear, the Jefferson candidate has fallen ill and Blake Truman pulled out of the running when he heard about your escape." He waves his hand at Fletcher.

"Coward!" I hiss.

"Yeah, well, coward or not, he's caused an imbalance in the Guild."

"How close family are Sienna and Andrew?" I ask, praying that the two Lincoln representatives are distant cousins.

"They're brother and sister," Vincent says. I whistle a low breath and he nods his agreement of my amazement.

"Shit!"

Fletcher looks mildly shocked at my easy use of profanity, but he says nothing, regarding me with hooded eyes.

"It gets worse," Vincent begins hesitantly and, when I raise my eyes to his, "Andrew has rallied the Guild against you. He's launching a global man-hunt to find you both and bring you in. You two are officially the world's most wanted fugitives." The news is not unsurprising, but it is a devastating blow. With all of Tempus after us there's no way Fletcher and I can stay here. It's too dangerous.

"Son-of-a-bitch!" I bite my tongue in anger. It would be difficult enough to access the Hall of Clocks with a Lincoln at the helm, but now I had the whole of Tempus breathing down my neck. Nowhere was safe. "We'll be gone by lunch," I promise a still-hovering Vincent.

"I'm sorry," he says, and he sounds it.

"It's not your fault, Vincent," I reassure him. "There's been bad blood between the Lincolns and the Kennedys since long before you were born."

"Yeah, why is that?" he asks. "All I heard is something about a theft between the families?"

"My father's pocket watch," I sigh. "It once belonged to Abraham Lincoln."

"The Abraham Lincoln?" Vincent's response reminds me so much of Aunt Elizabeth's that I laugh.

"Yes. He gifted it to my grandfather who served on his council and it was passed through Kennedy hands until it came to belong to my father."

"So?" Fletcher and Vincent speak as one.

"The Lincolns believe that the watch should have been returned to them when my sister... when we fell from grace. It's an heirloom, what with it having belonged to Abe and all."

"But your father didn't return it?"

"You obviously didn't know her father," Fletcher muses.

"Over his dead body, he said," I add.

"Okay..." I can see Vincent piecing it together in his mind. "No disrespect, but he did die, so why didn't you just return the watch then? That would've breached the divide between your families."

I lower my eyes, but to my surprise Fletcher answers the question.

"Because she didn't have it. She's never had it. I stole it from her father the day that he died."

Both Vincent and I listen, transfixed, as Fletcher recalls his most recently returned memory.

"I saw you go into the house," he fixes me with his midnight stare and I see a flicker of guilt in the depths of his gaze. "You held your head so high with your shoulders back, but I could see the regret. It rolled off you in waves. It pleased me and pained me all at once. When you came out you didn't look back. You didn't look anywhere except right in front of you and I slipped past you without you even realising it, close enough that I could've reached out and touched your hair."

I recall the blind pain of that day, the mortification of my father's final words. Fletcher could've tipped his hat and I wouldn't have seen him.

"By the time I got inside he was almost gone, but the sight of me roused him. Stubborn old bastard," Fletcher adds, and I can picture the scene all too clearly – Fletcher appearing at the foot of the bed like a wraith and my father's apoplexy at the sight of him, his face turning puce, his breathing coming in gasping rasps as he tried to formulate the words to express his hatred.

"He was calm," Fletcher says now, and I whip my head to face him, the image dissolving as quickly as it had come.

"Calm?"

"Yes," Fletcher nods, and the sunlight streaming through the open window falls upon the rapidly healing wound on his temple. "He called me Demon, so I guess he hadn't changed his mind about me, but he said it with resignation rather than revulsion."

"What else did he say?" I ask, clutching my hands together to still their trembling. Fletcher gives me a pitying look and I brace myself for what's coming.

"He said, 'You deserve one another'."

Tears of humiliation prick at my eyes and I press my lips together to keep them at bay.

"I'm sorry, Clarke."

"It's not your fault my father was an asshole."

"I was furious," Fletcher continues, giving me time to pull myself together. "I took the watch from his hand and it was like his life was linked to it. He succumbed shortly after. I watched him die."

The silence that follows is absolute, not even broken by a breath. It's as if all three of us have stopped breathing, stopped living, frozen in one single moment in time. And then Vincent starts to laugh and the spell is broken.

"So let me get this straight," he wheezes, turning to Fletcher. "Because you haven't given the Guild enough trouble the past hundred years, you're telling me you're also responsible for the feud between the Lincolns and the Kennedys?"

Fletcher gazes quizzically at him for a moment and then a broad smile splits his face in half. The absurdity of the whole situation is ridiculous and I join in, a hysterical giggle rising up in my chest.

"Well, when you put it that way..." Fletcher shrugs.

It's not long before the mood turns sombre once more. Vincent is right – with the Guild after us, Fletcher and I need to leave as soon as possible.

We pack light, limiting ourselves to one backpack each. In mine, I stow the envelope of cash Martha gave us and a few items of the clothing she gave me that I suspect will fit. The money won't last long now that we're fending for ourselves, but with both Fletcher and I almost qualifying as professional thieves, I'm not too worried.

"I hate to throw you out like this," Vincent says as we gather in the hall.

I lay my hand on his shoulder. "Don't be stupid. They'd find us here for sure. You've done more than enough."

"I'm glad you came, Clarke."

"So am I. And I'm sorry for how I acted before when you left the Hall."

He pulls me toward him in an awkward embrace, but I try to put as much emotion into that hug as I can. When we break apart, Fletcher is watching us with amusement.

Vincent clears his throat. "You're going to dump the car?"

"As soon as we're far enough from here that they won't suspect we came to you for help."

"Take this," he shoves a small card into my hand and I see a number scrawled on the surface in black ink. "It's a burner phone. Use it if you need to get hold of me."

I nod and then, on impulse, I hug him again.

"Well, I guess that's it." Vincent gently disentangles himself and opens the front door. Fletcher strolls through it and I follow him.

"Vincent," I turn back to find him brushing irritably at his face, "don't ever tell them I was here. No matter what you hear, or what they tell you, you stick to your story, okay? Tempus isn't above hurting you to get information and the Guild trades in so many lies and secrets it could be their official currency."

He stares at me, open-mouthed for a minute and then nods slowly, knowing that the advice is for his benefit, not my own.

"You take care of yourself, Clarke Kennedy," he murmurs, and then the door closes and Fletcher and I are officially on our own.

TWENTY-THREE
THE BIRD AND THE WIND

WE DUMP the car in the no-man's land between California and Arizona, still uncertain of where to go next.

"Where to?" I muse, more to myself than anything.

"I've never been to Vegas," Fletcher raises his brows hopefully.

"How would you know you've never been to Vegas? You have amnesia."

His memories are returning sporadically, a jumble of recollections that he is slowly piecing together, but there are still gaping holes in his history. At my words the familiar frown creases the skin between his brows.

"Well, I don't *think* I've been to Vegas..."

"Then we're definitely not going to Vegas." I take his hand as we walk toward the bus stop. "If you've never been there, my dial isn't there."

He grins. "Come to think of it, I might actually have been there." He raises his hand to his temple as if recalling something. "I remember a lot of bright lights and the sound of the slots."

"Nice try!" I laugh. "But we are not going to Vegas." I glance around and spot a mall a few streets down. "What we are, however, is running out of money."

Fletcher follows the line of my gaze and grins. "Are you thinking what I'm thinking?"

I throw him a wicked look as we head toward the mall.

"Leave it to me," Fletcher announces as we walk through the automated door.

"No way! Why should you get to have all the fun?"

"Because it's been a while. I've got all this money, now, remember? When do you think was the last time I got to do this?"

"For someone with so much money we sure are living the low life," I grumble teasingly. "Besides, I get the feeling that you still pick plenty of pockets even if you are rich."

Fletcher laughs, drawing the attention of a group of teenage girls near the entrance. In their short shorts and tank tops they eye him appreciatively. Having lived for so long, Fletcher and I have long lost the naiveté of our youth, and it's easy to forget that we don't look much older than they do.

"You look ridiculous in that hat," I say, taking my annoyance out on him. I snatch the newsboy cap from his head and ruffle his dark hair before he can protest. I catch myself staring at the cap in my hand.

"I can't believe you still wear these, after all these years."

"They look good on me," he replies easily, waving at the giggling girls who fall over one another to wave back. Thankfully we lose sight of them as we enter a popular department store.

"I think there's more to it than that."

"Oh really? Do tell."

Discreetly he swipes a leather wallet off a display counter. A second later, the wallet has disappeared, no doubt into a jacket pocket.

"I think deep down you were always the same person," I press up against him, slipping my fingers into his jacket and he grins as the wallet reappears on the counter. "You just hid it well."

We wander aimlessly up the aisles until I spot my target. Fletcher sees him too, a balding, reedy-looking man with his pants belted high up his waist and an air of importance about him. He is arguing with a store attendant, a small, nervous woman who is trying to be assertive, but is failing miserably.

"You remember what I taught you?" Fletcher asks as I stride forward confidently.

"Be the wind, not the bird," I recite the words from memory.

1916, *Flagstaff, Arizona*

"THE KEY to picking pockets is distraction," Fletcher's eyes were dark as the evening sky as he coached me through the tricks of the trade.

"You want to divert your mark's attention somewhere else, and, while he's looking over there," he waved his hand at a spot in the distance, "he's not focused on what's happening here." The hand came to rest on his breast pocket. I was beginning to really enjoy myself. Every time I stole from a member of the Guild, I felt a sense of retribution, as if I was somehow striking back at my father and the people who had taken Anna away from me.

"What kind of distraction?" I was still gazing at the spot in the distance that he had indicated, imagining a horse bolting unexpectedly or a fire breaking out in the tavern. Fletcher took my chin and turned my face toward him.

"You're taking it too literally, Clara. The distraction can be small, wily, and it can happen right in front of the mark's face." He was still holding my chin and I was, in turn, holding my breath at the intimacy of the moment, when Fletcher's face split into a smug smile. He held up a pendant, which twisted and spun, catching the light. I gave a gasp of surprise and my hands flew to my naked neck where the pendant had hung only seconds ago.

"How did you...?"

"Distraction," he reminded me, but his left hand still held my chin and I couldn't seem to focus on anything but the feel of his warm fingers against my skin. Fletcher fell quiet, his face so close to mine that his eyes loomed before me, growing steadily bigger as he closed the gap between us.

"Miss Clara!" I jumped at the sound of Hattie's voice. A big, buxom woman whose black braids had long turned grey, but whose liquid caramel eyes sparkled with mischief. Hattie, I felt, sympathised with my lonely childhood plight. Still, just because I'd overheard her badmouthing my father when she told the cook that he 'neglects that child', I doubted that Hattie would take kindly to finding me with Fletcher, unchaperoned. More likely she would set her razor tongue on me and threaten to tell father. The threats would be empty and painless, but her scolding would not.

"I have to go!" I whispered urgently to Fletcher. I wished I could tone down the pink flame of my cheeks but Fletcher didn't seem to mind.

"We'll continue our discussion tomorrow," he promised, tipping the familiar newsboy cap. Hattie called again, closer, and I could imagine I heard the crunching of leaves under her broad, flat feet. I squinted through the trees, searching for any sign of her white apron.

"Until then, Clara," Fletcher left the words on only a breath of wind because, by the time I turned back, he was gone.

The following morning – a Monday – found me pacing my bedroom in an impatient swinging of skirts. I knew that Fletcher had found work here in Arizona as an assistant to a cantankerous but renowned blacksmith, so it was hardly surprising that I was annoyed by his promise to continue our lesson when he knew full well he would not be available. The day passed slowly, and eventually, after taking my supper alone in the dining room, I retired to my room in a foul temper.

"Best place for you," Hattie remarked as I stomped up the stairs. "A good night's sleep might improve your temper."

Curled up under the sheets of my four-poster I felt ashamed of myself. Tomorrow I would apologise to Hattie and I would take to the streets on my own. I didn't need Fletcher's guidance or his permission!

I was almost asleep when the window opened and I stifled a scream of terror, recognising Fletcher's tall frame as he unfurled himself from the cramped opening.

"What on earth do you think you're doing?" I exclaimed, trying to still my frantically pounding heart.

"I made you a promise," he opened his arms gallantly, "so here I am. How fortunate we're not in Charleston – I don't think I could've made the climb."

"You can't be in here!" I hissed, ignoring the pleasant heat rising up my neck. "My father would..."

"Your father is currently thirty-seven dollars and fifty cents down in the cards and I have a feeling he won't be leaving until his luck turns." Fletcher laughed, which I thought was big of him considering that my father's gambling loss tonight was probably more money than he made in a month.

"Now," he cast around for a place to sit and then deposited himself comfortably on the Chippendale chair beside the window. I watched him shift his weight, hiding a smile. That chair was remarkably uncomfortable. Placing my hands primly in my lap, making certain that the covers were pulled up to my neck, I waited. After a time, he abandoned the chair and, instead, took a seat on the window sill.

"Now, where were we?" He laced his long fingers together and fixed me with a determined stare.

"Distraction," I answered immediately.

"Right," he nodded his approval. "Speaking of which..." he withdrew my pendant from his pocket and set it on the small bedside table between us, "I think it's best if I return this."

"It was my mother's," I said, reaching for it. "Anna wore it almost every day since Mother died. She gave it to me just before she left."

He seemed to sense my sadness and was eager to distract me.

"Let me help you with that." He took the pendant from me and got to his feet, leaning over me until I felt his fingers at the nape of my neck as he fastened the clasp.

He cleared his throat before speaking again.

"Now, once your mark is suitably distracted, you have to perfect the art of sleight of hand. Clumsy fingers will land you in trouble. You need a feather's touch," he wiggled his fingers between us and I mirrored his action, as if this alone proved I could be as deft as he. Fletcher chuckled, taking a seat on the edge of the bed. His weight drew the covers down, exposing the arch of my neck and the gentle swell of my breasts beneath my white batiste nightgown. Fletcher froze, seeming to remember himself, and then shifted so he could pull the covers back up, protecting my modesty. His hand lingered near my neck, tracing the lines of the pendant, and then, as if with a mind of its own, it edged nearer to my face.

"A bird can neither see nor touch the wind beneath its wings," he murmured, in his gentle baritone, "but the wind can carry that bird hundreds of miles without so much as ruffling its feathers."

"A feather's touch," I echo, trying to make sense of it and not to be so affected by his nearness. "I should be as light as a bird."

He tugged my braid, a secret smile shining in his eyes. "You are not the bird, Clara. You are the wind."

His fingers brushed against the curve of my jaw and then moved away, so suddenly that I had to stop myself from lurching toward him. I cleared my throat.

"What else?" I asked, trying to act, like him, as though nothing had happened.

"We don't steal from friends," he instructed simply.

"I would never!" I exclaimed, insulted that he would feel this rule even bore mentioning.

"Don't be so sure," Fletcher was uncharacteristically serious. "People change, feelings change. More importantly, tempers flare. I hope you never lose sight of what's important, Clara."

. . .

"YOU STOLE FROM ME," I murmur, coming back to the stark reality of the department store.

"What?" He gives a confused half-smile.

"You said we should never steal from friends. But you took the dial from my clock."

"I did," he murmurs, lost in thought. "I guess I lost sight of what was important."

Without warning, he gives a low curse.

"Your mark has disappeared."

I raise my eyes to find the store attendant looking thunderous. The reedy man is nowhere to be seen. I dart down the next aisle and the next, and finally track him down browsing a kaleidoscope of shampoo bottles. I walk up beside him and pretend to be examining them too. I stand far too close and when he steps away irritably, I move in again.

"Excuse me!" he huffs.

I grin sarcastically up at him. "You're excused."

His face reddens and he takes another step to the side.

"You should take this one!" I announce, reaching for a bottle and shoving it against his chest. His hands come up automatically to grab hold of it, and my fingers dart inside the gaping pocket of his trousers. *Gotcha*, I think as they close around the smooth leather of his wallet. What I don't anticipate is the manacle-like vice grip of his fingers around my wrist as I withdraw my prize.

"You're in real trouble now, missy," the man announces calmly.

"You might want to let me go," I reply, just as calmly. He feels the bite of my dagger against his hip and glances down to get a better look.

"You might want to open that," he replies, unconcerned, and he inclines his head at the wallet still trapped in my grasp. Awkwardly, I flip it open.

Shit.

The official police badge seems to mock me as I flip the wallet shut.

"I guess there's no way you'd just forget about this and let me walk away, officer?" I ask brightly.

"Detective," he corrects coolly. Over his shoulder I catch sight of a woman rounding the corner into our aisle. She is holding a young child by the hand and hasn't noticed our strange presence – the detective still grasping me firmly by the wrist, his other arm at his side, not wanting to make any sudden movements with my dagger at his waist.

"It appears we're at a bit of a stalemate," I say, watching as Fletcher steps in front of the woman and leads her away, speaking rapidly. She listens, meekly, as she follows him out of the aisle and I wonder idly what excuse he gave for temporarily denying her access to the toiletries. The Detective sees none of this, his back to them.

"I wouldn't call it that," the Detective huffs, "not when I have mall security at my disposal."

"Ah, but I have something better," I smile sweetly up at him and watch the confusion slowly crease his brow.

"I have him." I incline my head over his shoulder. He turns instinctively, but it's too late. Fletcher, in one swift, precise movement, brings his fist down on the man's neck, rendering him unconscious.

"Time to go," he says, as a dark shape emerges on the other end of the aisle. By the time the customer reaches the prostrate form of the detective, we are already out of the door.

"How was that being the wind, Clarke?" Fletcher hisses as we pass the same group of girls from earlier sauntering in the opposite direction.

"Hey," I snap, "I'll have you know I hardly ever get caught. You jinxed me."

His musical laugh sounds in time with the automated hiss of the external doors.

"You cracked under the pressure?"

"Something like that."

Later, we check into a roadside motel which is so antiquated they still make use of a guest sign-in book. No computer or tech of any kind is evident for record-keeping and I happily hand over one of my fake IDs with the room charge.

"That's daylight robbery," Fletcher grumbles about the exorbitant deposit as we make our way to the allocated room.

"Whatever do you mean?" I feign shock as I open the door and we are hit by stale air. "Do you think a place as classy as this comes cheap?"

I flip the light switch. The globe flickers once and then, with a tiny pop, promptly goes out. I collapse against the door in a fit of giggles while Fletcher opens the curtains, allowing the dusk light to filter through the window which he opens with a heavy grunt.

"And look at that view!" I announce, sweeping my arm toward the depressing parking lot and the railway track beyond. Fletcher comes to stand before me, blocking the dreary sight from view.

"Let me see," he murmurs, lifting my wrist. There is only a faint line remaining where the Detective bruised my skin, but he lifts it to his lips, kissing the gently beating pulse in the soft skin of my wrist. Butterflies burst to life in my stomach, fluttering wildly with no sense of direction.

"How does it feel?" Fletcher asks, his voice low and inviting. I gaze at his lips for a full ten seconds before I throw myself at him, and, over the next few hours, we forget everything but each other and barely notice the seedy state of the motel room.

TWENTY-FOUR

FOUR NAMES ON A CLOCK

I WAKE with Fletcher's arm draped across my chest. He is lying on his side facing me, his eyes open, his dark hair a mess. The five o'clock shadow has become a coarse beard but it does nothing to hide the smooth youthfulness of his face. As I become more awake I notice, for the first time, and without surprise, that the sheets are stiff and scratchy, but I have no inclination to leave this bed.

"Good morning," Fletcher murmurs, moving his hand to my waist and pulling me closer so that my body is pressed up against his, my hip fitting perfectly into the concave curve of his abdomen.

"Morning," I stretch lazily, brushing against him in the most intimate of places, and he groans good-naturedly.

"Minx." He kisses my temple and rests his lips there. It is a peaceful, beautiful moment, but we both know we will have to get moving again soon.

"Do you think you can manage to stay out of trouble today?"

"I'll do my best."

"Perhaps you should leave the hard stuff to me? You obviously haven't mastered the subtle art of sleight of hand." He emphasises the words by brushing his fingers down my skin, from shoulder to hip, the touch so light it sends a shiver down my spine and raises gooseflesh on my arms. His eyes have darkened, the blue almost black in the dim light.

"There was nothing delicate about your hands last night," I tease. He grins arrogantly and I can't stifle a giggle at his typically male pride.

"You didn't perhaps have an epiphany last night during that mind-blowing experience, did you?"

I watch as his smile fades, cursing my own stupidity. *Why did I bring it up now?*

"No," he admits.

"It's okay, it'll come back to you." I keep my voice light, trying to brush it off and get back to the playfulness of before, but I can see that's not going to happen.

His eyes slide to mine, still more grey than blue.

"Why do you want the dial?" he asks, as if it had never occurred to him before.

"I..." the question is so unexpected I falter. "It belongs to me."

"But what difference does it make if you have it or not," he fixes me with an unnerving stare before he continues, "unless you intend to repair your clock?" It's not really a question. We both know what he is implying and what the consequences would be. "You do, don't you?" he asks sadly, and, finding that I cannot lie to him, I nod. He turns away from me to lie on his back, our hips only barely touching. The loss of physical contact leaves me feeling cold and vulnerable. I stare down at my hands unable to justify my desire to die, not when it means leaving him alone.

"There's a boy named Cody Johnson," I begin tentatively. At this point I almost envy his amnesia but I know I'll have to explain it to him again. "A baby, actually. His name is branded on your clock. He's... in six months he's supposed to die."

Fletcher has gone still and I risk a glance to find him staring at me quizzically.

"Supposed to die?"

A sigh dances between my lips.

"His name is on your old clock."

"O-kay?" he draws out the word, still not understanding. It strikes me again how different he is now from the cruel man who hurled disdain at me in Charleston only a few weeks ago. Then, he had spoken of my involvement in Henry's death with icy detachment. Now, his eyes are warm and reassuring.

"Something happened to your clock when Anna damaged it, Fletcher. It doesn't work properly anymore. Names appear on it with a date of death, but the people don't actually die."

"They're immortal?" the concern creeping across his brow is genuine and my heart aches for him. I know he's going to feel responsible.

"Not technically. Because an immortal can't die, but they do."

"I don't understand...?"

"I kill them, Fletcher." It comes out harder than I wanted it too, the words hurled across at him, an echo of the anger I've harboured all these years for having to fix Anna's mess, an echo of the hatred I felt for Fletcher. It's not fair but I can't take it back. I can only continue and hope that he understands why I'm so determined to get that dial.

"They're anomalies," I explain quickly, "they're not supposed to live and someone has to make sure that the fabric of time doesn't unravel. I was the Clock Keeper. I'm a member of the Guild. My sister caused this mess. It's my job to set things right."

Fletcher doesn't say anything but he lifts his hands to his eyes, squeezing at his temples with thumb and middle finger, as if trying to relieve a blinding headache. When he finally lowers his hands, he looks straight at me, his eyes cutting into my own, and I fear for an instant that he has remembered something terrible – that he is going to attack me again. Instead, when he moves, his hands reach for me and he pulls me against him, so tightly I struggle to breathe.

"I'm so sorry, Clarke," he murmurs into my hair, his arms increasing their desperate pressure, his lips grazing my forehead. To my surprise, I find tears welling in my eyes. Never did I expect anyone to comfort me, or to understand just how hard it has been.

"I didn't know," Fletcher continues, his voice low and strained. "I had no idea this was happening, or that you... oh God, I can't believe you've had to deal with this all on your own."

There is no point in reminding him that he had known it was happening. The Fletcher who knew and didn't give a damn one way or another, is gone.

"It's not your fault," I say. Hearing how muffled my voice is in the crook of his shoulder, he releases me slightly so he can look me in the eye.

"Tell me," he says, kissing my eyelids and tasting the salt of my tears.

I pull away from him, brushing at the wetness on my cheeks and he lets me go, giving me space to compose myself, but he keeps a tight hold of one of my hands in both of his.

"Tell me," he says again. "I want to know. You don't have to carry this alone. Not anymore."

I exhale slowly and clear my throat, shifting the emotional block that has settled there.

"The first was a man named Viktor Ivanov. He was destined to die on the tenth of January 1964. The Guild had no idea then, that your clock had stopped working properly, but, after forty-six years of searching for you, I had become obsessed with it. I wanted to witness his death so I travelled to Moscow. Viktor worked for the Soviet Ministry of Education. He had three children – two strapping young men and a daughter who was in love with the son of a baker, a boy Viktor didn't approve of."

"I can sympathise," Fletcher murmurs and I smile weakly at his attempt to lift my spirits.

"Viktor's wife was ill at the time and he left work early to check on her. I knew he wouldn't make it home. It was only a twenty minute walk, but, from the moment he stepped out of his office building Viktor had exactly sixteen minutes left to live."

. . .

JANUARY 10, *1964, Moscow*

VIKTOR IVANOV HAD the determined stride of a man who knew his destination and saw no reason not to arrive there promptly. I found myself struggling to keep up with him as he marched along the street, my boots slipping on the slick ice. I had never known such cold and I pulled my coat tightly around myself, my head bent low as I followed Viktor through suburbia. He made good time, marching through the snow-lined paths as if he knew he had to hurry - as if he wanted to say goodbye before death came for him. Every few seconds I glanced at my watch, counting down the remaining minutes of his life. We were nearing his street when the moment arrived. Viktor paused, suddenly, and gazed up toward the sky. My breath caught in my throat but I kept moving forward, covering the distance between us in a daze. I was almost at his shoulder when he moved, and I cried out in alarm. He whirled around at the sound, uttering a guttural curse and then he stepped closer to me, his mouth forming words I didn't understand.

I stood before him, my mouth opened in shock, unable to answer the question he was demanding of me. I assumed he wanted to know who I was, or why I had snuck up on him, but the question itself was not the point. The point was that the man who was asking it shouldn't be alive to do so.

"I PANICKED," I tell Fletcher, remembering it with vivid clarity. "I didn't have time to think, or formulate a plan, I just reacted."

"Your daggers?" Fletcher asks and I nod, glancing automatically to where they are hanging casually over the back of the dressing table chair.

"Someone sounded the alarm," I continue. "I didn't even realise there were people around. I ran as fast as I could and took shelter in an empty schoolyard. By the following morning a composite sketch had appeared in every paper in the surrounding area. It was a decent likeness, but by the time it was printed I was already back on U.S soil."

"He was forty-eight?" Fletcher probes gently and I nod.

"He lived the longest. Since then, every person whose name appears on your clock has a shorter life span."

Fletcher's face shows visible signs of shock.

"What does that mean?"

"I honestly don't know. The Guild... the Guild thinks that your clock is deteriorating. That it's malfunctioning. They fear there may come a time when it goes blank."

"And if that happens?"

"Fletcher there's no way of knowing what will happen. The Sovereign didn't leave any notes on this type of scenario."

"The Guild must have a theory?" he asks sharply.

"They're probably wrong."

"What is it, Clarke? What's the theory?"

I heave a sigh and raise myself up into a sitting position. I look long and hard at him, not wanting to tell him what the Guild's concern are, but he doesn't yield, his face a determined question.

"There's a possibility that time itself will unravel, that the clocks will cease to record life." I don't mention that certain Guild theorists claim the clock will disintegrate in a singular explosion which will literally destroy the entire Earth.

Unfortunately, Fletcher is a lot smarter than I gave him credit for.

"They think the world will end?" he guesses.

He drops his gaze, his tone disbelieving and ashamed, and I raise my hand to his cheek, forcing him to look at me again.

"It's only a theory," I say, forcing a confidence I don't feel. The truth is, Cody Johnson is proof that the lives on Fletcher's clock are getting shorter.

Fletcher nods, half-heartedly.

"Tell me about the others," he pleads, but this time I think it is less for my sake than to distract him from his guilt.

SEPTEMBER 21, *1997, Paris, France*

IN THE SEPTEMBER OF 1997, Celine du Bois retired after fifteen years of dancing for the Ballet de l'Opéra Paris – the oldest national ballet company in the country. Celine had starred in every major production for the past ten years, but for the last four she had not been offered the starring role and had thought it best if she disappeared gracefully into the wings. Celine knew exactly what she wanted to do next and had already viewed the perfect studio from which to start her own ballet school, teaching young girls the poise and grace that she had mastered in her years on stage. At 9.30 on the morning of the September, 21st, Celine signed a two-year lease for the premises. By 9.42 she was dead.

I watched as Celine left the realtor's office, moving with the fluid grace of a life-long dancer. Her white-blonde hair was pulled up into a bun and her soft skirt swished delicately around her knees with every step. I was more prepared this time than I had been with Viktor Ivanov and alert to everything around me. I saw the taxi jump the red light, watched as Celine glided toward the street. In the instant that I moved, taking long, determined strides toward her, she seemed to hesitate, reaching down to rummage in her leather tote, as if she had suddenly realised she might have forgotten something.

She had half-turned back by the time I reached her side and, for an infinitesimal second, our eyes met. Hers were clear blue, wide-set and remarkably youthful. Out of the corner of my own I saw the taxi hurtling toward us. Without missing a beat, I placed my hands on Celine's shoulder and pushed, just hard enough to unbalance her. With a ballerina's impeccable footing, she skipped only a few steps, before righting herself, looking up at me with wounded indignation.

The taxi hit her from the side and, like a marionette, she was flipped over the hood. She bounced onto the roof and then crumpled in a heap on the street, plumes of white smoke billowing over her as the cabbie tramped on his brakes.

It took me only a few seconds to make sure that no one had witnessed me push her and then I was at her side. Celine stared up at me, her tiny body broken in more places than I wanted to count. Blood poured from her nose, and, as I watched, more dribbled from her ears, streaking her white hair scarlet.

"I'm sorry," I murmured, holding up her head. The indignance faded from her face, to be replaced by an infinite and accepting sadness, and I felt again the sting of tears on my chalk-white cheeks. Celine tried to speak but managed only a rasping slur. "I'm so sorry," I repeated, squeezing my eyes shut as the spasms slowly subsided and her body became still.

"SHE WAS THIRTY-THREE," I say, as I finish relaying the story. "Younger than Viktor, but we didn't think anything of it. Until Henry Abbott died at the age of nineteen."

Fletcher stiffens and I look up to find a frown creasing his brow, his eyes narrowed in concentration. I know that look well – it's the one he gets every time he remembers something new.

"There was a train," he murmurs. "Henry Abbott was hit by a train. He was going to commit suicide but changed his mind at the last minute."

"Yes."

"You pushed him back onto the tracks."

"Yes."

"I was there." His eyes clear as he focuses on my face. "I saw it happen. I wonder if I was there for the others, too."

"Probably," I sigh, and allow him to take me in his arms, drawing comfort from the warmth of his body against mine. "I can't believe how often you were watching without me knowing."

"I'm just sorry I was so cruel."

"You didn't know about the anomalies," I point out. "You probably thought I was a murderous bitch." Anyone watching me would've thought the same without all the information at hand. He rubs my arm with his strong hand as if he can massage away the pain.

"Henry was the last?"

"Yes. When Henry died, Cody Johnson's name appeared." I swallow a lump in my throat but when I speak again my voice breaks anyway. "He's only a baby, Fletcher."

"It'll be okay," he says. "I promise, everything will be okay."

We fall silent, lost in our own thoughts. Only when the sun has risen, high enough to send a shaft of light through the gap between the ill-fitted curtains, does Fletcher speak.

"Your clock hasn't changed."

"What?"

"Your clock," he repeats. "It still has your name on it."

"I know." I don't understand what he's getting at. "What about it?"

"They're not the same, Clarke. You and I aren't the same. You can be saved. You want the dial back so you can die, right? It's possible for you."

I can hear the pain in his voice but I can't deny it and his face falls.

"I'm tired," I admit after a long pause. "I don't even know what else to say, I'm just tired. I don't want to kill Cody Johnson. I need to know that I have a way out of this. I know that's selfish but..."

"It's not selfish." His voice is clipped but adamant and I know he doesn't want me to say anything more. "I want the same thing. The only difference is that there's no way the Guild - or anyone else - can help me."

I try half-heartedly to reassure him, but Fletcher insists I drop the subject and we don't bring it up again.

Another town, another mall, and this time everything goes according to plan. We regroup after a particularly successful morning stuffing our pockets with jewellery and cash. We discard all the purses and wallets, along with all identification and drivers' licences they contain, in a neat pile right outside the post office and then catch a bus heading east. Since our conversation this morning, Fletcher has been quieter than usual, but other than that he seems to have returned to normal. I rest my head on his shoulder and his hand lifts automatically to stroke my hair as he gazes out of the window, watching the world pass us by in a blur. My eyelids droop. I blink once, twice, and then I stop fighting sleep and let it take me.

When I open my eyes Fletcher is rigid in the seat beside me. I stifle a yawn and sit straight up, scanning the bus for any sign of danger. Finding none, I turn to find a strange look on Fletcher's face and I don't know whether he is angry, afraid, or disappointed.

"What's wrong?" I turn my head again, rechecking the passengers on the bus, but I find nothing and no one to be concerned about.

"I'm just thinking." He gives me a small smile and leans back in his seat. We travel in silence for a few minutes with Fletcher lost in thought, staring out of the window. I want him to look at me, I want to know what he's thinking, but I bite down hard on my lip and stare fixedly ahead.

It is almost an hour before the silence is broken.

"We're getting closer to Arizona," Fletcher remarks as we cross the Colorado River.

"I know." I don't know if I am deliberately taking us back to where it all began but there is a crossroad up ahead. I'm going to have to decide soon whether we continue onward or hop buses.

"We could still head north," I say, trying to lighten the atmosphere. "Take a jaunt to Vegas?"

"No." Fletcher sighs heavily, the exhalation coming from a place deep inside his chest. "We need to go back," and then, "I remembered where it is, Clarke. I know where your dial is."

TWENTY-FIVE
AN UNJUST PUNISHMENT

FLETCHER'S ADMISSION CHANGES EVERYTHING. I don't know how long he'd known the location of my dial before telling me, but I suspect it wasn't long. I also know how hard it was for him to confess. Fletcher is a far better person than I am. He would sacrifice his own happiness for mine. He's going to help me become mortal again leaving him alone for eternity. I still cannot believe the depths of his selflessness.

As it turns out we need to get back inside Fletcher's house. During the journey back to Flagstaff, which takes two further bus trips and a short cab drive, we speak very little. There is a chasm between us, my possible mortality weighing heavy in the air. Fletcher has his newsboy cap tilted forward, hooding his eyes and he gives nothing away, shutting himself off from me. My heart hurts, knowing how deeply this pains him, and I crave the intimacy we shared last night but the coldness emanating from him keeps me at arm's length.

Being back in Phoenix, so close to Tempus headquarters, also has us both on edge. We exit the cab a few miles from Fletcher's house. He stuffs a wad of stolen notes into the cabbie's hand, the tip so excessive that the man asks three times if we are sure he can't take us anywhere else. It's an understandable question, given that we've had him drop us in the middle of nowhere. Hoisting our bags, we start walking.

"No sign of the Guild," Fletcher whispers a few hours later. We have been watching the house from a safe distance long enough for my butt to go numb but we haven't seen any sign of movement.

"There's no sign of anything. It's too quiet. You have staff, Fletcher, where are they all?"

He squints toward the small guardhouse at the gate and narrows his eyes.

"You're right. Luke should be on duty. Unless he's fallen asleep."

I curse in frustration.

"He's not sleeping. They're here. Or at the very least, they're watching the house."

"It's not as if we didn't expect that," Fletcher points out.

"I know. It's just that things are even more dangerous now that the Lincolns hold so much power. At least Harrison and I had an understanding."

"Didn't that understanding include you bringing me into custody?" His attempt at humour is endearing, given what he has agreed to help me do.

"Well, initially yes," I retort, "but even after I betrayed the Guild, he still trusted my judgement."

"And I assume, by your tone, that Andrew Lincoln doesn't?"

"Andrew Lincoln hates my guts. I don't take it personally," I add at his arch look, "he hates all the Kennedys. I just happen to be one of the last so I bear the brunt of his loathing."

"I don't know how anyone could ever hate you." He winks at his own irony and I shake my head at the feeble joke.

"Do you know where Martha lives?" I ask, peering back at the eerily still house.

"Why?"

"I told her to get somewhere safe – to hide, until this was all over.

If we can find her, she might be able to tell us something that would help."

"Good thinking." Fletcher nods, backing away from the rocky boulders we've taken cover behind.

"Follow me."

"You know where she lives?" Despite it being my idea I'm quite shocked that the selfish, egotistical Fletcher of a few days ago actually knows where his housekeeper lives when she's not cleaning up after him.

"She hurt her ankle a few years back," Fletcher explains, as we follow a footpath littered with pebbles and sand. "I drove her home."

It turns out that Martha's house is nowhere near the mansions of the Foothills and we have to catch another cab to a far less ostentatious but more welcoming part of town.

Children spill out onto the street, their drab clothing doing nothing to dull the sparkle in their eyes. Rosy-cheeked and filled with the energy of youths who have yet to discover that their childhood paradise is not without flaws.

"You folks sure you're going to be all right?" the cabbie asks as we hand him the fare.

"We'll be fine," I snap, annoyed by his assumption that, just because these people are poorer than most, they might mean us harm.

"Thank you," Fletcher tries to ease the offended man's pride and hands him a generous tip.

"You shouldn't have done that," I say, scowling at the departing cab. "We don't have money to throw away – you're not rich anymore, remember."

"I'm still rich," he replies easily, enjoying my irritation, "I just don't have access to my money at this moment."

As we walk down the street, the lack of maintenance and shabbiness of the houses becomes more pronounced and I can't help but reflect on the fact that this is how Fletcher was living when I met him. Growing up in high society I had always felt suffocated, but I had become completely unselfconscious around Fletcher's friends once I realised they weren't going to rat me out to my father. Underfed and underpaid, they were in need of everything but spirit and I had never witnessed such naked joviality. They were uninhibited, unapologetic and undeniably good. Salt of the earth - my father had loved to use the term, and it was a saying I had often heard but never fully understood until meeting Fletcher and his friends.

"What are you thinking about?" he asks me now, with genuine curiosity.

"These people," I say, encompassing the neighbourhood with one insignificant sweep of my arm. "They remind me of you."

He looks pleased and I can't help but smile.

"I didn't think you'd be that thrilled, Mr CEO."

"Then you don't know me very well," he replies teasingly.

"That's it." He points at a modest white house just a few doors down. "That's Martha's house."

We are halfway up the neat garden path when a handsome youth of about sixteen comes flying out of the front door. His curly black hair is long and wild and an enormous skull pendant bangs against his chest as he runs toward us.

"Mister Fletcher!" he calls, wide-eyed and frantic.

"John, is that you?" Fletcher manages, before the youth reaches him and half-strangles him in an awkward hug.

"Mister Fletcher, I knew you'd come! Dad!" he yells over his shoulder, not giving Fletcher a second to speak, "Dad, it's Mister Fletcher!"

I cast a wary glance over my shoulder and scan the surrounding houses and the street in both directions. Fletcher, sensing my anxiety over John's own, quickly lowers his voice. "John, please keep it down!"

A SHADOW PASSES across the front door and I look up to see another man step through it. He's older than John, his dark eyes narrowed, mouth set in a grim line. He doesn't look particularly friendly, but Fletcher steps forward to meet him.

"Henry," he extends his arm. Henry shakes his head and gestures us inside.

I know the second I step inside that Martha isn't here. The housekeeper is meticulous to a fault and this house is in a state – dirty cups on every surface, coats not hung on the designated rack and draped negligently over the backs of chairs, shoes littering the tiny hallway. Henry closes the door behind us and deadbolts it.

"Henry?" Fletcher asks. "Henry what's wrong?"

The giant man turns from the door to face us. His black eyes pass over me for only an instant but I get the feeling he has already weighed me up and found me wanting.

"Do you know where my mother is?" he asks and I see Fletcher's face fall.

"She's not here?"

"She was arrested," John interrupts.

"John," Henry uses a father's voice, "go and clear a space in the living room."

The boy looks devastated but he doesn't argue.

"Arrested?" Fletcher probes and Henry nods.

"It happened a few days ago – a group of men pulled up in their dark SUVs and took her. She'd been acting strange ever since she came back from work." He leaves the implied question hanging, but my mind is already two steps ahead. The Guild. The Guild has Martha. Fletcher has obviously come to the same conclusion and, as our eyes meet, I see the guilt reflected in his.

"Mister Fletcher is there something I need to know? Is my mama in some kind of trouble?"

"No," Fletcher's voice rises, "no, Henry. She hasn't done anything wrong. I'm sure this is just a terrible mix up."

"And her job?" Henry asks, more quietly. I can hear that he is ashamed to be asking, but I gather Martha's income is essential to their family. "I assume you came here because she hasn't been into work?"

I can practically see the cogs of Fletcher's brain working. Martha's family know nothing of what's happened. All they know is that she's been arrested for an as-yet unknown crime and their biggest concern is that Fletcher is going to fire her over it.

"Your mother will always have a job with me," Fletcher says. "I'll go down to the station now and see what the problem is."

"I'd be mighty grateful, Mister Fletcher," Henry sounds as though a colossal weight has been lifted from his shoulders. "I've been down there a few times and they won't tell me anything. I don't even know if that's where they're keeping her. They haven't even told us what she's been charged with and we... well, we can't afford an attorney, Sir."

"I can," Fletcher announces boldly, for a man who is committing petty robbery just to survive. "I'll get to the bottom of this, Henry, I give you my word."

"Thank you." Henry shakes Fletcher's hand so hard it turns white in his grip. "I'm sorry for the inconvenience this has caused you."

"It's no trouble, Henry. None of this is your fault, or Martha's, for that matter. Your mother is a good woman – one of the best. I'll make sure she gets the justice she deserves." I see it then – the glimmer in his midnight eyes – and I can sense the anger radiating off him.

"We should go," I say, fearful that he might give us away if we stay any longer. Henry looks at me curiously, but he doesn't ask who I am and Fletcher doesn't volunteer the information.

Before we've taken a step toward the door, John reappears.

"I cleaned it up a bit, Dad," he announces eagerly.

"We can't stay," Fletcher says and his youthful face falls.

"Mister Fletcher is going to go and see if he can't get this mess with your grandma sorted out," Henry tells his son, and then, as if to prove the point, he unlocks the front door and opens it wide.

There is no reason to linger, so Fletcher and I bid our goodbyes and step outside.

"You want me to call you a cab, Mister Fletcher?" John asks politely.

"No, that's okay, we'll call one from the road."

Henry frowns, scanning the street, only now realising that we didn't bring a car.

"It was lovely meeting you!" I say, drawing his attention away from Fletcher, and by the time he waves confusedly in response we are out of earshot.

"What are you going to do?" I ask Fletcher. His face is like thunder and I have to take two steps to every one of his just to keep up.

"I don't know yet," he growls. "But I have to do something. We can't just leave her with them."

I nod grimly.

We make it about two hundred yards before they appear. A pair of black-clad men who step out onto the street ahead as if they have appeared out of thin air and fix their eyes on us.

If we had known Martha had been taken by the Guild, we would have known that they would be watching her house. Unfortunately, in our ignorance, we didn't, which is why we now face two members of Tempus who have obviously been charged with keeping an eye on the house in case we showed up.

"Well, this isn't good," I murmur, barely moving my mouth.

"I don't know," Fletcher answers lightly. "It could be fun."

"Tell me you're not going to do anything reckless," I plead. A second later, he is sprinting toward the two men, closing the distance between them in long, furious strides. I heave a sigh and pound the pavement after him.

TWENTY-SIX
JONATHAN HARRISON'S FILES

THE ELEMENT of surprise is crucial to the success or failure of any attack. Fletcher surprised the Tempus soldiers by rushing them head-on instead of trying to run. The Tempus soldiers, on the other hand, surprised us by having back-up. As three more soldiers joined the pair, I had no choice but to follow Fletcher into the fray. That he would be killed wasn't a concern, but I'd be damned if they were going to apprehend him after all the trouble I'd gone through to keep him out of the Guild's custody.

With Fletcher in their midst and fighting in such close quarters, the soldiers quickly abandon any attempt to use their guns. They have about as much chance of shooting each other as hitting either of us. I draw my daggers as I run, the reassuring steel cold against my palms. Fletcher's knives are slashing the air around us viciously, and I duck to avoid losing an ear as he brings his blade streaking downward, severing the tendons in one soldier's forearm. With the instantaneous loss of the use of his right arm, the man teeters away, his other hand clamped firmly on the wound to staunch the blood flow.

"Do you mind?" I hiss at Fletcher, jabbing out at another soldier. Anyone watching might think the blade had slipped beneath his arm, until, with another brutal shove, the tip of my dagger blossoms from his shoulder blade. The soldier screams in pain and stumbles backward, taking my dagger with him. Grabbing hold of the steel hilt, I press my sneakered foot against his stomach and kick out. My dagger wrenches free, but, before I can recover, I am seized from behind, a pair of muscular arms encircling my waist and lifting me clear off my feet. I toss the blade into a spin, catching it on the way down, and, with a short, swift shove, I stab my captor in the stomach. The man releases me instantly, his hands going automatically to the wound, his face a mask of stunned disbelief.

With only a fleeting thought for his welfare, I whirl around to find Fletcher involved in hand-to-hand combat with the last remaining soldier. I have no idea where the other two went, but I assume, because I can't see them, that they have fled. Chest heaving, I step toward the man I just wounded. He staggers backward, but I return both daggers to my waist holster and raise my hands in a gesture of peace.

"What's your name?" I ask. He glares at me warily. "Your name!" I snap.

"Truman," he mumbles, "Lawrence Truman."

I try to lift his shirt but his hands are cemented to his stomach.

"Any relation to Jason Truman?" I ask as I slap his hands away.

"He's my cousin."

I note the hiss of breath through gritted teeth and I wince at the amount of blood bubbling from the wound.

"It must be your lucky day," I say, stripping off my hoodie. "Jason Truman is one of my favourite people."

I quickly tie the hoodie around his waist, pulling it as tight as possible.

"Keep pressure on it," I tell Lawrence, and then I beckon Fletcher over. Without being told, he retrieves his backpack and hands me a clean T-shirt which I ball up and stuff beneath the hoodie.

"How did you...?" Lawrence jerks in pain as I yank on the sleeves of the hoodie to tighten it again.

"Don't feel bad," I say, sensing what it is he wants to know. "You've only been training a few years. I've trained under the Guild for a century."

"I guess I should count myself lucky," he wheezes, and he suddenly reminds me so much of his cousin that my heart aches.

"Clarke," Fletcher issues a low warning and I look up to find two of the men have returned. One is pointing a gun at my chest.

"Put that down," I say, my primary focus still on Lawrence.

"Go to hell," he spits at me.

"Already there," I murmur. "You need to lie down," I add, catching Lawrence's gaze. Without argument, he sinks to the floor. I help him down, until he is lying flat out on the ground. His face is pale against the gravel backdrop.

"I need your phone," I tell the man with the gun.

"You need to put your hands in the air," he corrects.

I breathe in deeply through my nose and then let the air out slowly before I get to my feet and round on the soldier.

"I can't die, you idiot," I snap, "but your friend here can, and he will if you don't give me your God-damn phone!"

"I have my orders," the soldier insists, unrelenting. A sheen of sweat has broken out on Lawrence's brow.

"We don't have time for this," Fletcher warns, but I'm not sure if he's talking about Lawrence's chances of survival or the fact that we should be getting as far away from here as possible.

"Who gave you your orders?" I ask and the soldier's chin lifts arrogantly.

"The Grand Master himself."

"Well that's convenient." My reaction takes him by surprise and the second's hesitation is all Fletcher needs. Before the soldier can blink, Fletcher has his knife pressed to his throat.

"Who the hell do you think I want to talk to, anyway?" I fume, jerking the gun from his hands and turning it on him. "Now get Andrew Lincoln on the phone."

I have only to mention my name and I am patched through to the Grand Master's secure line.

"Clara Kennedy," Andrew Lincoln's voice oozes disdain. "How lovely of you to check in after your disgraceful betrayal of the Guild."

"I haven't betrayed anyone, Lincoln. The Guild has no idea what they're doing. You would've seen Harrison's files by now – you know it, and I know it."

"You may have eighty years on me, but don't presume you know anything about the inner-most workings of Tempus. That honour is reserved for people who actually follow the rules."

I ignore him.

"Your people are hurt. Lawrence Truman needs immediate medical attention."

"I'll have a team sent straight away," he concedes. "Although I don't know why you care, given that you must be the one who injured him in the first place?"

"I don't want to hurt anybody!" I snap. "You may not believe me but I am trying to fix this mess and I have an idea that might just work. You don't have to like me, but I need you to trust me."

"Trust you?" he laughs. "Is this your idea of a joke? Because I have to tell you, Clara, if it is, you're not that funny."

"Jonathan Harrison trusted me."

At this, he actually laughs out loud, the sound distorting through the receiver.

"You think Jonathan Harrison trusted you? That he gave a damn about you? Tell me you aren't that naïve. In fact, why don't you come over to my office and I'll show you the files we have on you and your family – Harrison's footnotes make for very interesting reading."

That hurt, just as he intended. I meet Fletcher's concerned gaze and draw in a steadying breath.

"You're right, Lincoln, I have been around a lot longer than you. And do you know what those eighty years have taught me? That some people are just full of shit."

His voice turns acid.

"You may think you're above the hierarchy, but you are just the by-product of your sister's sins. As is Fletcher."

"I'd be careful not to insult my sister," I say, "given that yours is currently in the same position Anna was in when she screwed up. I hope Sienna doesn't stumble across any of your loved ones' clocks."

Leaving him with that thought, I hang up and toss the phone back to the soldier Fletcher has restrained. He catches it clumsily, Fletcher's knife at his throat hindering his movement.

"Time to go," I say and Fletcher shoves the man aside. "You hold on, Lawrence," I add, gazing down at the weakened man. "I would hate for your cousin to hear that I killed you."

We run, then, sprinting through alleyways, ducking under washlines and vaulting over rickety wooden fences until we are certain that no one could have followed us through the labyrinth of the path we've taken. We emerge from the village on the opposite side from where we arrived and Fletcher hails a cab.

"What do we do now?" he asks, buzzing with the need to act. "How do we get to Martha?"

It's hard for me to say what I do next.

"Martha will be stashed in the bowels of Tempus headquarters, Fletcher. We can't get to her."

"What? We have to – this is our fault. We can't just leave her there."

"Yes," I nod my agreement, "it is our fault. But there's another way to fix it. We're going to get that dial."

The cabbie drops us back in the Foothills and we take up our previous position watching Fletcher's house. Fletcher hasn't asked me what my plan is, but I think he's beginning to suspect.

"We make our move as soon as it's dark," I tell him. No matter how many times I've scanned the area, I cannot spot any Guild soldiers, but I know they're out there.

As dusk falls, my eyes burn with the effort of our ongoing surveillance and I slump down behind a rock. Fletcher is fiddling with one of his knives, balancing the blade on the tip of his finger. As

I watch, a red droplet blossoms on his fingertip, but Fletcher doesn't remove the blade.

"Are you okay?" I ask, only noticing now how withdrawn he is.

"I'm fine."

I shift closer to him. "You don't seem fine."

"You're leaving me," he shrugs. "it's not something I'm thrilled about."

"I'm not leaving you, Fletcher."

"You want to restore your dial."

"Yes."

"You'll die." His voice breaks.

"Fletcher," I gently take the handle of his knife and set it aside, wiping away the blood on his finger as I take his hand.

"Look at me."

He does, his midnight eyes locking onto mine. I lift my hand to his face, feeling the days old stubble under my palm.

"I'm not going to leave you," I promise.

"I know we haven't had much experience with death, but I'm pretty sure that your dying will include leaving me."

"I'm not planning on dying."

His head jerks up, and I smile at his confusion.

"I'm not going to simply restore my dial," I explain. "I'm going to turn it back."

TWENTY-SEVEN
THE STAINS OF TIME

"HOW DO you even know that's possible?" Fletcher is more animated than I've ever seen him, his hair standing up on all ends from the constant running of his hands through it. "It's never been done. What if it doesn't work? What if you drop dead before you can turn it back?"

"Well that's a nice thought."

"You know what I mean. You were supposed to die in 1984. I remember, because I bought a bottle of the finest scotch I could find to celebrate."

I burst out laughing. I can just picture the old Fletcher with his feet up, raising a glass to my clock, celebrating my would-be-death.

"I bet you counted down the days," I tease.

"I looked at that clock every night for a week," he winks, before turning solemn once more. "The point is you've lived a lot longer than you were supposed to. What if time catches up the second the dial is put back? I don't think you'd look as hot after decades of decomposing." He pulls a face and gags.

"Well we certainly couldn't have an open-casket."

"That's not funny."

"Yeah, I get that a lot. Apparently my sense of humour leaves much to be desired. Look, thirty-two years isn't much in the greater scheme of things," I say, trying to reassure him. "Time is infinite, so it's just a fleeting moment if you think about it."

"I don't want to think about it."

"Then don't. Let's just get the dial."

Fletcher isn't listening, a perplexed look coming over his face, his eyes fixed on something in the distance.

"Oh God," he drops his head into his hands.

"What?"

"I gave your clock back," he groans. "Even if we manage to get the dial from my house, how the hell are we going to sneak back into the Hall of Clocks with the whole of Tempus after us?"

"Yes, that might require a bit of planning," I say, "but let's just take this one step at a time."

"Okay," Fletcher gets to his feet, brushing the sand off his pants.

"Step one," he looks purposefully across to where his house is situated, nestled in the valley. "Let's get that dial."

Creeping under the cover of darkness we edge closer to the house. Fletcher leads me in a broad circle so that we approach the property from the back, cutting through a conservancy of trees and shrubs, which snag my hair and leave multiple scratches on our hands and arms.

"Dammit!" I curse, as I trip over a gnarled tree root and only just manage to stay upright with an impressive manoeuvre that I could never possibly hope to replicate.

"Always the bird," Fletcher grins, his teeth flashing white in gloom.

"I can be the wind," I grumble, taking extra care where I place my feet as we continue onward.

"This is the servants' entrance," Fletcher whispers, as we approach a small gate in the imposing white wall that encompasses his entire three-acre property. "They're no doubt watching the entire perimeter, but at least this is slightly less conspicuous than walking right up to the front door."

We crouch behind a natural hedge of shrubbery and scout the area.

"I don't see anyone," Fletcher murmurs.

"Me neither, but we know they're out there."

"Okay, I have an idea. I'll go in first and draw them out, then you can come running if trouble starts."

"When trouble starts," I point out. "There's no way you're going to make it inside without drawing attention to yourself."

"You might be surprised," he says, "and I definitely have a better chance of it than you do."

"Ha-ha," I mock-laugh, and then mumble under my breath.

"What's that?"

"Nothing."

"There's nothing wrong with being the back-up," he chuckles, proving that he heard me loud and clear.

I hold my breath as Fletcher ventures out of the cover greenery. He is utterly exposed for the few seconds it takes to reach the wall and then he disappears, blending into the shadows at its base. I can't help but be impressed. I'm struggling to keep sight of him and I have a general idea of where he is. With any luck, any Guild soldiers watching this section of the perimeter will have a hard time spotting him. My neck and shoulders are tense, but I don't move as Fletcher reaches the gate. I can only barely see the red glow of the keypad on the wall and then it is snuffed out as he stands before it and punches in a code. I wait for the creak of the gate but there is nothing and a second later Fletcher disappears inside.

I count to ten in my head, then twenty, then thirty, expecting all hell to break loose at any second, but the night is still. Unable to bear it any longer, I creep forward, toward the dark mouth of the gateway, a black rectangle against the wall of white and poke my head around the corner. There is no sign of Fletcher, but ahead, the rear of the house looms. There are a few lights on outside, illuminating patches of lawn.

Suddenly one of the patches moves and I zero in on the spot. A black-clad man is inching his way toward the open door which leads to the kitchen – the door Fletcher must have passed through only moments ago.

I am about to follow the dark form when another shadow breaks away from the light to my left. Three more men follow the first into the house. I give it a few seconds, to be sure there are no more and then I tiptoe after them.

The sound of a scuffle reaches me almost immediately. Snatching up my daggers, I find Fletcher in the kitchen, fighting a mass of black limbs. There are more than four opponents and I wonder how many snuck in before I entered the property. Fletcher must have been lying in wait, just beyond the open door and he is putting up a hell of a fight, as if galvanised by the invasion in his own home.

I leap onto the marble island in the centre of the kitchen and snatch one of the Guild soldiers by the hair, yanking him backward. His brown eyes glare up at me, his arms reaching over his head to try and get a grip on my arms, but I bang his head down hard on the solid stone, once, twice. The third time is the charm and his eyes close. He slithers to the ground in an unconscious heap and I turn my attention to the next threat. Unfortunately, it comes from behind me. A sharp yank on my braid and I fly backward off the counter, landing painfully on the floor. My daggers skitter across the tiles as a grim face looms over me. I register the balled fist only just in time and I roll out of the way to avoid getting my face bludgeoned.

The space is small, but I manage to twist my body and spin, so that by the time my legs kick out, I am perfectly positioned and I strike both of his kneecaps. I hear the satisfying crunch of bone and the man drops, ironically, onto his knees. The pain is too much and he flops to the side to take the pressure off, his hands cupping the shattered area.

I vault back onto the counter, using the height to my advantage.

Fletcher's hands are covered in blood, his knives lost in the fray, and a thin trickle is navigating its way lazily from the corner of his eye to the corner of his mouth. A soldier is backing away from him and I kick out at his head when he ventures too close. Fletcher meets my eye for a second over the chaos and grins. "Little bird," he mouths and then he is fighting once more.

It's all over within minutes.

"You'd think they would've learned their lesson the first time," Fletcher pants as we bind the soldiers' hands and feet with neckties I fetch from his closet. Seven men had been watching Fletcher's house – only three more than the number watching Martha's – and, knowing how easily we had overcome that group, one would think that Andrew Lincoln would take extra precautions.

"Harrison wouldn't have made this mistake," I say smugly.

"Well, then I guess we should be thankful he's no longer in charge." Fletcher yanks on the final tie and the soldier whose hands he is restraining gives a moan of discomfort.

"Stop your griping," Fletcher tells him as he retrieves his knives. My daggers are already stowed back in my waist holster.

"Demon!" the soldier spits at Fletcher's feet.

Fletcher heaves a weary sigh.

"Don't I know it."

He leads me up the stairs and back into his bedroom which is spotless. Martha's proficiency, no doubt, before she fled. The white sheets are pristine, no wrinkles daring to disturb her handiwork.

I watch as Fletcher gazes up at the painting of me. The way he looks at it makes me feel almost shy.

"It's beautiful," I say.

"Yeah." He stares at it for a few more seconds and then, with a determined resolve, he steps forward and lifts it off the hook.

"What are you...?" I trail off as he lays it on the floor, my eyes following his hands as they trace the clock in the background. His fingernails plunge into the paint and I breathe out an astonished exhalation of air. As the paint peels away, leaving only stained canvas behind, the dial of the grandfather clock remains unspoiled. Fletcher's tanned fingers curl around it and, with a swift tug, it comes away in his hands, art becoming life.

I cannot formulate rational thought. It was here all along. I saw it with my own eyes – I sat in this very room and admired it. Fletcher holds it out and, with a trembling hand, I take it from him. It's warm and the familiar thrum of life emanates from it. The gold glows through where the paint has been rubbed away. It is surreal, holding my life in my hands, and the brevity of it brings tears to my eyes. Fletcher wipes them away, leaving dried paint smeared across my cheek.

"Thank you," I croak, raising my eyes to his. He doesn't answer as he lowers his dark head and brings his lips to mine in a kiss that is as tender as it is desperate.

TWENTY-EIGHT
THE LAWS OF ATTRACTION

THERE IS nothing left for us to do but get into the Hall of Clocks, which is, of course, impossible. With no concrete plan and no place to stay, Fletcher suggests we look up an old colleague of his. The way he says it gives me the distinct impression that this is a last resort, and I wonder why he's so hesitant to lean on this colleague for help.

Until I meet her, that is.

We reach Tucson late the following day. Walking through the University of Arizona's campus, we draw a few curious looks from loitering students, but Fletcher doesn't seem to notice. He knows exactly where he's going and, sure enough, five minutes later we reach the Physics Department.

"Lucy's one of the world's most respected physicists," Fletcher explains as we enter the building. "She conducts a lot of her research here. I just hope she's in town."

We pause outside a lab and Fletcher raps on the door.

"Go away!" a high-pitched voice yells from within.

Fletcher grins and raps again.

I hear the thudding of heavy footsteps and the door is yanked open.

Luciana Gonzales is a diminutive woman with the copper skin and caramel eyes of a new-born fawn. Fletcher mentioned on the bus ride here that she's in her mid-forties, but her skin is unlined, save for a slight creasing around her enormous eyes. Her brow is slightly too heavy to be classically beautiful, but the word stunning comes to mind as I gaze down at her. She looks more like a Hispanic sitcom actress than a professor.

It's also obvious that she is furious at being interrupted, but, as her eyes light on Fletcher, her face splits into a dazzling smile.

"Fletcher Kincaid," she says in a voice like honey and mist. "As I live and breathe."

"Hi Luce," Fletcher drawls. Lucy's gaze takes me in with one appraising sweep from head to toe, and then she nods. I'm not sure whether it's a greeting or an approval and I get a gnawing suspicion that perhaps there's more between them than Fletcher implied. I shoot him an arch look as Lucy beckons us inside.

"Fletcher seems to have left his manners at home," Lucy says as we gather around a lab table. "Luciana Gonzales." She sticks out a hand and I grip it firmly.

"Clarke Kennedy."

Her eyebrows shoot up her forehead and she gives Fletcher a crooked smile.

"Any relation to *Clara* Kennedy?"

"Lucy," Fletcher issues a low warning.

"Well actually," I look quizzically between the two of them. "One and the same."

Lucy looks gobsmacked. Her eyes flicker between the two of us, a range of mixed emotions reflecting on her open face, and then she bursts into peals of laughter.

Fletcher looks decidedly uncomfortable.

"I'm assuming you know who I am?" I ask dryly.

"Oh I know exactly who you are," she grins, "I'm just amazed Fletcher finally got around to admitting the truth to himself." She gives Fletcher a look that clearly means I told you so.

"He wanted to kill me, didn't he?"

"I think that would've been too painless." She winks. "But all that anger and hatred wasn't difficult to see through. I assume you two have finally gotten it together?"

I look confused and she rephrases.

"You're together?"

I nod.

"About time. And don't worry," she adds to Fletcher, "I won't take offence. I always knew I was a rebound."

I gape at the two of them and Fletcher's cheeks redden.

"You two...?"

"Years ago," Lucy brushes it off lightly. "I got too old for Fletcher in the late nineties. Since then, our relationship has been purely professional."

"Maybe we could keep it that way, now, Luce? Professional, I mean." Fletcher asks, clearing his throat.

"Am I embarrassing you, Fletcher?" she looks positively thrilled at the prospect. "That's a first! Anyway, I'm sure Clarke wouldn't be upset about something that happened when she no doubt wanted to imprison your sexy ass. Right Clarke?"

I honestly don't know whether I love or hate this woman. She has absolutely no filter, which, if it wasn't for the nature of the subject matter, I would find refreshing. As it is, though, I can't help but feel a pang of jealousy. It's obvious that she and Fletcher have a history that runs deeper than a simple physical relationship. She teases him as if she's known him forever – as if they share some secret bond that I cannot compete with.

Fletcher, sensing my unease, quickly steers the conversation back to why we are here.

"Lucy knows all about the Guild," he admits. "She's particularly revered for her work in the fields of quantum gravity and general relativity." He continues, even more sheepishly, "She was trying to help me find a way to become mortal again. Obviously she's never seen my clock but she has studied yours."

"Mine?" I feel as embarrassed as I would if he'd mentioned she'd studied my underwear. Fletcher studiously avoids my eyes.

"And did you find anything?" I ask, turning to Lucy, who is watching us in unabashed amusement.

"Of course I didn't. The entire concept of the Hall of Clocks and the Sovereign are steeped in, well, for want of a better word – magic. You cannot explain, study or quantify it. It simply is."

"Then why are we here?" I demand of Fletcher.

"Because I want to know if Lucy has any theories on what would happen if time was turned back."

"You're planning on turning back time?" I wouldn't have thought it possible for her doe eyes to open any wider.

"Basically."

"Wow." She slumps onto a lab stool to process this.

"Is that bad?" I ask.

"Well, usually I'd say that would be very bad, but, in this instance, from what Fletcher's told me, the timeline we are living now is the anomaly. You would be setting it right."

"Would there be any dire consequence?"

"You're asking me? You're the one who works for Tempus."

I narrow my eyes at Fletcher, but his only response is an unconcerned shrugging of his broad shoulders.

"I'm asking you," I tell Lucy seriously.

"I honestly couldn't tell you, Clarke. Time travel may be a recognised concept in fiction but it has no support in theoretical physics, unless you count the Einstein-Rosen Bridge hypothesis."

"The what?"

"Wormholes," Fletcher interjects, reminding me that he and Lucy have spent a lot of time working on this together.

"Okay, but we're not talking about wormholes or hypothetical time travel. We're talking about turning time back."

Lucy whistles.

"I'm going to miss knowing this is an actual possibility."

"What do you mean?" Fletcher asks.

"If Clarke does what she's hoping to do, neither of you will ever set foot in the twenty-first century. I'll never meet you..." she trails off, becoming thoughtful. "Which means I'll spend my life researching something that is utter crap. Dammit!"

"You won't know it's crap, though," Fletcher points out wryly.

"True." She sighs. "I guess that's something."

"So, back to me turning back time..." I prompt.

"We have no idea what will happen," Lucy repeats, "but I figure it's probably safer than leaving the world on an alternate course."

She's lost us both and she seems to realise it. Leaping off the stool she snatches up a red marker pen and brushes past me to pull down a massive whiteboard.

"Let's just say, hypothetically, that this is the path time would've taken if Anna hadn't interfered."

She draws a straight line and marks it A to B.

"Now," she draws a line from point A at a 45-degree angle and ends it with a C. "This is the alternate timeline created when Anna..." she gives me an apologetic look, "when Anna did what she did. If you can go back to here," she circles point A with a frantic red circle to emphasise, "you can correct the anomaly and, theoretically, you should reset time back onto its original course." She highlights the first line with a few strokes of the marker.

"How?"

"That's the tricky part." She rams the lid of the marker back on with a pop. "You have to stop Anna from destroying Fletcher's clock."

I slump down on the stool she so recently vacated.

"How? How am I supposed to do that?"

"I can't tell you that."

"Hang on," Fletcher interrupts, speaking for the first time in a while. "There's no way to be a hundred percent certain of the precise point in time we go back to. There aren't any markings on the clock – Clarke would have to take an educated guess."

"Rather safe than sorry," Lucy murmurs. "I'd err on the side of caution and make sure you give yourself some breathing room."

Fletcher is staring intently at the rudimentary diagram on the board.

"What happens if we get there before point A?"

"I," I say quietly.

He swings around to look at me.

"I," I repeat. "I'm going back in time, Fletcher, not you."

"Yes, but I can help. I'm the only one who will know what you're trying to do..."

"No," Lucy cuts him off, "you won't. God, as far as doomed lovers go, you two are positively Shakespearian. It took you a hundred years to admit your true feelings for each other. What a pity you won't get that long this time around."

"What are you talking about?" Fletcher snaps, but Lucy doesn't answer him. Instead, she focuses entirely on me.

"If you really intend to turn time back," she says, "you alone will have knowledge of it. You," she turns to Fletcher and gives him a sympathetic look, "won't remember any of this."

I can sense that Fletcher is fuming and I am grateful when Lucy offers us a place to stay at her apartment. Fletcher is deadly quiet during the drive.

When we arrive I take the most luxurious shower of my life, washing away the smell of sweat and dirt from my hair and skin. Inspecting my body for the first time in days, I am surprised to discover bruises on my arms and legs, and that the toenail on my right foot is completely black and hanging on by a thread. I find a pair of nail scissors in the vanity above the sink and have just set about cutting it away when there's a knock at the door.

I pull the towel more securely around me.

"Come in."

The door opens to reveal Fletcher's dark head.

"You done?"

"Yeah, it's all yours."

Without any modesty, he strips off his clothing and dumps it in the laundry basket.

"Luce has gone back to the lab," he announces casually as he steps under the steaming spray. "She has some work to finish up but she said she'd grab us some dinner on her way back."

"I'm starving," I admit. He's left the shower door open and I watch the overspray speckling the tiled floor.

Fletcher pulls his head back out of the water to look at me, perched on the edge of the ball and claw tub.

"I want you to promise me something," he says, and his tone is so serious I pause my attack on the wayward toenail.

"What?"

"You have to tell me, Clarke. Promise me you'll tell me how you feel when you go back. I don't want to go through life without knowing."

"Fletcher..."

He cuts me off.

"I know, okay? I know that there won't be much time. I know how I died, and I can accept that. But I don't want to die never knowing the truth. I want to hear you say it."

"I love you," I say simply, but he shakes his head, sending out a spray of water.

"No," he says, "you don't get to do that. I want to hear it in 1916."

"What if it alters the timeline?"

He steps out of the cubicle, his naked body rearing above me as he reaches over for the towel on the rail. I'm relieved when he wraps it around his waist, but the way that he looks at me sets my blood on fire.

"I don't give a damn about the timeline," he snaps. "You're going to set things right, which is all we can ask for, but I refuse to die believing you don't feel the same way about me as I do about you. Promise me, Clarke."

I get to my feet, my heart thumping in my chest.

"I promise," I lie.

I don't know if he believes me, so when he opens his mouth to question my reply, I do the only thing I can think of to distract him. I drop my towel.

By the time Lucy arrives we are ensconced on the well-worn leather sofa. Fletcher borrowed Lucy's razor and she nods at his clean-shaven face over a bag of Chinese takeout.

"Better," she says, dumping her purse on the table in the hall with an almighty clatter. "What did I miss?"

"Not much," Fletcher says. "We're still trying to figure out how to get inside the Hall."

"The Guild will have all the access points heavily guarded," I say, as Lucy unpacks the food onto the table. "There's no way we are going to be able to get through to the Hall."

"You know that canyon better than anyone. Are you sure there's no way to sneak past them?"

"No. The only way to access the tunnels is to come at them from the River."

"You couldn't climb down? From the top?

"That would be suicide."

Lucy snorts and we both turn to look at her.

"Suicide?" she grins, "I don't think you could really call it suicide seeing as how you can't actually die."

I meet Fletcher's eye. I can practically read his thoughts.

"Not going to happen," I say firmly. "We'd wake up, but we'd be too banged up to climb into the tunnels, let alone fight off an army of Guild soldiers."

"Then there's only one thing we can do," Fletcher says, grabbing a carton and a set of chopsticks.

"What's that?"

"We need to find some reinforcements of our own."

TWENTY-NINE
INADEQUATE REINFORCEMENTS

"IS THAT ALL OF THEM?" Fletcher sounds disappointed as he peers over my shoulder at the list of ten names I've compiled.

"Actually, no. These three are dead," I scratch out the first three names. "And these three," I circle them, "are all over seventy. I don't think they're going to be able to help us."

"That leaves four," Fletcher sounds as unenthusiastic as I feel.

"There's no guarantee that any of them will come," I remind him.

He places his finger on the last name.

"Vincent will."

"I need Truman." I've been insisting on this for the past few hours but Fletcher isn't keen on the idea.

"It's too risky. He's Guild, through and through."

"So are all the Clock Keepers."

"Yes, but they see things differently. They've lived in that Hall, they respect time more than anyone. Plus, they've got to know you as a friend. The Guild's biggest mistake was leaving them in isolation." He lowers his voice. "Anna is proof of that."

It's the first time Fletcher has shown empathy for Anna, and a warmth flushes over me as he continues.

"If Anna hadn't been abandoned – if she'd had someone to speak to, to guide her, she might not have done what she did. You were the only person who was allowed to visit the Hall and then only once you were immortal yourself and they charged you with finding me. Another mistake," he adds with satisfaction. "You were the only person these people interacted with for ten years - ten very lonely years. I'm willing to stake my life that they will show you more loyalty than they will the Guild. Vincent's our proof."

"I haven't spoken to these people in decades," I point out.

"Neither will the Guild have. You say that Clock Keepers get to retire after their stint in the Hall?"

I nod.

"They're only called on if the Guild needs something, but I've never heard of Tempus having anything to do with them after they leave."

"Exactly. They'll still put you first. Tempus used them and discarded them when they had served their purpose."

"You don't understand the Guild mentality, Fletcher. It doesn't matter what Tempus does, we are blindly loyal to the cause."

"The cause being to protect time?"

"Yes."

A smirk tugs at his lips.

"Isn't that exactly what we're trying to do?"

Fletcher is right. Andrew Lincoln and most of the Guild regard Fletcher and I as the enemy, but we share the same goals. To right the wrong. It's the reason I switched sides and teamed up with Fletcher in the first place.

"Now we just have to convince them," I muse, scanning the too short list of names.

"Exactly."

"I hate to burst your bubble of positivity," Lucy says, "but you're going to need a lot more than four people if you're going to stand a chance."

"She's right," I tell Fletcher. "I know you don't like it but I'm going to have to talk to Truman."

"Not yet," he replies, holding up the piece of paper. "First we tackle these."

I fish the card Vincent gave me from my backpack and we head back to the University campus. It's dark and there are very few people around, but Lucy waves us through the security boom with a flash of her ID card.

"Are you sure we can trust this kid?" Fletcher asks, as she leads us to a small building. It's on the opposite end of the campus to her lab.

"JT is a genius. He hacked my personal computer at the beginning of the year and I threatened to have him expelled."

"Did you report it?"

"Hell no," Lucy laughs. "A kid with that kind of talent deserves an education. I did, however, make him hack my ex's phone records and send them to his wife."

"You are a terrifying creature," Fletcher chuckles, while I try to keep from reacting to Lucy's unapologetic admission of sleeping with a married man.

"Takes one to know one," Lucy says.

JT meets us inside the bowels of the IT department. He looks nothing like a computer geek. Instead, his branded T-shirt strains across biceps double the size of Fletcher's and his hair is slicked into a trendy comb-over.

"Ms Gonzales!" He greets Lucy with not an ounce of the resentment I would expect.

"Hey JT." She gestures at one of the workstations. "I need you to send a message to a mobile phone without it being traced. You up for it?"

"Do I have a choice?" he retorts, but it's obvious he's pleased. For a hacker, the permission of his college professor to indulge in his favourite pastime must be a dream come true. His fingers fly across the keys and a second later he looks expectantly over his shoulder.

"The number?"

I recite it from the card.

"What do you want to say?"

We have already decided that Flagstaff, over two hours away from the entrance to the Hall, won't be a safe bet. Ironically, we have chosen somewhere even more dangerous. Jacob Lake, a small, unincorporated community on the Kaibab Plateau in Coconino County is known as the Gateway to the Grand Canyon, and, more importantly it's only forty-five minutes from the Marble Canyon. Nestled in a ponderosa pine forest, the community is difficult to access, and, as a sleepy backwater town, the Guild pays it little attention, but it's the fastest way to reach the Hall.

"Jacob Lake, Friday. Bring other CKs if possible," I tell JT.

Friday is three days away. It'll only take Fletcher and I seven hours to reach Jacob Lake, and ten for Vincent, but, in the event that he does manage to rally any of the others, they'll need time to make arrangements and to travel.

"You having a party?" JT asks as he punches in the message, "Because I can think of far more exciting venues."

"JT," Lucy warns. He rolls his eyes but obediently hits send.

"You want me to keep the line open in case he replies?"

"No," I shake my head. I don't want to risk any further contact, or the chance that the Guild could accuse Vincent of giving me information. This way, the conversation is entirely one-sided. "He'll either be there or he won't." I tell Fletcher.

Our backpacks are in the car, and we decline Lucy's offer to come back and spend the night at her place.

"We shouldn't stay in one place too long," Fletcher tells her. "It's safer if we keep moving."

"I guess this is it, then."

To my amazement, she gives me a bone-cracking hug.

"Good luck," she whispers in my ear, "It was an honour to meet you."

"Thank you," I say, but I'm not sure exactly what for.

The hug she gives Fletcher is longer, more lingering, and I see her brushing glistening tears from her eyes.

"I'll miss you," she admits with a hiccup.

"No, Luce, you won't." Fletcher squeezes her arm and smiles down at her. "You can't miss someone who never existed."

Lucy drops us on the main road and we hail a cab to take us to the bus stop.

"I miss my cars," Fletcher complains as we settle in for the trip north. "Public transport leaves a lot to be desired."

"There was a time you had to walk everywhere," I remind him.

"True," he concedes, pulling the newsboy cap over his eyes. Despite his grumbling, he's asleep in minutes, while I stare out at the night sky and try to imagine how we have a hope in hell of succeeding.

Fletcher is still sleeping when the bus hisses to a creaking halt.

"Fletcher!" I shove his shoulder and he groans, one arm flopping over his eyes. "Fletcher, this is our stop."

I lift his arm and two doleful eyes glare blearily up at me.

"Rise and shine," I announce cheerily, keeping the rising tension out of my voice. Fletcher follows me off the bus and gazes around. I see the moment he realises, by the rigid set of his shoulders.

"Clarke, this isn't..."

"I know." I cut him off. "But we still have two days and this is important."

"Clarke!" his fear for my safety is making him angry. "Truman is not going to turn on the Guild. We shouldn't be here. You're no use to anybody if you get caught."

"I'm not going to get caught."

He rubs his hand through his hair in frustration.

"How do you plan on even making contact?"

"I know where he lives," I say. "It's almost dark – he'll be home soon."

"You're going to go to his house? That's your plan? Are you crazy! Do you have any idea what a risk that is?"

"Actually, I don't think it's any riskier than everything else we've done so far. Sure, the Guild were watching your place – and Martha's - but what reason could they possibly have to keep an eye on loyal Tempus members? There aren't enough of them to spread themselves so thin, and besides, the entire Guild would go into a frenzy if they knew they were being watched. Lincoln's not that stupid."

He gives me a look that says otherwise.

"Okay, he's pretty stupid, but he's not going to risk antagonising the entire Guild when he's only just become Grand Master."

I bite my tongue to keep from saying anything more while Fletcher considers this. Eventually, he heaves a weary sigh.

"Where does Truman live?"

THIRTY
WAKING JASON TRUMAN

TRUMAN SNORES. And not just your run of the mill gentle purr, but a chainsaw-esque, roof-raising, window-rattling grate of air that makes me want to send a letter of apology to his neighbours.

Standing at the foot of his bed I try to stifle a giggle. Fletcher shoots me a look of such intense disapproval that I sober immediately. It was almost too easy to gain entry into Truman's house, but of course, having an expert lock picker helped.

Fletcher casts me one last warning look and then rounds the side of the bed. Almost leisurely, he pulls one of his knives from his holster and then, with a final questioning look at me, which I respond to with a nod, he brings the blade to Truman's throat. Truman wakes with such a start that if wasn't for Fletcher's restraining hand on his chest, he would've sliced his own neck open. The second he feels the bite of the blade, he slumps back onto the pillows, wide-eyed and fearful. I feel bad for him. Truman is a computer geek – he's not equipped to deal with violence of any kind.

"Stay calm," I say, stepping forward to switch on the bedside lamp. Truman recognises my voice before he even sees my face.

"Clarke?" he sounds hurt, vexed that I would come into his house and have someone put a knife to his neck, considering how we've always gotten along.

"Don't scream, okay?" I ask and he nods, wincing slightly as the blade gives him a too-close-for-comfort shave. Fletcher withdraws but he stays within arm's reach, ready to intervene if Truman tries anything. Which he won't. I can tell by his eyes. He's more curious than alarmed. Rubbing at his throat, he glances up at Fletcher and then does a double take.

"You're taller than I thought you'd be," he says.

I sit on the edge of the bed.

"I'm sorry I had to break into your house but I didn't know how else to reach you."

He nods.

"I figured as much. I've been wondering if you'd get in contact. I've been leaving the garage unlocked just in case."

Fletcher looks as if Truman has just announced he set his own hair on fire.

"We came in through the back," I admit, but before I can tease Fletcher about not needing to pick that lock after all, he looms before me, the knife back at Truman's throat.

"Fletcher!" I hiss. "What the hell are you doing?"

"He left the place unlocked to make it easier for you to find him?" he snaps. "That sounds a little convenient, don't you think. Unless the Guild suspected Clarke would come to you?" he prompts, increasing the pressure of the blade until a pin prick of blood wells on the edge of it.

"Stand down, Fletcher," I warn.

"This reeks of a trap."

"It's not a trap," Truman's voice is hoarse as he tries to speak without moving his adam's apple. "Although, you might've gone a little easier on my cousin, Clarke. He almost died."

Annoyed, I reach forward and pull Fletcher's hand away. Truman sucks in a deep breath and massages his throat.

"Is he always this violent?" he asks me.

I pull a face.

"Not always. How's Lawrence?"

"He'll live. It was nice of you to call for medical assistance."

"You don't seem too upset about the fact that I stabbed him."

"He's not my favourite cousin." Truman regards me intently and then shrugs.

"It's Lincoln's fault more than yours. Lawrence didn't want to enlist in the combat unit, but the new Grand Master has deemed it necessary to introduce a year's compulsory service."

"What?"

"Yeah. Lawrence shouldn't have been out there in the first place. Not that you're forgiven," he adds grudgingly.

"For what it's worth, he attacked me first."

The memory is too much for Fletcher, who clenches his fists at his sides.

"So he says." Truman eyes Fletcher apprehensively. "Maybe you should just get to the point of why you're here, then, lest we test his temper any further?"

Fletcher makes a threatening sound and then moves back to stand beside the window, his fingers pulling back the drapes as he scans the garden below.

"Truman, before Harrison died, did he mention anything to you – about what I was doing?"

"No, why, what are you doing?"

I sigh. This would've been so much easier if Harrison had confided in the others.

"I'm trying to do exactly what the Guild instructed me to a century ago."

"Didn't they charge you with finding Fletcher?" Typical Truman, everything by the book. "Because you seem to have succeeded in that department."

"Finding Fletcher was only a small part of the bigger picture."

"Yeah, to make him mortal again," he agrees.

"I know how to make that happen."

To my relief he doesn't look at all surprised.

"How? I mean, I know the Guild like to pretend they have a clue as to how to do it, but given that catching Fletcher Kincaid isn't going to make any difference to his irreparable clock, I've never really believed that."

"Not as stupid as you look," Fletcher remarks drily.

"He's lovely," Truman tells me and I smile.

"He grows on you."

"Can we get back to the point?" Fletcher asks. He's like a caged tiger, bristling with unease.

"Andrew Lincoln wants us in custody," I say quickly, "but he's blinded by his own hunger for power. Harrison trusted me – he was giving me time to put my plan into motion. Unfortunately, he didn't have enough time to give. I know you have no reason to believe me, but I'm asking you to anyway."

"Actually, I can believe that," Truman announces casually. "By all accounts and appearances, Harrison made out like finding you two was the Guild's top priority, but shortly after you disappeared, he called off all active search teams and he told me to stop monitoring the airwaves. Of course, the second Andrew Lincoln was voted in, the entire Guild was put on high alert. I think he's more desperate to find you than he is concerned about the Hall, given that he's instituted his sister as the Clock Keeper. That girl's about as stable as this one." He jerks his thumb in Fletcher's direction.

"That's why I'm here," I say quickly, trying to avoid another argument, "I can't do anything with the Guild on my tail. I need people I trust to work with me."

"You trust me?" He looks between Fletcher and I, sounding enormously pleased with himself.

"*She* does," Fletcher corrects.

"I do," I say. "And I may be making the biggest mistake of my life, but I was hoping you might be able to convince some of the others to help me too."

Truman pulls a face.

"I don't know, Clarke. Lincoln may not be my first choice, but he is the Grand Master. I don't know if anyone would stand against him."

"What is the purpose of Tempus?" I counter.

"To protect time."

"Exactly. That's precisely what I'm trying to do. Andrew Lincoln – the Guild, for that matter – have no idea how to fix this, but I do."

"Prove it."

"What?"

"You're asking me to trust you. To choose between you and the Grand Master of Tempus. At the end of the day, I believe in the oath. I believe in protecting time, and that our duty is bigger than any one person. It's bigger than you, bigger than me, bigger than Lincoln. I trust in Tempus and the purpose of the Guild. Give me a reason to believe I should trust that you will do what you're promising."

It's the most emotive speech I've ever heard him give, and the enormity of the true meaning of serving the Guild crashes down on me. For so long we have been divided, but Truman has just reminded me why I was so blindly loyal to Tempus. It was never the Guild itself that compelled me. It was the honour and the duty. The belief in our purpose. And that hasn't changed. Only now I see a better way to do it than what has been dictated. I know better. And I alone can fix it.

Truman and Fletcher are watching me intently.

"I can't help you if I don't believe you," Truman prompts. "How are you going to fix this?"

"With this." I pull the dial from my pocket and hold it up so it catches the light of the lamp.

"Clarke," Fletcher growls, furious that I am revealing our plan to a man who could sell us out and make it impossible to achieve.

For once, however, Truman is at a loss for words.

"Is that...?" he breathes.

"Yes. It's my dial. You said it yourself – Fletcher's clock is irreparable. It can't be fixed. So I'm going to use this to turn back time and prevent Anna from ever destroying it in the first place."

For a few heart-stopping seconds there is absolute silence and then Truman is spurred into action.

"This just might work!" He is more animated than I've ever seen him. "The Guild can't fix Fletcher's clock. We've had years to study it, but it can't be done. Your plan, however..." he trails off, overcome with the possibility.

"Could work?" I improvise.

"No," he grins, "it *will* work. We've been so focused on Fletcher's clock that we overlooked the fact that yours is the one with the power. I mean, technically, we could turn back any clock, but no one has been alive long enough to pre-date 1917. If only we'd thought of it years ago we could've set things right almost as soon as it happened."

"We didn't have my dial," I remind him.

"We wouldn't have needed it. We could've picked any clock at random and gone back. Why didn't we think of this before?"

"Because of the oath," I say gently. "We don't interfere. It's our cardinal rule."

"I think we might have made an exception," Truman says, "considering your sister did it first."

His words strike a chord within me. I hadn't even considered the fact that in turning back time I would not only fix Anna's mistake, but I would clear my family's name. The disgrace of the Kennedys would never exist. The thought leaves me reeling.

"Clarke?" Fletcher's voice pulls me back. "We really need to go."

I nod.

"Truman?"

"I'm in," he answers without hesitation. "And I'll try to get as many others on board as I can. Only those I believe are loyal to the oath."

"I need to get into the Hall. They're going to try and stop me."

"We won't make it easy for them," he says grimly and I can't help but feel warm at the 'we'.

"The longer we delay the more chance we have of being caught. So only tell them at the last minute. Can you do that?"

"I head up the tech department of the most powerful organisation in the world," Truman says. "What do you think?"

"I think I'm glad I came here."

"I can't make any promises, though. I can enlighten them, that's it, then it's up to them."

"Let's just hope enough make the right choice."

"They better." He pales. "Because this is mutiny. You better succeed, Clarke," he adds. "because if you don't, we'll all have to deal with the consequences."

We leave shortly after, but not before I tell Truman that we're convening in Jacob Lake and that we're planning to enter the Hall on Saturday night, shortly after nightfall. It's only three days away. Truman promises to do what he can and Fletcher and I slip back out into the night. We have a bus to catch.

THIRTY-ONE
THOSE WHO CAME BEFORE

THE SMALL TOWN of Jacob Lake consists of the Jacob Lake Inn, a restaurant, gift shop, bakery, general store, gas station and a visitor's centre. Fletcher and I bypass the Inn and take up residence on the rustic campground. The cabin-style room doesn't allow for cooking, so we grab a few food items from the general store – a loaf of bread, a packet of verging-on-stale jerky and a few bags of chips. It doesn't make for the most nutritious meal, but we are too exhausted to care. The enormity of what we are about to attempt is taking its toll on us emotionally.

Cramped together on the tiny twin cot, I struggle to sleep until Fletcher stalks out and returns half an hour later with a hoard of freshly laundered linen. I don't know whether he paid for it, or whether he helped himself, but I don't really care because I can finally get some rest. Fletcher falls asleep with his back to me, but it's not long before he shifts in his sleep, his arm coming around me and pulling me closer.

Friday dawns a glorious spring day and we head into town.

"Do you think he'll show?" I ask Fletcher. There's no way of knowing whether Vincent will respond to the text we sent him.

"I don't know, Clarke. He's your friend, not mine."

Fletcher has been irritable since we arrived and I suspect it has less to do with the daunting thought of accessing the Hall and more to do with the fact that I'm going to be turning back time and returning to a place where this relationship we're building doesn't exist.

By midday my hope is fading fast.

"You didn't specify where we were meeting," Fletcher says, relenting slightly in the face of my despair. We've been sticking to the outskirts of town, keeping an eye on the foot traffic, which has, so far, consisted of a small group of middle-aged hikers and a lone man with dreadlocks and tattoos banding both legs, who is smoking something suspicious-looking.

"It's not exactly a big town." I point out. "We'd know if he'd arrived."

"Come on," Fletcher is on the move. "Let's stake out the access road. That way there's no chance we'll miss him."

It's late afternoon by the time we spot a lone car approaching. It's the first vehicle we've seen since we arrived yesterday and my impulse is to run into the road and flag it down, but I quell that impulse. There's a chance that the Guild might be on to us and, if so, whoever is in this car could just as easily be a foe as a friend. We take a shortcut through the trees and watch as the inconspicuous grey sedan pulls up in front of the inn.

"Two people," Fletcher murmurs and, squinting, I see that he's right. The shadow of two heads is visible through the back windshield. I hold my breath as the doors open, and then, with a cry of delight, I rush forward, recognising the small figure who gets out of the passenger seat opposite Vincent.

"Aunt Elizabeth!" I fly into her arms, my heart thumping in my chest. "What are you doing here?" As thrilled as I am to see her, this is not the safest place in the world for her to be.

"She insisted," Vincent explains, coming around the car to stand beside us. He's obviously expecting a lecture, given his contrite expression.

"I took the bus out of Flagstaff when I got Truman's message," Aunt Elizabeth tells me firmly. "And Vincent had no choice but to pick me up or leave an old woman stranded in the middle of an unfamiliar town with nowhere to stay."

I hear Fletcher chuckling behind me and Vincent shakes his hand, grateful for the reprieve.

"You're a Kennedy all right," Fletcher says, holding his hand out to Aunt Elizabeth. Her wise eyes give him an intense once-over and then she slaps his hand away, going in for a hug instead.

"You must be Fletcher," she mumbles into his chest, dwarfed by the sheer size of him.

"Guilty as charged, Ma'am." He tips the newsboy cap in a perfect imitation of the Fletcher of my youth.

"It's lovely to meet you," Aunt Elizabeth pats his cheek fondly. "Although you have given my Clara a hard time."

Fletcher hangs his head in shame.

"Well, all's well that ends well, I guess," Aunt Elizabeth relents. "Now, where can young Vincent deposit my things?"

Fletcher offers to take her back to the cabin.

"I'll stop at the check-in and book another cabin," he says. I'll obviously be bunking with Aunt Elizabeth and I grin at the thought of Fletcher and Vincent crammed into the tiny double cot.

"You might want to book a few more," Vincent says. "We're expecting company."

Wide-eyed, I round on him.

"You got them?"

He looks surprised that I might have doubted him.

"Every single one."

Vincent had managed to round up all three of the previous Clock Keepers who were still alive and young enough to help. They had convened in Flagstaff and convoyed to Jacob Lake, but Vincent had insisted they stagger their arrival, just in case the Guild were watching. At my reassurance that Jacob Lake is safe, he calls them in, and, within the hour I am reunited with friends I haven't seen in decades.

Rebecca Jefferson is the least changed, given that I last saw her just over ten years ago and she's not yet thirty, but the passage of time is far more evident on the faces of Eric Harrison and Jacob Cleveland.

"It's been a long time, Clara," Jacob drawls, holding out his weathered hand. Seeing him thirty years older than when we last met, I feel an ache in my chest. Vincent was right. These people were my friends and I had cut all ties when they had left the Hall, when they no longer served any purpose.

My guilt is knocked for a six, however, when a pair of intelligent blue eyes peers at me out of a face almost as wrinkled as Aunt Elizabeth's.

"Joanna?" I ask, not daring to believe this sixty-something woman is the same young Clock Keeper I befriended in the late sixties.

"Hello Clara," she says and her voice is unchanged. She takes in my youthful eighteen-year-old face and heaves a sigh. "And to think I used to be the pretty one."

"Joanna, what are you doing here?"

The fact that she's closer to seventy than sixty is eclipsed by the fact that she's a Lincoln and what I'm asking requires her to stand against her own family.

"If you're referring to the fact that I happen to be a Lincoln, I'd prefer that you didn't judge us all by the standard young Andrew is setting," she warns primly.

"Okay," I say, "but, even so, and I say this with the utmost respect, you're in no condition to..."

"Sixty-six is hardly an old woman, Clara!" she snaps before I can finish. "There's life in these old bones yet. Who knows, I might find a new husband while I'm here." She winks at Eric, who's not yet turned fifty.

I have no words to argue, so instead, I simply thank them all.

"I'm so grateful to you for coming."

"You were there when we needed you," Jacob reminds me. "It's only right that we return the favour. Now tell us where you want us and then we can figure out how to get you into the Hall."

The camp site is a lot busier with six extra bodies milling around.

"I can't believe you brought Joanna," I murmur under my breath to Vincent.

"Hey, your message said to bring old Clock Keepers. She fits both descriptions. Besides, you're lucky I didn't bring Patrick Truman. I can't say I didn't think about it - we need all the help we can get."

"Patrick Truman is almost eighty!" I laugh. "But you're right, we do need numbers, so I called on a younger Truman for help."

Vincent whistles through his teeth.

"Is that wise? Truman's practically tied to the Grand Master's chair."

"Not the current Grand Master, apparently. But I guess we'll find out soon enough."

"What do you want us to do?" Rebecca gets right to the point as we gather in a messy circle around the fire that Fletcher has started. The spring days are warm enough, but as soon as the sun sinks below the horizon it cools down quickly.

"To be honest, there's not much you can do," I say. "I don't expect a single person here to physically endanger themselves..."

"Bit late for that," Joanna pipes up. "Besides, at my age, there's nothing left to do but wait to die. I quite like the idea of going out fighting. Unless you can offer me a better way to go, Eric?" she waggles her brows suggestively, and Fletcher leads the chorus of guffaws while Eric tries to hide his unmanly blushes.

"We've all been trained by the Guild," Vincent says when they finally settle down. We know how to fight."

"I know that and I appreciate your courage and your volunteering, but I would prefer it if you didn't die on my watch."

"If you succeed, we won't," Rebecca points out, "but if you didn't plan for us to fight, what exactly did you call us here for?"

There's an edge to her voice and I suspect that Rebecca is less forgiving of my decade-long absence than the others. I can understand her anger – after all, besides Vincent, Rebecca is the Clock

Keeper I was closest to, during her service. I had promised to keep in touch and hadn't spoken to her since.

"You all underestimate how revered the Clock Keepers are among Tempus. Those at the top may feel you are a means to an end, but, for the rest of us, the Clock Keeper epitomises everything Tempus stands for. Your sacrifice is legendary."

"I doubt that," Vincent grumbles, pulling a Mars bar from his satchel.

"It's true," I insist. "Look at Anna. How many Grand Masters have made colossal mistakes and bad judgement calls but they aren't persecuted as my family has been. Anna wasn't the first person in Tempus to make a mistake, but it was all the worse because no one expected it of her – of a Clock Keeper."

"You make a good point," Jacob says, and the others fall silent, thoughtful.

"I believe," I say, taking advantage of their silence, "that if you speak, if you stand up for this, they might hesitate. They might falter."

"Giving you enough time to storm the Hall," Rebecca murmurs. Her dark hair is a curtain, hiding her eyes.

I nod.

"That's all I'm asking for. A little time."

"Even if you manage to get inside the Hall how will you get past Sienna Lincoln?" Rebecca is once again on the offensive. "She's not exactly like the rest of us. That's one Clock Keeper you won't convince, and, from what I hear, she's no easy opponent."

"Sienna Lincoln will not lay a hand on Clarke," Fletcher's voice is low and menacing.

"You'll go with her?" Aunt Elizabeth asks. "To the Hall?"

"Yes."

Aunt Elizabeth gives a shaky sigh of relief and I wonder how she can put such faith in a man she's only just met.

"We don't know what we're going to encounter tomorrow," I say, "and there's no way to plan for it. All we can do is act in the moment and pray for the best."

There's a sombre silence as everyone digests this.

"You had me at legendary sacrifice," says Joanna.

Fletcher and I stay by the fire long after everyone else has gone to bed. I rest my head on his shoulder as his long fingers gently stroke the crook of my arm.

"We won't know if Truman rallied any troops until we get there," I sigh. Truman had only been given the date of our supposed raid, so, unlike the Clock Keepers who came through Vincent, and Aunt Elizabeth, who had been notified early, we won't have a clue if any people responded to Truman until we get to the canyon.

"Do you think you should've asked them to convene here?"

"No. He was right about delivering the message at the last minute. That way, if anyone betrays us, the Guild will have less time to act."

"Are you worried?"

"Not about myself. You and I will survive this regardless of the outcome. It's them I'm afraid for." I incline my head in the direction of the cabins.

"You know what's funny?"

"What?"

"I don't know what scares me more – failing, or you actually getting this right. Spending the rest of eternity with you isn't the worst thing I could imagine."

"If our theory about your clock holds true, eternity might not be as long as we think," I point out.

Fletcher nods in unhappy agreement.

"And then there's Cody Johnson."

My blood runs cold at the mere mention of the baby's name.

"And then there's Cody Johnson." I echo.

We watch the flames flickering until they slowly dwindle and only the red glow of the embers remains. Fletcher doesn't put more wood on the fire, but he draws me closer to him, wrapping the side of his coat around us both.

I turn to look at him and our lips meet, sweetly, naturally. The kiss is gentle and unhurried, but, as it deepens, I can feel his desire mingled with desperation. I thread my hands into his dark hair, pulling him even closer, but, just as I am about to suggest we take a stroll out into the woods, he pulls back. His breathing is ragged, his breath warm on my face, but his dark eyes hold mine as he presses his forehead against mine.

"Don't you forget," he growls. "You promised me, Clarke. Don't you dare go back on your word!"

"I won't," I whisper, tilting my lips to capture his once more, and closing my eyes so he won't see the deceit shining there.

Later I crawl into bed beside Aunt Elizabeth, being careful not to wake her. I have just closed my eyes when she speaks.

"I can certainly see why you love him," she says.

I open my eyes to find her smiling at me, her hair glowing white in the moonlight filtering through the window.

Shaken, all I can do is nod and bite my lip to keep from crying.

THIRTY-TWO
RUNNING OUT OF TIME

“YOU’RE NOT COMING!” I am practically yelling. We are due to leave for the canyon’s edge in five minutes and Aunt Elizabeth is refusing to get out of the car.

“I am going and that’s final.”

“Stop being so stubborn!”

“I’m a member of the Guild, Clarke. Just like you, just like everybody else. Do you really think I travelled all this way to stay behind and wait to find out if everyone made it?”

“Aunt Elizabeth, please! I can’t focus knowing you’re out there with us. I can’t have that kind of a distraction.”

She locks her eyes on me.

“I am exactly the distraction you need,” she replies through gritted teeth. “Because if I’m out there, in danger, you will do what you need to do to get this done.”

I curse, turning my back on her and walking a few paces to steady myself before I say something I’ll regret later.

“She’s right.” Fletcher appears at my side as if by magic.

“What? Have you lost your mind too?”

“Clarke, the only way to make sure she stays safe is to make sure none of this ever happens. If Elizabeth is the incentive for us to succeed, I'll take it."

"What if something happens to her?"

"What if something happens to any of them?"

It's a brutal reminder that not only one life is at stake.

"You're letting your family ties get in the way of your common sense, Clarke." Joanna has joined us, her shrewd eyes giving me a healthy dose of judgment. "Imagine if I did the same?" The fact that she's going up against her own blood is a poignant reminder of the sacrifices everyone here is prepared to make, and if they are, then who am I to play hypocrite?

"We need to go," Fletcher urges. Both engines are running, the whole team is ready to depart.

"Dammit!"

"Let's get this done." He places his hand briefly on my shoulder.

Wordlessly I stalk back to the car and slide in beside Elizabeth, slamming the door behind us.

"You'll thank me later," she promises cheerily, patting my knee.

Of course we walk right into a trap.

Our descent into the canyon is slow-going, our older companions needing help down the rugged terrain. Still, we make it as far as the water's edge when, without warning, we find ourselves surrounded.

"Clara Kennedy," a deep voice booms, reminding me so startlingly of Jonathan Harrison that I squint through the darkness, expecting to catch sight of him. Instead, a younger version of the previous Grand Master steps forward. He has the same eyes and heavy-set shoulders and I would stake my life that he's a Harrison.

"You're under arrest," he intones darkly, jerking the rifle in his hands to draw my attention, in case I haven't noticed it already.

"For what?" I ask arrogantly.

He seems to hesitate, obviously not expecting me to question his orders.

"For crimes against Tempus," he starts to recite them as if ticking them off a memorised list. "For harbouring a fugitive. For betraying the Guild. For going against the direct instructions of the Grand Master."

"Okay," I relent. "I'll admit I'm guilty of at least two of those things."

It's almost comical to watch as he tries to work out which two I'm referring to before I decide to save him the trouble.

"I haven't betrayed the Guild. It's your new Grand Master who's done that."

"And how exactly do you figure that out?" a hateful voice sneers.

I barely catch Joanna's mumbled 'Oh shit' when Andrew Lincoln himself steps out from the shadows.

I feel Fletcher go rigid beside me as he senses the power of the new threat, but I put out a hand to stay him.

"The Guild's purpose is to protect time," I say, raising my chin defiantly.

"Yes?" Lincoln says. "You don't need to educate me on what the Guild's purpose is, Miss Kennedy, I'm well aware of it. Perhaps your father might've educated your sister as well as he so obviously did you."

"You leave my sister out of this."

"Why? Your sister betrayed Tempus too – just as you have. It seems the Kennedys are determined to drag their name even further into the gutter."

"What do you want, Lincoln? What are you hoping to gain by locking Fletcher and I up?"

"I want what everyone wants. I want to send both of you into the ground where you belong."

"But you can't, that's the whole point. Fletcher and I are immortal – there's no way to kill either of us."

"Perhaps," he concedes, "but I'd certainly like to try."

If I didn't already know how evil this man was these words cement the fact in my mind.

"So you want to kill us, over and over?"

"I'm not a monster, Miss Kennedy. It's not something I want to do for pleasure. You both should've died a long time ago."

"You're right." My agreement sends a twitch around his mouth and his smile falters. "Fletcher and I were supposed to die. Which is exactly why I'm here."

"If you think that you're somehow going to convince me that we're on the same side, after harbouring Fletcher Kincaid and keeping him from us, you're sorely mistaken."

"Bingo." I hear Rebecca's softly spoken word and I can't help a smug smile spreading across my face.

"I'm not trying to convince you," I say cordially, gesturing at the soldiers who have us surrounded. "I'm only trying to convince them."

Lincoln recovers quickly.

"Convince them of what?"

"Of the fact that I'm not your enemy. I want the same thing you do – only, unlike you, I actually have an idea of how to do it."

Out of the corner of my eye I see the young soldier who looks like Harrison lower his rifle. Only an inch, but it's a good sign.

"Oh you do, do you?" Lincoln sneers. "Conveniently now, after all this time, you've figured it out. Why do I get the feeling this is some lavish plot to save your own skin?"

"My skin doesn't need saving. I've lived longer than I ever wanted to. It's your life on the line now."

"Time is unravelling," Vincent announces, stepping forward to stand beside me and addressing the entire crowd. A few murmurs run through it and this time there's no mistaking it - the rifle drops even lower, no man wanting to point a gun at one of the Clock Keepers.

"I served ten years in the Hall," Vincent continues boldly. "Fletcher's clock is running out of time."

"We know this!" Lincoln spits, but if the faces around him are anything to go by, many people didn't.

"We're down to a matter of months," I say. "How long before it's weeks and then days and then hours?"

"Many lives end mere minutes after they're born," Lincoln counters.

"Randomly, yes. But Fletcher's clock isn't random. You've read Jonathan Harrison's notes," I add sweetly, throwing his own weapon back at him. "What do they say about the Guild's theory on the complete unravelling of time?"

"The Sovereign wouldn't let that happen."

"The Sovereign?" I bark. "Really – have you spoken to him lately? The Sovereign gave us life and then left it in our own hands. He charged us with protecting time and we failed. My sister failed," I add, as my chest heaves with emotion. "The Sovereign isn't going to save us. The world will end, Lincoln, if you don't let me fix this."

"She's right," Vincent says.

"She is." Rebecca steps forward and one by one so do Eric, Jacob and, to my horror, Aunt Elizabeth.

"Look, personally I wouldn't mind if the world ended, but I do feel incredibly sorry for all you lovely young men," Joanna adds, as she too, steps forward.

"Who the hell are you people?"

There are a few gasps of shock from his own men as Andrew reveals his ignorance.

"They're the Clock Keepers," I say, a note of pride in my voice. "From the past fifty years. You might not believe me," I tell the soldiers, "but surely you must believe them?"

I watch as it slowly dawns on Lincoln that this is a battle he may not win. Before I can further convince his army, he acts.

"Enough! Seize them – all of them!"

The crowd is too big to keep track of, but it seems torn. A substantial group steps forward, as one, to follow his instruction, but at least half remain where they are.

"Not so fast, Lincoln."

I feel a bubble of hope well in my chest at the sound of Truman's voice. I look up, in the direction of his voice, to find a crowd gathered on an outcrop just above us.

"Would you look at that?" Vincent murmurs beside me. There must be at least twenty people with Truman.

"What are you doing here Truman?" Lincoln demands.

"The right thing," Truman retorts snappily, with none of the respect he paid Jonathan Harrison. I can't help but feel the old man would be bursting with pride if he could see Truman now.

"Clarke is right!" Truman addresses the soldiers spread out below him. "And, even more importantly, she has a plan. I suggest we all get out of her way and let her get on with it."

"Over my dead body," Lincoln snarls, and, before I know what is happening, he snatches up the young soldier's rifle and aims it at me.

"No!" Fletcher bellows. An instant later his body slams into mine, knocking me to the ground as the boom of the rifle shot resonates around us.

In the roaring echo that follows, the protective shield of Fletcher's body is gone as quickly as it came and I look up to find him grappling with the rifle in Lincoln's hands. The gunfire is a catalyst and suddenly, fighting breaks out among the crowd. Soldiers are fighting soldiers, the Clock Keepers diving into the fray, as Truman's Guild members swarm down from the rocks. Stunned, I gaze around, and then I see her and a wail bursts from my chest.

I'm at her side in two strides, my eyes taking in the rapidly blooming rose of red spreading across her chest.

"No!" I yell, dropping to my knees and cradling her in my arms. Aunt Elizabeth's eyes are open, but the youthful glint is fading fast.

"Stay with me, please, stay with me," I beg.

She takes a gurgling breath and tries to raise her hand, but I snatch it up in my own.

"Don't try to move," I plead, my other hand hovering over the wound. "I don't know what to do. Somebody help me!" I yell over my shoulder, but my words are drowned out by the intensity of the battle waging around us.

"I don't know what to do," I sob again, tears streaming from my eyes and making my vision blur.

"Yes you do." It's a faint murmur, but I hear her. Despite everything, her words rise above the noise.

I gaze down at her face, her eyes narrowed in agony as her body bleeds out. Her bloodless lips open again and I lean closer, so close that I feel her faint breath on my ear.

"It was a privilege knowing you Clarke. I'll miss you this second time around."

"Please," I say, tears flooding my mouth, leaving a salty tang on my tongue. "Please don't die."

"Go," she says simply. "Go, and I won't."

With one last shuddering breath, her body goes still.

Rough hands seize my shoulders and I give a bellow of rage, my hands going for my daggers.

"Clarke!" Fletcher's voice pierces my addled mind. "We have to go!" He drags me to my feet and I stumble against him.

"I'm sorry," he says, "but we can change it. You know we can change it."

I nod, wiping the wetness from my face as we charge toward the river. There is no time to waste and I'd rather not see any more of my friends hurt, or dying. None of this will matter unless we get to the Hall. The planks of the small jetty tremble under the weight of our pounding feet and then I leap into the dinghy as Fletcher unties the rope. By the time he climbs in beside me, the engine is fired up and I haul on the tiller. The little boat lurches forward, careening through the water as we leave the chaos behind us.

THIRTY-THREE
A NEEDLE IN A SEA OF CLOCKS

I CLIMB the wall of rock with such single-minded purpose that I reach the hollow entrance to the caves faster than I ever have before. Even Fletcher struggles to keep up, but he follows me through the labyrinth of tunnels without a word. As we reach the edge of the inner canyon, however, he pulls me back.

"I'm going down first," he says, leaving no room for argument. I step aside and he lowers himself over the edge. A moment later he's sucked into the darkness and I begin my own descent.

The dim glow of light from the hall illuminates our advance. I can hear every beat of my heart, every exhalation of breath, as we walk toward the Hall, but no one bars our entry. It's almost too easy. I have walked this path so many times before but always with a friend waiting for me. I have never felt so unwelcome. Fletcher halts me at the doorway and gestures that I should wait. Watching him step around the archway and into the Hall, I can only marvel at the fact that we are so close to achieving our goal. Nothing is going to stop me now, I vow.

I peer around the doorway and see Fletcher standing in the

antechamber. There's no sign of Sienna or any other members of the Guild.

"It can't be this easy," Fletcher whispers as I join him, but I've already seen that our trip has been futile.

"It's not," I say, and then, indicating the place where his clock is hanging and the empty space beside it, "they've moved my clock."

We both turn at the sound of footsteps, instinctively raising our daggers. Not that they'd do any good against the black military rifle Sienna Lincoln is holding.

"Hello Clarke," she says, her murderous eyes even more terrifying than her brother's.

"Put down the gun, Sienna," I reply, with more than a touch of righteous anger that she would threaten violence in this place. "The Hall is sacred – you can't possibly intend to fire it in here."

"I'll do what I have to." She peers past us, toward the entrance. "Where is my brother?"

"He's still upriver."

I notice with a sense of satisfaction that her hands are shaking.

"How did you get past him?"

"He was distracted. A fight broke out. There are people who oppose his decisions."

"Then he will punish them all. That's mutiny."

"The Guild is divided, Sienna. Your brother may not be the Grand Master for much longer so why don't you put down the gun and we can talk."

"Talk? What could we possibly have to talk about?"

"Where you've hidden my clock, for starters."

Her eyes flit to the empty space on the wall.

"You noticed, did you?" she says with a twisted smile. "Well, I may as well tell you you'll never find it and save you the trouble of looking."

"It's not far," I say calmly, but I bend my knees slightly and drop my shoulders.

Sienna doesn't notice.

"Oh really? And how do you figure that?"

"The dust on your feet."

Just as I expected, she glances down to look, the rifle lowering automatically, and I make my move, bursting into a sprint. I hear Fletcher's cry of alarm and, as if in slow motion, watch Sienna's head jerk up in shock, the rifle drawing level again. I dodge to the right, barely missing getting my head blown off as her finger tightens convulsively on the trigger, and then I bring my fist flying forward and punch her full in the face.

Sienna spins almost a hundred and eighty degrees but she doesn't drop the rifle. Before she can regain her footing, I kick out at her hand. I hear the crunch of fingers breaking and the rifle clatters to the floor, but Sienna isn't giving up that easily. Spitting with rage, she launches herself at me. I drop to the ground, sweeping my leg in an arc as I go. The impact knocks her to her knees and a second later, Fletcher has her in a headlock.

I get to my feet and snatch up the rifle.

"Where's my clock, Sienna?"

She spits at my feet and I press the barrel into her temple creating a spiral of skin.

"Company's coming," Fletcher murmurs. I hear the muted clang of boots on iron. Someone is coming down the ladder.

"Where is it?" I hiss, but Sienna only laughs bitterly.

"I'm not a Kennedy," she says. "I'm not a traitor."

I nod grimly, and then, spinning the rifle around I knock her out with a brutal blow to the head.

"Now what?" Fletcher asks, gazing disdainfully down at Sienna's prostrate form.

I shove the rifle into his hands.

"Now we find that clock."

He doesn't argue but, as we exit the antechamber, the Hall stretches out before us.

"I'd forgotten how big it is," Fletcher breathes. "How the hell are we going to find it in this?"

"It won't be far. Lincoln didn't expect us to make it here or he would've posted guards. He expected to arrest us before we even made it to the water. I'm guessing Sienna had half an hour at most to stash my clock."

The sounds of footsteps are growing louder and we plunge into the cover of the maze of clocks. The humming is louder here, drowning out the sound of our pursuers. With any luck, they'll get so horribly lost we won't even see them.

"I hate to be the bearer of doom and gloom, but even with only half an hour, there are a million places she could've hidden it." Fletcher whispers as we weave through the aisles.

"Nope," I grin up at him, "Only one."

"How do you figure that?"

"Her feet," I remind him. "Did you see the dust? Her feet were covered in granite schist mingled with flecks of quartz. Garnet coloured quartz," I add smugly.

"Okay?" he looks utterly mystified.

"There's only one place that has that particular sand. Come on!"

It takes us fifteen minutes to reach the place where I'm certain Sienna has hidden my clock. I've narrowed our search down, but it will still be like finding a needle in a haystack.

"The second she regains consciousness she'll lead them straight here," Fletcher says.

"I know. Maybe we should split up. I'll take this aisle. You take that one. We'll meet at the end."

My adrenalin is pumping as I race down the endless aisle, frantically scanning the walls. A sea of clocks swims before my vision, identical, the heavy thrumming in the air pressing down on me as I look for something – anything - out of the ordinary. It takes a good five minutes before I burst from the other end, but I don't stop. Instead, I fly down Fletcher's aisle. I come across him a short way in.

"Anything?" he asks urgently.

I shake my head.

"We'll never find it like this," he says, his brow knitted in thought.

I recognise that expression – it's the one he gets when he's on to something he can't quite put his finger on, so I force my feet to still, fighting the urge to act.

"She didn't have a clock!" Fletcher announces suddenly.

"What?"

"Sienna. Back in the antechamber she wasn't holding a clock."

"So?"

"So she didn't swap yours for another. The clock's not on the walls, Clarke."

Our eyes lock for only a second and then we both spring back into action. I return to my aisle and we search again, sweeping the dusty ground with our feet.

I am halfway down the third aisle when I hear footsteps heading our way. At almost the same time, Fletcher's voice yells from one aisle over.

"Clarke! I found it!"

My feet practically fly over the dusty floor kicking up small eddies of glittering red dust. As I round the end of the aisle I spot a group of men hurtling toward me from the direction of the antechamber, but they're at least a minute away.

I screech to a halt and drop to my knees before Fletcher, who is holding my dirt-stained clock.

"She tried to bury it," he murmurs, dusting the red powder off the centre pin.

I pull the dial from my pocket and lower it to the golden pin in the centre. My name gleams just below it, a gilded reminder of the death I eluded. With fumbling hands, I place the circular hollow of the dial over the pin.

"Eighty-four years," I mumble, studying the smooth clock-face and doing a mental calculation.

"So 1916 should be around here." I place my forefinger on the spot and then shift it almost imperceptibly anti-clockwise. I need to make sure I turn it back enough. We only get one shot at this. My thumb moves over the pin.

"Wait," Fletcher's big hand covers mine, giving me pause. The sound of footsteps is drawing closer, but I lift my head, meeting his dark eyes. Fletcher doesn't speak. Instead, he lowers his head and kisses me – passionately, desperately. It's over before I'm ready for it to be over.

"Don't forget," he murmurs. I watch his eyes drawn to something over my shoulder and I know the guards have reached us. I feel tears well in my eyes, see the shocked understanding dawn on Fletcher's face and then I close my eyes.

"I love you Fletcher," I whisper, and then I press down, clicking the dial into place. Fletcher's warm hand covers mine as I turn it back.

THIRTY-FOUR
MY FAITH IN FLETCHER

1915, *Charleston, West Virginia*

FLETCHER'S EYES look exactly the same – intense, deep as the midnight sky, and holding my own with a question. I blink, once, twice, and slowly I become aware that our surroundings have changed. It's light out – almost too bright after the claustrophobic darkness of the Hall – and the sun hurts my eyes. Fletcher's white shirt is grubby, his newsboy cap frayed along the rim. We're in the orchard in Charleston, the distant chirp of a hummingbird the only sound until Fletcher says softly:

"I want to give you something new to pray for in Church on Sunday."

Like a lightning montage, images bombard my mind; a painful, frenetic overflow of information that drives the air from my lungs and almost splits my skull apart. As quickly as it happens, one single memory erupts to the fore, so vivid it overshadows all the others, smothering them in darkness. It's this moment – this exact moment, as it happened in 1915. This is the moment that Fletcher kissed me for the first time. And, as quickly as the certainty of that fact hits me, I stumble to my feet and flee.

My bedroom is exactly as I remember – the damask upholstery and solid wood furniture. My vanity is cluttered with the evidence of my innocent, unaffected life. I shut the door and lean back against it, taking a few deep, steadying breaths. It worked; only just. If my calculations are correct the Guild will come for Anna tonight.

A light clink of stone against glass draws my attention to the window. Crossing the room, I flinch as another stone hits the glass. Fletcher is standing, half-hidden, behind the trunk of a red maple tree below. *Oh God.* I lift the window shutter and peer through the leaves. I can only just make out the dark thicket of his hair.

"Go away, Fletcher!" I hiss.

"I need to talk to you!"

"No!" I slam the window resolutely and draw the drapes. A second later I almost jump out of my skin as my bedroom door opens.

"Why on earth is it so dark in here?" Anna asks, breezing in as if it's the most natural thing in the world. For a full thirty seconds I am so dumbfounded I simply stand there, taking her in – beautiful, spoilt, and very much alive – and then my emotion overcomes me.

"Clara!" she yelps as I throw myself into her arms. "I can't breathe!" The sound of her laughter is like touching heaven with your bare hands and drawing it into your heart.

I loosen my grip but I don't let her go.

"What's gotten into you today?" she asks. Like mine, her eyes are more green than grey when she's amused. I want nothing more than to gaze into them for the rest of the day, to spend time with her, time I wouldn't have believed possible, but I can't. Taking her hands I squeeze them tightly. The amusement fades from her face as she takes in my panicked dismay.

"Clara? Are you all right?"

"No." I shake my head, steeling myself. "Anna, you need to pack up your things. Not too much and nothing that father would notice in a hurry."

"Pack? Why would I pack – are we going somewhere?"

"We're not going anywhere. You are."

"Father hasn't mentioned anything..."

"Anna, this has nothing to do with father. He mustn't know you've left."

Her mild concern is building into genuine fear.

"I don't understand..."

"The Guild is coming," I blurt out. "They're coming tonight – for you. You're the new Clock Keeper, Anna. You've got to run."

The blood drains from her face, leaving her pale and trembling. I catch her as she collapses and lead her to the bed. Not for the first time I find myself wishing that my sister wasn't such a delicate flower.

"It can't be true," she whispers. Fear does what it does best and tries to deny what it's hearing. "It's Christmas Eve," she adds, "father would never..." As quickly as denial raises its ugly head, Anna dismisses it. Of course he would. And I would never lie to her. She knows that.

"How do you know?"

"I just do. There's not much time, please, Anna, go and get your things ready. I'm going to get you out of here."

With a jerky nod she rises off the bed and pats her cheeks.

"Where am I going to go?" she asks in a small voice.

I grit my teeth and raise my chin, giving her a confident smile.

"To Fletcher. He's going to take you somewhere safe."

The mention of his name dissolves any reservations she may have had. Lifting her skirts, she hurries from the room.

I steal into father's study with a ball of nerves in my stomach, until I remember that I am no longer the terrified, innocent girl I was when I was last here. Straightening my back, I move around his desk to sit in the pompous leather chair and take up a pen. His writing pad proudly bears the Kennedy name across the top. With a lump in my throat that has nothing to do with fear, I draft a letter to Fletcher.

. . .

MY DEAR FLETCHER,

These past months you have shown me kindness and compassion for which I will be forever grateful. It pains me to tell you that we can no longer see one another, but I must ask of you a favour. You may be inclined to refuse, but I must stress that this will be an act of kindness and mercy that will surely save my sister's life.

My father has consented to her being taken away, to a place where she will be alone and unhappy for ten long years. I cannot allow this. Anna is neither strong, nor brave, and I fear that, if she is sent away, I will never see her again.

My father will look for her, so I must ask you to take her far from here – somewhere where he can never find her. You should also know that Anna is very fond of you and I hope that perhaps the two of you can make a life together.

I know that you can protect my sister and I beg of you, if you care for me at all, to do this final thing for me. They will come for her tonight. If you are willing, meet her in the orchard at sundown.

Yours,

Clara Kennedy

I DROP the pen with a heavy heart and read it through. It's not quite right – years of progression have affected my language, and I'm pretty sure it sounds off - but there is no time to worry about it and I think it's close enough to pass. I seal it with wax and, to be sure he knows it came from me and not another girl trying to play a ruse, I seal it with the Kennedy seal.

I find Hattie in the kitchen barking instructions at cook. By the size of the order, Hattie has obviously already been told to expect company for dinner. The gall of my father – blindsiding us as he did – fills me with anger and courage.

"Hattie," I say, getting her attention. "I need you to deliver a letter for me."

She frowns at the strange request.

"A letter, Miss Clara?"

"Yes, Hattie, a letter," I snap. I shove it into her hands before she can question me further. Her big brown eyes drop to the name on the front, but, with a pang I remember that she doesn't know how to read.

"It's for Mister Fletcher," I add casually.

"Fletcher Kincaid?" Hattie's voice could scrape bark off a tree. Her hairline and eyebrows pull together as if there's a party they're both desperate to attend and I feel my face grow hot.

"Now, Miss Clara, it ain't right for you to be sending no letters to a man like Mister Fletcher," she scolds. "Why, if your father..."

"Hattie!" I snap, and her head jerks up in surprise. "I am a mistress of this house and I am giving you an instruction. Now deliver this letter to Mister Fletcher immediately!"

Hattie curtseys without even realising she's doing it. She's never curtsied to Anna or me before, reserving the custom only for father's benefit. I can see the hurt in her wary eyes as she turns to go, but I don't back down. I follow her to the kitchen door and watch as she sets off down the path before climbing the stairs to Anna's room.

"I said to pack lightly!" I groan as I sneak back inside Anna's bedroom. There are two full-size luggage cases, a smaller vanity case and a hatbox – a hatbox - on the floor! Anna is folding items of clothing and pressing them into the suitcases. If it wasn't for the constant tremble of her hands, I would be forgiven for thinking she was packing for yet another trip to Paris.

"This is packing lightly," she stammers, gazing around helplessly.

"No," I insist, "it's not. Firstly, you don't need this." I toss the hatbox back into her wardrobe. It's followed by one of the larger suitcases and the vanity case. Hoisting the last remaining suitcase onto the bed, I turn to face her.

"This is it. This is all you're allowed."

She purses her lips in dismay, but she doesn't argue. With a newfound determination, she starts sifting through the items, separating them into two distinct piles.

"Good girl," I say encouragingly.

Anna's hands hover over the suitcase.

"You sound different," she says eventually. Her suspicion is fuelled by curiosity, but deep down she doesn't really want to know, and it's not something I would ever want to burden her with.

"Everything is fine, Anna."

"Will Fletcher really come for me?"

"I believe he will."

"What if he doesn't?"

"Then I'll find another way to keep you safe."

She nods, discreetly wiping at her eyes before resuming her methodical packing.

By the time I descend the stairs an hour later, Hattie is back. Her heavy jaw is set, the soft flesh of her underarms swaying as she stirs an enormous pot of soup. The steam rising from inside it has deposited tiny droplets in her braided hair.

"Did you...?"

"I delivered your letter," she barks, before I can finish. "Is there anything else you need doing, Miss Clara?"

She won't meet my eyes. She wants me gone from this room.

"No," I admit, edging away from her. "Thank you Hattie."

"What do you mean, you're not coming with me?" Anna gasps. We are standing at the back door, away from the hustle and bustle of the kitchen.

"I can't." I say firmly. I know for a fact that father will arrive home shortly, along with the two members of the Guild and I need to distract them.

"Just head for the orchard. Fletcher will find you there."

"What if he doesn't?" She starts to cry. "I'm scared, Clara."

I take her in my arms, cradling her head like I would a child's.

"I know you are," I murmur in her ear. "But you need to be brave now. Fletcher will come, I promise you."

"How can you be sure?"

"Because he'd never let you down," I say. My heart repeats the mantra, but in its purest form. *He'd never let* me *down.*

I watch her pick her away across the lawn until she's swallowed by trees and shadow. I lied to her. The Guild weren't coming for her tonight, they were simply coming to announce her selection. Still, I didn't want her to witness what I planned to do, and, being Anna – typical spoilt, self-indulgent, glorious Anna – she was so concerned about escaping her fate that she never once stopped to consider who would take her place.

I am waiting patiently at the foot of the stairs when they arrive. If father is taken aback by my loitering in the hall, he hides it well.

"Clara," he booms, his voice carrying through the house. "These gentlemen are here from the Guild..."

"I know exactly why they're here," I say, my voice tight, clipped, "but Anna is not going to serve as the new Clock Keeper."

My father's face turns puce, but before he can sputter a response I continue.

"Anna is gone, Father, but don't despair, Tempus will have a new Clock Keeper because I will be taking her place. And before you even think about sending Tempus to find her, you should know that if ever Anna sets one foot in that Hall, her actions will have consequences you couldn't even begin to imagine."

THIRTY-FIVE
A MORTAL PROMISE

1916, *The Hall of Clocks, Grand Canyon, Arizona*

I'M sick to death of the dark. Of all the things I hate about living in isolation, the lack of electricity is the worst. I know that eventually the Guild will install closed circuit power, gas and even rudimentary plumbing, but that won't happen until long after I'm gone from this place.

In the two months that I've been here, serving as the Clock Keeper, I've had time to think, to reflect on the journey that brought me here. Memories are my constant companion.

I still think I did the right thing. Knowing that Anna is safe – that time is safe – makes it all worthwhile and keeps the guilt over what I did to Fletcher at bay, and, whenever thinking of Fletcher becomes too painful, I picture instead my father's face that night. Something in my words terrified him. Perhaps, deep down, he suspected what had happened, or perhaps he was simply stunned that I stood up to him, but he had agreed to let me serve in Anna's place, and, as far as I knew, he hadn't gone looking for her.

I had undertaken the month-long journey to Flagstaff on my own. Father had decided to stay behind, in Charleston, and I doubted I would ever see him again. I planned on retiring after my decade of service, in the grand tradition of Clock Keepers, preferably with enough money to set up a business. I might not be living in the twenty-first century anymore, but, as a member of Tempus, sexism didn't come into play, and I had a feeling life insurance would be a lucrative investment.

I wander through the Hall often. The humming of the clocks calms me and serves as a reminder of why I'm here. That, and the gold object I carry close to my heart, on the locket I wear permanently around my neck.

I am sitting at the small desk, playing absent-mindedly with it, when I hear the soft ping of leather on iron. I cock my head, listening intently, and, sure enough, the sound intensifies. Someone from the Guild is making their way down the ladder. Soft footfalls follow and I rise from my chair to greet the visitor, delighted to have company. Only it's no Guild member who walks through the door. I freeze, unable to move or speak as I gaze across the space between us.

His dark hair is windswept, his blue eyes sombre, and, in his hand, a crumpled letter with a broken but familiar seal. He is not supposed to be here – he's not supposed to remember - but he does. He wouldn't have been able to find this place if he didn't.

"You made me a promise, Clarke," Fletcher says. There is no condemnation in his voice, only bitter regret and sadness. His eyes go to the object at my throat and my hand tightens over it convulsively.

"I figured as much," he says. "When I didn't die last week, I figured you must have taken it. Isn't that kind of defeating the whole purpose of everything we did? I thought you weren't supposed to interfere."

I finally find my voice.

"You're not immortal, Fletcher. I just... put you on pause. I'll put it back eventually."

"Aren't there people who are supposed to be living in my place?"

"Probably. But, after everything we've sacrificed, I decided I was allowed to be selfish. Just this once."

"Why bother? You obviously have no intention of growing old *with* me, so what does it matter?"

"It matters because you're alive, and I can't bear the thought of you not being alive. And," I admit, "I needed you to protect Anna."

"Ah, Anna." He holds up the letter and waves it around. "I must say, that was one hell of a favour to ask, considering the circumstances. You betrayed me and then expected me to do you a... what did you call it..." he scans the page. "A favour?"

"I didn't know how else to save her. And I thought..."

"You thought that by refusing to kiss me in the orchard, combined with my losing all memory of us, I might fall in love with her?"

He comes closer, taking long, certain strides and tosses the letter onto the desk.

"I'm a little disappointed by your lack of faith in me. In *us*."

"There wasn't supposed to be any us. I thought you wouldn't remember."

"But I did."

"How?"

"That's a good question and one I've had a lot of time to think about. I can only assume it has something to do with the fact that my hand was covering yours when you turned time back. I guess we did it together, so we both remember."

I cast my mind back to the moment we reappeared in the twentieth century.

"Why didn't you say anything?"

"In the two seconds you gave me? All I wanted to do was kiss you – well, actually, I wanted to do a lot more than that, but I thought I was being romantic, replaying our first kiss. It didn't work out so well. You bolted out of there like a frightened rabbit and then refused to speak to me when I came to your window."

"But then – when you got my letter...?"

"When I got your letter I realised what your plan was and, I hate to admit it, but it was a good one. So I took Anna and fled Charleston. As soon as she was settled I headed out here. I didn't know if I'd make the journey – what with D-Day coming up – but I didn't dare risk coming to find you without making sure Anna was safe first."

"You left Anna? Where?"

"In Charlotte, North Carolina. My mother had cousins there and," he grins, "it turns out one of her sons looks a lot like me. Anna is very happy, I assure you."

"She's safe?" It's a rhetorical question but I ask it anyway.

"She is. And the Kennedy name is restored. You did it, Clarke. You did everything you wanted to do."

"Not everything," I confess.

Fletcher steps closer, his body only inches from my own.

"What else did you want?"

"I never wanted to lie to you. Betraying you broke my heart."

"The promise?"

"The promise."

"Tell me now."

The warmth of my feelings for him washes over me in a wave, threatening to consume me, and, for the first time, I let it.

"I love you, Fletcher. I have loved you for a hundred years and, with any luck, I'll get to love you for-" I cock my head, doing the math, "-at least another sixty-five."

"Less a day," he murmurs, reaching for me.

As his arms come around me, I lean back, searching his face.

"A day?"

"Yeah," he nuzzles my neck, kissing the dial hanging between my breasts. "You're going to have to put this back before you die."

His mouth claims mine then and I melt against him, the possibility of a full and happy life lighting me up from the inside. I had resigned myself to a life without him – a life without my best friend, a life without love. The fact that he is really here after everything we've been though is beyond belief, but, as my hands trace the hard contours of his chest and rise to plunge into his dark hair, pulling him closer against me, there is no denying he is real - a man of flesh and blood, no longer immortal, but destined to live a long and healthy life.

"I love you," Fletcher says between the breath of his next kiss, and the words send an arrow of heat straight to my heart and set the world alive with possibility.

Our journey begins now.

We will live. We will love. And finally, we will die.

THE END

AUTHOR'S NOTES

This story was inspired by an online article I found during the course of my research which tells of a front-page story in the *Arizona* (Phoenix) *Gazette* on the 5th April 1909, which reported an archaeological expedition in the heart of the Grand Canyon. The original story claims that the expedition was funded by the Smithsonian Institute and that an underground network of tunnels containing various ancient artefacts was discovered. The article was anonymous but identified two of the archaeologists involved: a Prof. S. A Jordan and a G.E Kincaid. The Smithsonian Institute later stated that it had no Jordan or Kincaid on record.

Further research turned up conflicting answers as to whether Kincaid did indeed discover the entrance to a lost city in the Grand Canyon and so, instead, I decided to simply enjoy the mystery surrounding the events and let the world of fiction take over.

Whether there is any substance to the article, or whether it was simply a hoax, or a late April Fool's joke is up to you to decide for yourself, but the point is that the article stuck with me and I used it to add an element of the bizarre and unexplained to this story. I did, however, alter the publication date to 1917 to fit in with my timeline.

Herewith the original story, as found on the internet:

EXPLORATIONS IN GRAND CANYON

Mysteries of Immense Rich Cavern being brought to light,

Jordan is enthused

Remarkable finds indicate ancient people migrated from Orient

The latest news of the progress of the explorations of what is now regarded by scientists as not only the oldest archaeological discovery in the United States, but one of the most valuable in the world, which was mentioned some time ago in the Gazette, was brought to the city yesterday by G.E. Kincaid, the explorer who found the great underground citadel of the Grand Canyon during a trip from Green River, Wyoming, down the Colorado, in a wooden boat, to Yuma, several months ago.

According to the story related to the Gazette by Mr. Kincaid, the archaeologists of the Smithsonian Institute, which is financing the expeditions, have made discoveries which almost conclusively prove that the race which inhabited this mysterious cavern, hewn in solid rock by human hands, was of oriental origin, possibly from Egypt, tracing back to Ramses. If their theories are borne out by the translation of the tablets engraved with hieroglyphics, the mystery of the prehistoric peoples of North America, their ancient arts, who they were and whence they came, will be solved. Egypt and the Nile, and Arizona and the Colorado will be linked by a historical chain running back to ages which staggers the wildest fancy of the fictionist.

A Thorough Investigation

Under the direction of Prof. S. A. Jordan, the Smithsonian Institute is now prosecuting the most thorough explorations, which will be continued until the last link in the chain is forged. Nearly a mile underground, about 1480 feet below the surface, the long main passage has been delved into, to find another mammoth chamber from which radiates scores of passageways, like the spokes of a wheel.

Several hundred rooms have been discovered, reached by passageways running from the main passage, one of them having been explored for 854 feet and another 634 feet. The recent finds include articles which have never been known as native to this country, and doubtless they had their origin in the orient. War weapons, copper instruments, sharp-edged and hard as steel, indicate the high state of civilization reached by these strange people. So interested have the scientists become that preparations are being made to equip the camp for extensive studies, and the force will be increased to thirty or forty persons.

Mr. Kincaid's Report

Mr. Kincaid was the first white child born in Idaho and has been an explorer and hunter all his life, thirty years having been in the service of the Smithsonian Institute. Even briefly recounted, his history sounds fabulous, almost grotesque.

"First, I would impress that the cavern is nearly inaccessible. The entrance is 1,486 feet down the sheer canyon wall. It is located on government land and no visitor will be allowed there under penalty of trespass. The scientists wish to work unmolested, without fear of archaeological discoveries being disturbed by curio or relic hunters. A trip there would be fruitless, and the visitor would be sent on his way. The story of how I found the cavern has been related, but in a paragraph: I was journeying down the Colorado river in a boat, alone, looking for mineral. Some forty-two miles up the river from the El Tovar Crystal canyon, I saw on the east wall, stains in the sedimentary formation about 2,000 feet above the river bed. There was no trail to this point, but I finally reached it with great difficulty.

Above a shelf which hid it from view from the river, was the mouth of the cave. There are steps leading from this entrance some thirty yards to what was, at the time the cavern was inhabited, the level of the river. When I saw the chisel marks on the wall inside the entrance, I became interested, securing my gun and went in. During that trip I went back several hundred feet along the main passage till I came to the crypt in which I discovered the mummies. One of these I stood up and photographed by flashlight. I gathered a number of relics, which I carried down the Colorado to Yuma, from whence I shipped them to Washington with details of the discovery. Following this, the explorations were undertaken.

The Passages

"The main passageway is about 12 feet wide, narrowing to nine feet toward the farther end. About 57 feet from the entrance, the first side-passages branch off to the right and left, along which, on both sides, are a number of rooms about the size of ordinary living rooms of today, though some are 30 by 40 feet square. These are entered by oval-shaped doors and are ventilated by round air spaces through the walls into the passages. The walls are about three feet six inches in thickness.

The passages are chiselled or hewn as straight as could be laid out by an engineer. The ceilings of many of the rooms converge to a center. The side-passages near the entrance run at a sharp angle from the main hall, but toward the rear they gradually reach a right angle in direction.

The Shrine

"Over a hundred feet from the entrance is the cross-hall, several hundred feet long, in which are found the idol, or image, of the people's god, sitting cross-legged, with a lotus flower or lily in each hand. The cast of the face is oriental, and the carving this cavern. The idol almost resembles Buddha, though the scientists are not certain as to what religious worship it represents. Taking into consideration everything found thus far, it is possible that this worship most resembles the ancient people of Tibet.

Surrounding this idol are smaller images, some very beautiful in form; others crooked-necked and distorted shapes, symbolical, probably, of good and evil. There are two large cactus with protruding arms, one on each side of the dais on which the god squats. All this is carved out of hard rock resembling marble. In the opposite corner of this cross-hall were found tools of all descriptions, made of copper. These people undoubtedly knew the lost art of hardening this metal, which has been sought by chemicals for centuries without result. On a bench running around the workroom was some charcoal and other material probably used in the process. There is also slag and stuff similar to matte, showing that these ancients smelted ores, but so far no trace of where or how this was done has been discovered, nor the origin of the ore.

"Among the other finds are vases or urns and cups of copper and gold, made very artistic in design. The pottery work includes enamelled ware and glazed vessels. Another passageway leads to granaries such as are found in the oriental temples. They contain seeds of various kinds. One very large storehouse has not yet been entered, as it is twelve feet high and can be reached only from above. Two copper hooks extend on the edge, which indicates that some sort of ladder was attached. These granaries are rounded, as the materials of which they are constructed, I think, is a very hard cement. A gray metal is also found in this cavern, which puzzles the scientists, for its identity has not been established. It resembles platinum. Strewn promiscuously over the floor everywhere are what people call "cats eyes", a yellow stone of no great value. Each one is engraved with the head of the Malay type.

The Hieroglyphics

"On all the urns, or walls over doorways, and tablets of stone which were found by the image are the mysterious hieroglyphics, the key to which the Smithsonian Institute hopes yet to discover. The engraving on the tables probably has something to do with the religion of the people. Similar hieroglyphics have been found in southern Arizona. Among the pictorial writings, only two animals are found. One is of prehistoric type.

The Crypt

"The tomb or crypt in which the mummies were found is one of the largest of the chambers, the walls slanting back at an angle of about 35 degrees. On these are tiers of mummies, each one occupying a separate hewn shelf. At the head of each is a small bench, on which is found copper cups and pieces of broken swords. Some of the mummies are covered with clay, and all are wrapped in a bark fabric.

The urns or cups on the lower tiers are crude, while as the higher shelves are reached, the urns are finer in design, showing a later stage of civilization. It is worthy of note that all the mummies examined so far have proved to be male, no children or females being buried here. This leads to the belief that this exterior section was the warriors' barracks.

"Among the discoveries no bones of animals have been found, no skins, no clothing, no bedding. Many of the rooms are bare but for water vessels. One room, about 40 by 700 feet, was probably the main dining hall, for cooking utensils are found here. What these people lived on is a problem, though it is presumed that they came south in the winter and farmed in the valleys, going back north in the summer.

Upwards of 50,000 people could have lived in the caverns comfortably. One theory is that the present Indian tribes found in Arizona are descendants of the serfs or slaves of the people which inhabited the cave. Undoubtedly a good many thousands of years before the Christian era, a people lived here which reached a high stage of civilization. The chronology of human history is full of gaps. Professor Jordan is much enthused over the discoveries and believes that the find will prove of incalculable value in archaeological work.

"One thing I have not spoken of, may be of interest. There is one chamber of the passageway to which is not ventilated, and when we approached it a deadly, snaky smell struck us. Our light would not penetrate the gloom, and until stronger ones are available we will not know what the chamber contains. Some say snakes, but other boo-hoo this idea and think it may contain a deadly gas or chemicals used by the ancients. No sounds are heard, but it smells snaky just the same. The whole underground installation gives one of shaky nerves the creeps. The gloom is like a weight on one's shoulders, and our flash-lights and candles only make the darkness blacker. Imagination can revel in conjectures and ungodly daydreams back through the ages that have elapsed till the mind reels dizzily in space."

ABOUT THE AUTHOR

Melissa is an award-winning author, copywriter, and lover of the written word. She is published in both S.A and the U.S.A and offers professional copywriting services and author coaching.

For ten years she owned and operated her own specialized logistics company until she woke up one morning and decided it was time to put her English degree to good use.

Melissa lives with her husband and three teenagers, none of whom take her seriously.

She also writes romantic suspense as Lissa Del and contemporary romance as Rachel Rhodes.

For more information, visit www.melissadelport.com

ACKNOWLEDGMENTS

As always, my husband Murray must be applauded for living with a writer. It can't be easy, but he has it down to a fine art.

An enormous thank you to my long-standing (and long-suffering!) editor, Catherine Eberle of Word Weavers, who has been with me since the very beginning and without whom I would still be writing cliched characters and terrible transitions.

Wendy Bow of Apple Pie Graphics, friend and cover designer, for your infinite patience and your vision.

Ian Tennent, who could probably have written at least ten more books if I didn't bother him seventy-five times a day. You are truly my Yoda in this crazy craft. Thank you for all your guidance and advice.

And finally, to all my readers, the biggest thanks go to you. Because, let's face it, without you I wouldn't be writing.

www.ingramcontent.com/pod-product-compliance
Lightning Source LLC
Chambersburg PA
CBHW020913310726
48980CB00011B/871/J

9780639844701